STINGER

Kenneth Varner

VarnerBooks Publishing

220 Bayou View
El Lago, TX 77586

STINGER

Copyright © Kenneth Varner 2014

VarnerBooks Publication 978-0-9889602-8-2

ACKNOWLEDGEMENTS

Again, I have to recognize the critical part Bob and Judy Fahy played in putting this book together. Their edits and Comments were so extensive that I thought I'd never see the end of them. I'm lucky that, as friends, they haven't sent me a bill for God knows how much money to pay for the hours they spent on this text.

I do need to mention my wife of fifty six years. Barbara, manages to put up with me even though paying for the initial printings is burning a hole in her budget.

You've often seen the caveat that any resemblance to real people, living or dead is purely coincidental. Well that's not the case here though all the names and a lot of their activities have been changed just in case I actually sell copies of this book instead of giving them all away to friends.

The people behind the characters did in fact exist though most though most of them would probably chuckle at their part in the book. Many of the historical events portrayed did actually take place, though not always in the time frame of the book, and many of the people upon which the characters are based were real. I did not however feel the need to stick strictly to the literal truth as to how they were involved. The point of all this is to say that the resemblance to real ones is not coincidental but is definitely fictional. For instance the persona behind Isaac's character didn't marry or, as far as I know, even make a pass at Joanne's. They, however, would probably get a real laugh at some of the things I had them do.

I hope you caught the word FICTIONAL above. Not all of the events were. The missile skin sections being sent to a German furnace, the action to remove nuclear weapons from French missile sites and the actions at the sites happened mostly as shown (barring the attempt on Scarborough's life). Our troops did, literally strip their bases in France of almost everything useful and the C123 engine problems at Ramstein AFB happened almost exactly as portrayed. That includes the "Flight of the GI's and the truck tarp."

Any rate, don't spend a lot of time trying to figure out what's real and what's not. Just remember the book is listed under the FICTION section. Kenneth Varner

A MODIFIED HISTORY LESSON

In recognition of the "Truth in Labeling" law, (if there isn't one pertaining to books like this there should be) I need to point out that the title of this book, Stinger, is historically incorrect. The word Stinger though has a lot more visual impact than the title of the actual missile involved in this book – the Redeye block I, block II or Block III or the last version, Redeye II. The Stinger is a name given to a later version of that missile system that gained fame years later in Afghanistan, when a Texas Congressman arranged for Afghan rebels fighting the Soviets to get the things. Development of methods to protect troops in the field from ground attack aircraft was begun almost twenty years before the nightly news showed pictures of Soviet aircraft leaving Kabul Airport spewing Infrared flares in all directions to ward off US built Stinger missile attacks, The Redeye II had no such fame. Even the name itself was usually buried in official governmental gobbledygook.

The development of the small Shoulder Fired Antiaircraft Missile System was a tortured one. The advent of Jet fighters meant that weapons of the time, mostly machine guns were no longer very effective against low level, fast moving jet attack aircraft. First conceived in 1959, the first test firing of a man portable antiaircraft rocket was in 1961 with only limited success. Between 1965 and 1966 modifications improving the target acquisition capability were made and during this period several other changes were made, purportedly because of a request from Denmark for a more powerful motor and warhead. The result was a missile officially designated eventually as the Redeye Block II.

In 1967 a new and more powerful version of the original Redeye missile was developed. Initially it was called the Redeye II and only later the "Block III" (the name did not become "Stinger" until 1972). During this long development period the Redeye variants were the subject of much controversy. An important question, lodged by the Air Force was how to assure that US close support aircraft would not be shot down by jittery Army GI's armed with the things. This was a serious problem since after an infantry unit has suffered a powerful strafing attack the next thing that appears in the sky around them is going to get their undivided attention. As a result, the "Stinger" acquired something that the Redeye didn't have – IFF, or Identification, Friend or Foe. This improved safety for friendly air force close support aircraft since the system would not attack an aircraft broadcasting an IFF signal. Of course no system is ever perfect so the new system meant that the supporting fighter was SAFER, but not completely

SAFE.

Now, IFF was a very closely guarded system and allowing it in the hands of foreign nationals would present a danger to the success of the weapon system. For example, Stingers that were issued to the Afghan rebels to use against the Soviet Hind Helicopters almost certainly had such systems removed. After all, there were no friendly aircraft as far as the Afghans were concerned. This is a big problem today since a number of those same Stingers are still in Afghan rebel hands today – without IFF - and our aircraft are not now their friends either.

Basically, the system is a small five foot long guided missile with a "target seeker", a rocket motor and a warhead. It is fired from a tube by an individual soldier and it acquires a target using a compressed gas cooled seeker head that "sees" the signature of a jet engine or on a bright sunny day, even the heat reflected off the aircraft skin and once fired, homes the rocket in on the target. Upon impact the warhead detonates usually with fatal damage to the target. For the Afghan rebels this was usually a Soviet Hind Helicopter. Small arms fire had proven useless against this heavily armored helicopter. The Stinger solved that problem.

It also created problems in resupply for the Soviet troops too. Not long after the Stinger arrived in country, newsreels showed Soviet cargo aircraft leaving Kabul Airport spewing Infrared flares in all directions – a sure sign of the fact that the Stinger was in service

There is a Soviet version of this weapon introduced in 1959, called the Strella 2 or the more common NATO designation SA 7. It had roughly the same capabilities as the original Redeye but had s less complex and less capable target seeker. NATO was able to revise their aircraft paint to minimize its effectiveness still further. It, however has remained a peril to aircraft for years and is wide spread over the world.

PROLOGUE

February 1966

I could feel the twinges in my leg by the time I reached the E ring and the Brigadier's office. I wondered if assigning the Department of Army Inspector General to the most inaccessible office in the whole damned Pentagon was deliberate.. I knew from personal experience that nobody in the military wanted to admit that the DAIG, or would never do so publicly, was anything but a pain in the ass so it was certainly possible. Oh well, I was sick of doing nothing. Even a desk job would be better that listening to a damned doctor tell me to "rest a bit longer". I pushed open the door. Sharon Jackson looked up then jumped up. She came around her desk and gave me a big hug. "Oh God, Arthur you look great. How's the leg?" The legs great but if you let Bill catch me making out with his wife he may break the other one."

"Captain, it's bad for your career to suck up to a Colonel in a General's office. If you must suck up do it with the General. Come in Arthur before I have to bring my aide up on harassment charges." I watched as Arthur came toward me and noticed he managed not to limp but couldn't completely cover up the fact that he favored his right leg. Considering how close that wound had come to having him lose it he was lucky. However, even taking a short cut across the atrium going from one end of the Pentagon E ring to the other was a hell of a walk fro someone fresh out of a hospital. As I closed the door, he stood at attention in front of my desk. "If you insist on standing till I sit down, I'll have to return to calling you Colonel." Arthur grinned as he lowered himself into the chair but managed not to hit the seat before I did. When he laid the files I'd given him on the desk I simply asked "Well?" "You're right sir, there's no direct evidence of conspiracy on the part of the troops in France but plenty of odd coincidence. Do you really think De Gaulle will go through with his threat?" I nodded. "Most of the spook community is convinced of it. That's why that folder takes on additional importance. He's making noises about closing all NATO bases in France. If that happens we're going to have a massive mess over there. Presumably, we'll have some time to do the job but if we don't it'll be chaos. Those discrepancies will be chicken feed to the material losses then. It's bad enough if those are just book keeping errors but if, as I suspect, somebody's raiding the armory then this move will be like giving them the key to the candy store. I'm arranging a transfer for you to Germany, preferably to Communication Zone HQ or maybe as liaison to the flyboys at Ramstein Air Base. Don't know what it'll be just yet but probably in the security area since that was your original Military Specialty.

March 11, 1966

I came back into the apartment and closed the door before starting to massage my damned leg. I was going stir crazy on so called Limited Duty and being limited to a half mile slow jog didn't help. I'd be even more pissed at the doctor if it wasn't for the fact that I couldn't even make that without stopping to rest half way through. Oh well, I'd already poured corn flakes in a bowl when I noticed the light on my phone. Limping over to it I punched the red button. "See me Arthur!" There was no mistaking Brigadier Morrison's clipped voice. Well, so much for breakfast.

"About time you showed up", Norman muttered, obviously angry. "Couldn't let Captain Honey outside smell my sweat." He leaned back with a sigh. "Well DeGaulle did it – or will. The son of a bitch is due to make a speech today, taking France out of the NATO military command. According to the spooks he'll demand we take all US forces out of the country – timetable unknown. They weren't sure if he intends to get out of the alliance entirely – probably not, he has nuclear ambitions since he tested his first nuke. We're not too sure just how many big bombs he has." He shoved a packet across the desk to me. Those are your transfer orders as Deputy Security Chief at COMZEUR. In a pinch they'll get you there but no one is really sure where they're going to move or even if the command will remain at all. Communication Zone HQ may go with to NATO in Brussels. So I'm changing the transfer to Ramstein Air Force Base as Chief of the Army Support Detachment there. Check with the Liaison office at Rhein Maine when you get there. I've authorized a staff car to pick you up. If the new orders are not there go on to Ramstein and check into the BOQ there till they come in. No sense in going all the way to France or Belgium then having to double back. It's closer to the really big bullets we're most worried about anyway. Also, it's easier to arrange quarters for you there. Both the airbase and Kaiserslautern have some available. Knowing you though, you'll probably prefer the living on the economy instead of in military housing.

I nodded as I skimmed the data packet. We discussed a few

more questions I had and I got up to leave. "By the way" he muttered. "You'd better get that leg back in shape pretty quick. You're liable to have to do some fancy footwork on this job."

Friday December 1, 1966 Ramstein AFB

He'd been right on target. It had been Chaos in the nine months since the French Fuehrer had pulled the plug on any NATO military presence in his country. Naturally, the Seventh Army didn't believe he'd actually insist on them leaving till the last minute. Then, in September the entire resources of the European Command had been turned over to the task of removing it's presence from France. Every vehicle in the command capable of carrying even the smallest load was pressed into service for day and night missions to one or another US Military base in country. Even dead lined vehicles were put into service if there was the slightest chance that they could make the trip there and back. The roads into France from Germany were littered with broken down trucks as the mechanics couldn't keep up with repairs.

Most of the equipment was now gone leaving only empty buildings where they'd been stored. The GI's, angered by their perception of the "traitorous French" had even torched the steel supports from any that they could manage to remove and take with them. The French countryside was now littered with empty, totally useless, US installations. The army had even sent large fighting units to assure the removal of nuclear warheads from French Missile sites. Now, though the problem I'd been sent over here to investigate was becoming more evident as the receiving reports for French munitions arriving at German ammunition installations began to trickle in. everyone had expected the massive confusion in general supplies movements but Ammunition was a much more tightly controlled commodity. Some problems could be expected but none like what were appearing.

I was puzzling over a report of, John Logan, one of my undercover people in Marseilles when I heard the phone ring in the outer office. The report about a mysterious ship unloading an equally mysterious cargo at the port was worrying – not the mystery so much as the fact that supervising the unloading was an officer of the Direction du Renseignement Militaire. Why was the French Military Intelligence Directorate, the DRM involved with a Syrian ship with close hold paperwork? Just as I sat back to consider it, Fraulein Von Bauman came in. "Sir," she said, a frown on her face "you have a call. He wouldn't give a name just said that he used to work for you and was one of your worst WAG's." I had to chuckle. I hadn't even known Isaac Hamlin was in country.

(Oct 23 1967 last US flag in France is furled)

STINGER
CHAPTER 1

Friday 2 December 1966

I was bogged down in paper and determined to unbog myself before I went home today. The had started within minutes of checking in at the depot and after this morning's hair raising trip over the mountain from Muenchweiler. It had snowed last night and the road so slick that I hadn't been sure I'd make it in one piece. I promised myself I'd be taking the long way home tonight. Even if I got away at 1600 hours, this time of year, it'd be a dark drive home across the mountain from Fischbach Kaserne to my apartment in the Muenchweiler Hospital complex. Since then it had been nothing but one flap after another. The first one this morning had hit me before I was even able to sit down. One of the newly assigned Warrant Officers over in the Maintenance and Assembly building was trying to throw our inspector out because she didn't have the proper clearance or "Need to Know". He couldn't believe that Robin was at least as well, and probably better, trained than he was. She also had a higher clearance than he did. I knew because I'd seen his records. His last posting was to a motor pool and his Secret Restricted Data hadn't finished processing yet. Then, when I, perhaps not too politely pointed this out, he insisted that all of my Surveillance DACs be taken off the "Critical Skills" list for the same reason. I tried my best to keep from busting his chops but had managed a shrug and a mentioned that I'd always wanted to take a few days and visit East Germany. He'd blustered for me to go ahead. He obviously didn't know that no one with our clearances would be allowed through Checkpoint Charlie. Hell, we weren't even allowed into West Berlin unless we flew or went on the Military Duty Train.

The whole thing had started because he'd wanted to throw some "Fertilizer" − according to him − out in the trash so it could go to the Pirmasens power plant for disposal. At that point, Robin had shown me the data remaining on the containers. The stuff was old, probably World War Two vintage and had been badly handled. Most of the stock number and other identifying data had worn off the six forty pound containers except for the last two digits of the four Federal Stock Class ones. They were a 7 and a 5. That said Demolition Material to anybody with a conventional ammunition background. A background that, unfortunately this new Warrant Officer didn't have. He pointed out that the remaining letters on the nomenclature were "NH4_N__ CRA_____ CH____". He insisted that it was Amonium Nitrate Fertilizer. It had taken a call to from him to the Depot Commander to stop his diatribe. Even so he wouldn't believe me – or at least admit to believing me that what he looked at was dangerous.

Next it was the Chief Warrant, CWO Backarice, who got in just before noon and we had to go through the same drill all over. I sighed because it wasn't a new problem. The sign on the gate to the ammunition area said "No Civilians Beyond this Point" and every time we got a new guard or WO we had to go through the same problem to convince them that no matter what the sign said, that "WE WERE THEIR CIVILIANS". Anyway, I was so disgusted at repeatedly being cut off trying to explain why this wasn't fertilizer that I finally told them, OK if they wanted to get rid of the stuff so badly, we'd take it out to the old demolition ground and burn it ourselves. The nasty grin on the young Warrant and the worried look on his Chief's face said that the CWO was suddenly suspicious of my retreat and wondering about the wisdom of being loyal to a subordinate without being certain of the facts in the case. It was enough to almost make me smirk. I was careful not to, though. I'd learned long ago that with an obstinate asshole, the best way to convince them they were wrong was to let them see the results of their assholishness.

By 1300 hours, we were all at the Demo Ground and Mister Mueller had nodded to me that he had primed the charges with blasting caps. Of course we both knew what they were, World War II Cratering Charges. I'd been tempted to have him slip a bit of Comp C4 in too but decided against it. By the time that the time fuse was laid, we'd acquired quite a following. Most of the Depot staff had found some reason to be at the Demo Ground this afternoon. Carrying a fuse lighter, I told everyone they'd better move to the barricaded bunker. The snotty young WO asked if I was still trying to scare everyone. Fed up, I turned to him and said, "Kid, are you willing to bet your life on the off chance that I'm wrong? In case you weren't out of diapers when it happened, in 1947 a ship load of Ammonium Nitrate fertilizer exploded in Texas City Texas. It leveled the city. There were almost six hundred known dead and over eight thousand wounded. The figures are not exact because a number of the victims were literally vaporized! A lot of others were decapitated and this damned stuff isn't fertilizer! You can stand out here and watch like an asshole if you like but I'll guarantee I'll be in the bunker. Now it's time to shit or get off the pot!" With that I lit the fuse and ran like hell. That was perhaps a bit theatrical since I knew I'd laid out at least three minutes of time fuse but it galvanized Warrant Officer Two Pierce. He was less than a second behind me.

We had felt the explosion in our feet before our ears even got the message. The ground actually rolled from the shock and clods of dirt fell atop the bunker with loud thumps. Every man in the bunker stood still in a state of shock except for my Surveillance Crew. While the earth was still shaking, I said, "Now for a lesson in explosives. Each one has its own characteristics. Ammonium Nitrate is a slow explosive. It's an earth mover. What you're going to see when we go out there is why they call these things Cratering Charges. Imagine a runway or building after an explosion like the one you just heard. Our more common explosives such as Composition C4, RDX, HMX and PETN all have uses, some spectacular but they can't touch that Ammonium Nitrate even in fertilizer form for moving earth. Imagine a big guy letting another big guy hit him on the shoulder. He might or might not get knocked down. If he let the guy push against his shoulder really hard, sooner or later he's going on his ass. That's the difference in a high explosive like C4 and a so called low explosive like Ammonium Nitrate."

"Those are just some of the better behaved, trust worthy, explosives and the only ones we in the military use today. Nitro Glycerin is well known to be so unstable a simple shock can set it off but, of all the ones you may come in contact with the there are two that a will cause a trained EOD man will to shiver before approaching. Black Powder and old Nobel dynamite can never be trusted to act in a predictable manner. Never under any circumstances, mess with either one. I'll guarantee that I never will because you can't trust them. Now let's go out and see the results of trying to burn our fertilizer – and remember this was from only six forty pound charges."

All the depot staff had stood in awe, staring at the monstrous hole almost five feet deep and fifteen feet across. One by one, they'd slowly slipped away with few comments. The Chief almost grabbed his Warrant Officer by the ear and dragged him away. I muttered to the Depot Commander that he could expect some phone calls when he got back to his office- that we'd probably shaken the ground all the way to France. Major, trying to keep a grin off his face, muttered in reply, that

"Well France is just across the back fence. I'm more worried about the prople in Pirmasens. I assume that you are satisfied with your little temper tantrum". I gave him a grin, albeit a sheepish one and told him that "Of course I was."

It was now an hour later and I was again back at my desk and yet again caught myself shuffling paper and staring at the dimple on the wall we had made with a drill and concrete bit. We'd tried to bore a hole in the wall to hang a manpower chart. If the Germans had done nothing else they had mixed hellishly dense concrete for the substantial dividing walls in their munitions facilities. The concrete bit had simply burned up trying to penetrate the damned stuff. As a result everything we had to hang on the walls was hung with "Green Tape." I don't know who invented it but it was used to seal up munitions containers was practically indestructible and would stick to anything.

As a result of my musing it was becoming obvious that I wasn't going to get my paper work done today. I sighed but didn't even look up as Thomas Byrnes and Herr Mueller came in. The sound of Tom's voice, though, got my attention. Tom was an Ammunition Inspector short timer - due to rotate back to the states in a week and not given to flights of imagination but the waiver in his voice spoke of extreme agitation. When I saw his face, I knew it was gonna be a long day. "We've got a problem, Squatter," he said. He took a deep breath and said. "We're short four Redeyes." An inventory glitch wouldn't put that look on his face - even one involving the newest little missile in our arsenal. "Short?" I asked. "Like they ain't no missiles in two of the boxes" he answered.

That got my attention. How could that be? Hell four highly classified missiles missing meant hell to pay. I knew I should have gotten into the inspection bay sooner. It wasn't every day we got this kind of weapon in to inspect – and this one had a maintenance job to do on it that required special test equipment. Our test equipment had only come in last week. I took my own deep breath. No doubt there was going to be somebody's ass to pay for this and I knew whose it would be if the Surveillance Division Chief at AWSCOM, Howard Dawson had his way. My mind went into overdrive. I managed, though, to get up without knocking my chair over - rather proud of myself for that - the shock of his announcement had been enough to keep me sitting long enough for my mind to get into gear. After all I had a reputation for a cool head under fire. It was the only reason I was over here in the first place. I knew the senior Inspectors hadn't wanted me but my anger

14

at their teletype that they had no "facilities" for ladies over here had earned me the nickname Tom had called me when he came in. I'd fired back a message telling Dawson I could "squat with the rest of the boys."

When I walked into the bay, there were ten metal storage containers lined up. "Why ten?" I asked the boys. "Well," Tom said, we couldn't get the things to run on our test equipment. The thing's not very well made. The missiles don't even fit on it properly. We had a total failure from the test samples we'd set out in the magazine. I decided to pull another sample before I called you. This time, we busted open a pallet and took the samples off the bottom. I smelled something wrong right away. Herr Mueller came and told me that four of the containers were way light. As soon as we got them in here, we opened them. There they are." He pointed to two boxes with the tops lying beside them. I suppressed a gasp of surprise at the sight of the containers. Inside were the supports the weapons should be lying in but nothing there. No gas coolant bottles either. Also, something else about them was wrong. I asked Herr Mueller to open another container. I wasn't surprised at the sight of the weapon in the new container.

"Better call McLauren?" I told Tom, managing to delete the expletive I would prefer to use for that asshole Missile Command Project Manager. He was even worse than Dawson. Tom picked up the phone and called the orderly room. I heard him say that we "had a problem with your material." He put down the phone. "On his way." he said. "He'll be going for a secure line to MICOM when he sees this." "It figures." I mumbled stalking out of the office to keep from blowing my stack. I thought I'd drop my teeth when I saw those weapons. There had to be a lot more going on than we'd been led to believe. No way in hell that the Federal Stock Number on those containers could be a simple error. Evidently, no one expected anyone over here to notice the differences in the weapons otherwise, McLauren would never have agreed to allow a receipt inspection. The damned fool, though, should have known that these things wouldn't ever pass a proper missile test. Hell they wouldn't even fit in the test set. Come to think about it, he might not know the difference either. This whole thing reeked of a spook operation. "ll hell was gonna break loose.

An hour after, I had, dutifully stared at four empty shipping containers that should have, but didn't, contain four, "Man Portable, Redeye Surface To Air Missiles." I had given the Atom – shit I've got

15

to remember that since that screw up last month when the painter had messed up the sign at the gate of Husterhoh Kaserne, AWSCOM is no longer ATOMIC but ADVANCED Weapons Support Command. Stupid change as if everybody in Germany didn't already know what the "Advanced Weapons" were. All because somebody let a picture of our sign get printed in a newspaper.

Anyway, before giving division a heads up, I'd gone over all the paper work that had come in with them and talked to the crew who'd unloaded them. There was no way they could have been stolen on this post. Everybody and his dog had been around to watch the receipt and storage of the things. Our project was a very visible one - at least locally. We were tasked to dismantle the things, remove the IFF - Identification Friend or Foe equipment, reassemble and test them. I cursed myself. If I hadn't been so tied up with getting settled in, that requirement alone should have set off alarm bells. The Redeye didn't have IFF. It was a special mission project and had a priority seldom seen on a non nuclear job and after that first look I wasn't surprised. This was a high level job by one of the alphabet agencies, CIA, DIA, NSA or perhaps a new one had been created in the last few hours. Enough of that - I couldn't put off my report any longer. No doubt, McLauren had already screamed to Missile Command and it wouldn't take long for the shit to roll downhill. I leaned back in the chair and waited for the inevitable.

Since it was another of the innumerable German holidays leading up to Christmas, I picked up the ringing phone. There was only one grating sentence, "Hamlin? Let me have Dawson! There's a problem - with our project." It was Joanne Scarborough. "Uh-oh!" I thought. Joanne was a hell raiser at times but she was invariably polite except when provoked. Of course Howard Dawson our Chief of Surveillance was a constant thorn in her side and she almost never asked to talk to him. This had to be a barn burner. I turned to Dawson and nodded at the phone, "Fischbach." Dawson looked up with a long suffering look on his face. "What's that bitch want now?" He grunted. I shrugged and he picked up the receiver. I put the receiver back to my ear as he muttered a very disgruntled "Yeah." It was no wonder Joanne disliked him. He made it obvious how little he thought of her. The SOB had no reason either. She was one of the best inspectors in the program and everybody knew it. He just didn't like women in a position of authority. I caught my breath as Joanne in carefully clipped tones gave her report. Since the line wasn't secure, it was a bit vague but the facts were clear. "Our downgrade operation has hit a snag sir" she said, sounding a lot calmer than I suspected she was. "We're missing at least four of the major components." I thought Dawson was going to drop the phone. "Oh Shit!" I thought. "How the hell can you lose something like that?" Dawson, practically screamed. "I was there when you received the damned things - all of them!" Joanne's voice was the epitome of cool. "We received the right number of boxes" she said. "It's just that a four of them – at least so far four - are empty."

I thought Dawson was gonna have apoplexy. "Lock the place down! Hamlin will be down there in an hour! In the meantime, I'll have Farlow send down a team. I want a full report before anything goes out on this." "Well sir," Joanne said quietly - no doubt with a nasty grin on her face. "The MICOM manager went to the orderly room an hour ago with fire in his eyes. No doubt he's already reported it to Redstone. He's due back here when he's finished." Dawson began to curse and slammed down the phone. "I'll be down as soon as I can get there Joanne." I muttered as Dawson sat behind his desk still cursing. "Better bring some Vaseline Isaac" she chuckled. "All our asses are due for a reaming on this one." I had to laugh at that and at the use of given name for the first time. That earned me a glare from Dawson. How could that girl keep her cool in a case like this I wondered? "Better watch your step down there Hamlin. I knew that damned bitch was trouble the minute I heard her name." Dawson Growled as he got up to leave the office. Presumably he was going to see the AWSCOM Commander. I was careful to keep from saying what I thought of his opinion, just nodded and got up to head for the parking lot.

As I came in the door to the Fischbach Army Depot Surveillance Office, the Depot Commander, Major Compton, was there standing, nervously, to one side. He looked like a man in dire fear of his job. Joanne and McLauren were leaning across her desk, almost nose to nose, facing each. I chuckled at "how little cool" she was showing. Both their faces were red as they shouted at one another. "I tell you they were expended in training!" McLauren shouted. Joanne glanced at me as I entered and straightened up and took a deep breath before she said, quietly, "Mister McLauren, there has never been a range exercise involving a Redeye yet in this theater - AND THOSE DAMNED THINGS AREN'T REDEYES!. You mean to tell me they fired four SAM's from the parade ground of Fleigerhorst Kaserne? - At

17

what?" "I don't care how they fired them" he shouted. "The Missile Lot report lists them as expended in training - and they are Redeyes! The stock number says so." Joanne looked at me and smiled a very unlady like smile. "Hello mister Hamlin" she purred, menacingly. "Why don't you explain to Mister McLauren what he can do with his f −" stopping to take a deep breath, finished the sentence "useless missile lot report? I've tried to explain how it wasn't worth the paper it's printed on but he seems to take umbrage at that." I had to suppress a grin. No doubt, her description of the inadequacy of that report had been a bit confrontational - especially to one of the major proponents of it.

It was, unfortunately, what was termed in the business, "an exception report." This meant that each quarter, units reported only changes in their stockpile. The problem was that any small mistake in transcribing a serial or lot number created another missile on paper. Compounding the problem was the simple fact that the job of ammunition officer in a unit was the one most likely to cause grief to an officer's career. As a result, it was given always to the most junior, and therefore, most inexperienced officer. They never stayed in the job beyond the time that a more junior lieutenant came in, making for a major turmoil in the position Army wide. Mistakes were endemic to the report. By the time three or four reports had been submitted our missile stockpile - on paper - usually grew by thirty or forty percent. It had to be completely redone on an average of once a year. MICOM however refused to recognize this fact. The suggestion, that an Ammunition Surveillance Inspector, who normally stayed around for three years and was familiar with those type reports, take over reporting was treated as an attempt to increase our turf- the idea of which, MICOM liked even less.

"I'm sure, Miss. Scarborough, that Mister McLauren is well aware of the lack of accuracy in that report." I said, solemnly. "There have been, at least, seven, letters from SMC headquarters on the subject." McLauren turned on me. "And all of them rebutted decisively" he growled. I shrugged. "I'll accept the rebutted part. Miss. Scarborough is right, though. It's impossible for those weapons to have been fired in training since they arrived here. Also, if Ms. Scarborough says they aren't Redeyes, I think we have a problem. I'd suggest you contact your headquarters and let them know a report is on its way up the chain from AWSCOM." Turning to Major Compton, I told him that Dawson had "suggested a lock down" of the depot until Major Farlow arrived to take over the investigation. He nodded as, exasperated,

McLauren turned on his heel and jerked open the door. Compton followed him out of the office

When McLauren had stomped out of the building, muttering his opinion of the Advanced Weapons Support Command and taking the major with him, Hamlin suggested that he and I take a walk. I guess he wasn't sure just how secure the depot offices were. Outside he asked, "Well Miss Scarborough, what have you found out about our problem. "You might as well call me Squatter." I muttered, fully aware of how much was at stake. "Everybody else does." He glanced down at me with a raised eyebrow. "Squatter Scarborough" he chuckled. "Has sort of a ring to it - a takeoff on Trapper John in Mash?" He let a moment pass by then added, "- or like a certain indelicate teletype?" Surprised that I could still be embarrassed about that damned teletype, I couldn't help a blush. "I was pissed." I muttered. "With good reason" he chuckled. "However, if I could call you Joanne, I'd be happy for you to call me Isaac. After all, you did less than an hour ago." I glanced, suspiciously, up at him. "I don't call the boss by his first name and I sure, as hell, don't flirt with him."

Shit! Where the hell, had that come from? I must be more shook up than I thought. He laughed out loud, though. "Well, since I'm not your boss and you haven't tried to flirt with me yet, I don't see your problem." I had to drop my face to keep from laughing - the first one today and I had to suppress it. I looked back up at him. Everything I'd heard about Hamlin was good - except that he was supposed to be a love em and leave em guy with the ladies. He had a reputation as a straight shooter, though. I had to admit that he wasn't bad to look at either - not exactly handsome but pleasant looking. I wondered if he was really so tall or that I was just so damned short. I also wondered how he managed to get along with his panty waist boss day in and day out. I decided it was time for me to get out of this damned mess. "Well," I muttered. "We've got a lot more problems than a couple of missing missiles. They're not the right ones. We got an update on the Redeye in Overseas Refresher. It was only an hour class and I was the only one in it because I was to have this job where we were going to rework them. Also, you should know -" I caught myself before I finished that remark. I wasn't sure he really should know about my briefing on materiel shortages in the command.

That was a new twist, or was it? I remembered what she'd shouted at McLauren. She had more on the damned thing than I did. I

19

wondered if Dawson had as much. "I suppose there's a point to that." I said then remembered -. "Should know what?" I asked. She hesitated then shrugged. "In the class they pointed out that the Redeye was just the first of a type. We have built another model - based on some modifications the Dutch asked for. The Redeye doesn't have IFF but the Dutch missile does. It's not been officially named but is generally referred to as the Redeye II or Redeye block III. It's also longer than the Redeye with a more powerful engine and a lot more capability. The speculation was that we would build our own version of the Dutch missile. Tentatively it was to be called "Stinger." When I got here I just glanced at the job requirements for the missile and didn't pay close enough attention since they weren't here yet. I got a surprise today when I realized they wanted us to downgrade the things. Why were we taking the IFF capability out of a missile that didn't have it in the first place? I feel like an idiot for not remembering that before today. The missiles in our shop are dead ringers for the Dutch "Redeye II" they showed us pictures of it in Savanna. Besides that, they don't fit on our test equipment because they're several inches longer." All I could say was "Shit!" "I take it you didn't know" she said. "Did Dawson?" I had to admit that I didn't know the answer to that.

AOK then" she murmured. "Just how do we handle this? The things are, obviously, marked wrong. The Federal Stock Numbers are for the Redeye. I doubt if the Redeye II even has an FSN, or if it ever will. Now how can Missile Command have a lot report that says the Redeye II's we have are actually Redeyes and that four were expended in training that never happened? Isaac, we're in the middle of a spook operation here. What happens if we file a report normally – that we have missiles that are not supposed to exist but that, at least four of the ones that can't be here are missing? Do we blow a big black operation? Is Dawson involved? Surely no one in their right mind would let that asshole in the loop."

Damn! That last just popped out. Me and my big mouth. I thought I'd covered up the slip I'd made before. I looked up to see how he took it. He was frowning. "Sorry." I murmured. "I don't suppose you want that to go in the report" he said, quietly. I couldn't help a blush of embarrassment. Then he grinned "even if it would be an accurate assessment of the situation. Don't let yourself be fooled by him, though. He's been around a long time and knows how to work the system. He can bury you if you give him a chance." I let out a breath I hadn't realized I'd been holding. "Let me think about it" he muttered. "You just put together a normal report as you would on any materiel shortage. Use the stock number on the boxes. Come to think about it you might add that the weapons don't fit the test gear. Nobody over here has to know that you would recognize the things. Considering the type item involved, I'd try to take my time to be sure I had all my, I's dotted and T's crossed. Handle it as Top Secret. In the meantime, when I get back to the office, I'll make a few calls. Don't let McLauren or the Colonel bully you into hurrying up. Hopefully, I can get you something definitive before the pressure gets too bad. No matter what, don't let anybody - and I mean anybody - get you in a box over this. I promise I'll get you some guidance by close of business tomorrow." I looked up and studied him really hard. He was asking me to put my neck in a noose if he screwed me over. Well, it wouldn't be the first time I'd been out on a limb. I nodded. He grinned, an almost boyish grin. "I won't let you down" he promised and strode off.

I had a lot to mull over on the way back over the mountain to Pirmasens. I had to accept the fact that Scarborough knew what she was talking about. The question was what to do now? Ass Hole Dawson would surely gum up the works. He wasn't about to stand his ground against McLauren, and MICOM wasn't going to acknowledge what was going on. Should we let sleeping dogs lie? This whole mess was the kind of thing that ruined careers - no matter what I did. If I went up against the boss I could get screwed good. My next performance report would put me in the toilet. If I didn't and the whole thing blew up, I'd have a choice of disavowing what I knew - and letting Joanne take the heat - or admitting I did know and didn't tell my boss. Shit!

By the time I got back to Headquarters, I'd decided that I had to live with myself. When I walked in the office door, Dawson was in a rage. "Hamlin!" he shouted. "What's that bitch down there think she's doing? That MICOM man is about to have a fit over the way she talked to him." Without thinking, I pointed out that her logic was impossible to refute. There had been no chance for those weapons to be expended in training. "God Damn It!" He roared, when I added that she said they weren't REDEYES but STINGERS. "Those are MICOM missiles. They know what they are and she needs to shut her mouth and let them take care of the problem!" I took a deep, calming breath. I wanted to say what I thought of how MICOM would "take care of it" - but I didn't. "Well, her report will be up here in a day or two and you can do

21

with it what you want." He looked at me, suspiciously. Apparently he decided against screaming at me further. "Yeah." he muttered. "I'll give that damned thing the attention it deserves." The thought flashed through my head, "I'm sure you will, ass hole." I was smart enough not to let the words get out of my mouth. "Well, I guess I better go and try to calm the Colonel down. Maybe now he'll realize I was right all along when I told him we didn't need that lesbian bitch over here." I resisted the urge to shake my head, instead waiting till he left the room before picking up the phone.

It was seven o'clock and it was already dark as only Germany can be on a December night. We were already going to work and coming home in the dark. I was just finishing up my plate of sauerbraten at the Forstmeister Gasthaus, in Kaiserslauten, when Arthur Montgomery leaned back in his chair and said, "OK, Isaac. I don't think you called me up after two years just to have a dinner with me. What's eating you?" I glanced around the place. We were the only people there, it being a bit early for the Germans to eat dinner - especially on a Wednesday night. In another hour the bar and the whole place would be packed. Keeping my face down as if fascinated by the remains of my sauerbraten, I asked "What do you know about a shipment of deliberately mismarked man portable, non type standardized, shoulder fired missiles being worked on in one of our depots?" I looked up in time to watch the storm cloud pass over his face. Finally, he growled, "Enough to know that you shouldn't be talking about such a thing - especially to me." "Well, I just thought," I said quietly "that somebody besides myself and three others should know that four of the damned things are missing, that a report to that effect is being prepared, and that a cover up of the whole thing is starting." He glared at me a moment then said, out loud "why don't you come over to my place for a beer. The nights still young yet."

An hour later, we were in his apartment which - he told me as soon as he'd closed the door - was swept for bugs daily. Sitting on his couch swilling a liter of Stuttgarter Hofbrau I gave him the story. "Son of a bitch" he muttered! "What a damned cluster fuck! You sure she knows the difference in those missiles?" I told him that, since I'd never seen one, I had to assume that she knew the difference. His frown deepened then with a deep breath, he continued. "Well, I guess I can take care of the MICOM end. How about your inspector down there?" I shrugged "she's good people. She's also, though, a tough broad. She won't get involved in a cover up even if it means her career." Then I added that I wouldn't stand for anything happening to her over this, either." Arthur raised an eyebrow. "You hot for the girl" he asked? "I could do worse. She could hold her own in a roomful of beautiful women. It's not her looks you see - it's something else. Maybe it's the way she holds herself - I'm not sure I'd describe her as beautiful but you can't miss her in a crowd." I chuckled, "but she works for me and her reputation has her with a temper to match that bright red hair - besides, I've seen no indication that she'd be interested in a pass." "But you'd like to make one?" "It'd be pretty unhandy due to the working situation." I temporized. "What's her clearance?"

"I went over her file before I left today. She's got a TSRD just like me, and her BI was redone just before she came over here." He mulled that over before muttering "well a Top Secret is pretty good and a Background Investigation for Restricted Data is almost as tight as for an SCI- which, by the way, we'll probably have to reinstate for you - and maybe have to get one for her too. Let me work on it. In the meantime, don't let her make that report." I thought it over. "Make sure she doesn't suffer and I'll do it. We've got another problem, though." "Yeah" he muttered, "Dawson. He sounds like he'd love to use this to get rid of her - even at the cost of flapping his jaws." Then he grinned. "What, you suppose he'd do if a priority requirement came down for a temporary GS 11 slot at Ramstein, came down?" I chuckled. "I'd say Fischbach would need a new Surveillance chief. One thing, though. I think Squatter would balk if it were a Safety Officer Slot. That has a bad - and deserved – reputation with the Air Force as a Career program dumping ground. It's gotten so bad that the Air Force has taken to checking out potential candidates with their own people and offering them a position without going through the Career Office. There's also the problem of replacing her at Fischbach. Ignoring the fact that she's the best branch chief we've got, we've got nobody else who knows anything about that missile except her." Arthur thought that over a moment.

"Well, what if we moved her up here to the Army Support Detachment at Ramstein?" "You gotta be kidding! Scarborough as a spook? She can't tell a lie worth a damn. Her face always gives her away." "Well, we need to get some control over this situation, what if we got rid of Dawson? " That caught me by surprise. "Can you clear it through our Career Office? He'd be an even bigger problem to replace. GS 13's take some special handling." He thought that over a bit longer. "What about promotions?" he asked. "If your man at COMZ was transferred, then Dawson could take his place. Are you in line for promotion?" I was in shock at the nonchalant way he talked about moving people around like chess pieces. "Damn it Arthur!" I muttered. "Before you start making plans for my career, I want to know what's going on." He leaned back in his chair and studied me, impassively. "Your SCI has just been reinstated. You do remember what happens if you don't play by the rules with Special Compartmented Information, don't you?"

Shit! Of course I knew. I managed to keep my mouth shut though. "That last job you did for us was handled pretty well. I even wanted you recruited but the powers thought you'd be more use to us if we left you where you were in case we needed you again. Looks like, for once, they were right. As to your question, I don't know. That's what Compartmented means. I was tasked to keep an eye out for irregularities in our supply system over here. Scarborough was also giving a cursory briefing on it since she was going to AWSCOM. Something funny is going on and everybody knows it. They just don't know what it is. US munitions and supplies are disappearing and we can't figure out how it's happening - now this. It sounds too coincidental to let pass. I'll try to get some guidance but, in the meantime, keep the lid on this problem." I didn't like the sound of all that and I guess it showed, because he added that he'd make sure that neither I nor "the girl" got stuck with "egg" on our faces.

As soon as I got home, I called Squatter and told her to hold up her report a day or so - and asked for a date.

CHAPTER 2

Saturday December 3 1966

I was a little nervous as I went to answer the door. One last glance in the mirror, said that I looked alright for the early Christmas party at the Pirmasens Officers club. About the only dressy things I'd brought over was my Alittle black dress" and it was the latest style here on the continent but was a bit short for my taste. I'd planned to do some shopping on the economy but hadn't gotten around to it yet. Also, I was a bit leery about a "date" with Hamlin. I'd hesitated, when he'd called last night, and asked for one - until he'd mentioned that he knew I had a "problem" with dating him - with emphasis on the word "problem" and a significant pause after it. I got the message. He had a reputation as a "lady's man." Word was that he'd been divorced once for running around on his wife with a flaky blond almost young enough to be a daughter and a second time from the flaky blond who decided that a young lover was preferable to an older one. Apparently, he'd been pretty torn up about both marriage failures and took the blame for both of them. Maybe he, actually, had a conscience - or maybe it was just hurt pride and a ploy to make him sound good to guys. Whatever it was, I wasn't sure I wanted to get involved with him - especially since he was one of my bosses. When I'd continued to hesitate, though, he'd said that we "needed to talk". It was about time. I'd thought. All I'd heard from him about the problem at the depot was to hold my report another day or so I'd agreed.

Now I took a deep breath and opened the door. He raised an eyebrow and said, "Hey! Not bad Squatter. You clean up real nice. There's gonna be some dirty looks from the wives this evening. They don't care much for having gorgeous broads working around their husbands." I didn't know whether to whack him or blush. I compromised, settling for, glaring at him and then, simply thanking him. When I picked up my coat from the chair, he took it and held it for me to put on. "I'm not sure this is such a good idea. The wives I don't worry about. I don't like the guys to get the wrong idea." I remarked. He chuckled. "You mean like you were sucking up to the boss?" "Something like that." "Well, it may get worse before it gets better," he said enigmatically. I raised an eyebrow at that - and watched his face become serious. "Later." he murmured.

He held the door of his Mercedes for me and I struggled to keep the hem of that damned skirt from riding up to the tops of my stockings as I got in. To cover my embarrassment when he got in, I said, "OK, Hamlin. What's this all about?" He glanced over at me, his eyes dropping ostentatiously to take in the length of exposed thighs before he answered. Then his answer had nothing to do with the question. "The only good thing about winter," he said, conversationally, "is that there are no bugs outside.A I shook my head in disgust. "What the hell -A then it dawned on me what he was saying. Startled, I blurted "you mean, you think this -." That was as far as I got before his finger pressed against my lips.

Joanne had sat, fuming, all the way from her apartment in the Army hospital complex at Muenchweiler to the Pirmasens O club. As soon as I opened the door, she got out - revealing a lot more of her extraordinarily legs in the process - and growled, "OK, now! What the hell's going on?" "Let's stretch our legs." I said, as I considered those legs in my mind. She was probably five four or five but over half of her was leg. Unable to cut off my thoughts I couldn't help adding, "If you're legs aren't too cold, that is." "Forget my legs" she grunted, scowling at me. She did let me take her hand and put it on my arm as we begin to walk down the sidewalk. "First," I said, with a grin, "No one will ever forget your legs" then added as her frown deepened,A - there's going to be a few changes around here - making my campaign for your favors more complicated." She bristled at that. "Ignoring your pitiful attempts so far, I presume, Dawson is going to get rid of me." I chuckled. "Yes and no. It's actually the other way round. Dawson doesn't know about it yet - probably Monday. It appears that Dawson and I both are going to be promoted. He'll still be my boss but he'll be over at Zweibruken. I got word this afternoon it's being cleared by the Career Office. He'll probably find out when he comes in on Monday. Don't know if he'll be pissed at not being able to harass you or happy to not have to put up with you. Probably, he'll just take it as recognition of his ineffable genius." She kept her angry eyes glued to mine as she thought that over.

"So I'll really be working for you?" "Nominally." I told her. "You'll still be working for the Surveillance division, but you're gonna have two bosses. The other is the head of The Surveillance Division at Ramstein." Her frown deepened. "Since when do we have -A "We're not the only Surveillance bunch in the services." I interrupted her. Her mouth dropped open. "You mean like cops or -A "Or spooks?" I

26

finished for her. Her frown reappeared. "Shit" she grunted. "Real spooks?" "Real as they get." I said. "It's the Chief of that Division you'll be working for but still be in the program and assigned as Chief of Surveillance at Fischbach but will get TDY orders to act as a munitions consultant to the Army Support Detachment at Ramstein. He's a good guy and a friend of mine." Her eyes kept boring into mine.

"So the scuttle butt is true. The word, when I came over here was that you were a spook" she said. I laughed. "A sort of pitiful excuse for one" I admitted. "I once did some business with them, strictly as a consultant. Mostly the extent of my cloak and dagger work was to spend a year in DC watching film of the various May Day Parades in Moscow and reading reports from Military Attaches. Then I'd write up an assessment of what the new weapons and munitions capabilities might be." That wasn't quite the extent of my labors but it'd do for now.

As we turned back toward the O club, my mind was working a mile a minute. I wondered what he'd done when he wasn't "mostly" working parades. I decided to let it go because I was also surprised to recognize a minor feeling of disappointment at the fact that I'd be working, directly for him. "Get over it Joanne!" I thought to myself. "No man is worth getting tangled up with - certainly not one with a past as checkered as this one." Just before we got to the entrance, I asked what this had to do with the Redeye shortages. He looked down at me with a frown. "Let's just say, for now, that your report shouldn't differ too significantly from whatever stupidity McLauren commits to paper." That really frosted my ass but I guess I could live with it. Obviously, something beyond my pay grade was going on, and I'd decided I could trust Hamlin - at least as far as the job went. "I take it I was right that those missiles are involved in a black operation." He shrugged. "Truthfully, I don't know - but, like you, I think that's a fair assessment." "So, for all normal things, I'll report to you and spooky things to him. Is that it?" He mulled that a bit as we neared the O club door. "I think -A he said, "that, for now, you'll probably report everything to me. I doubt Montgomery will want you contacting him too much. Once you're over there things will, no doubt change." "Montgomery?" I asked. He held the door closed a moment. "He's the chief of the Support Office in Ramstein, attached to the admin staff as I mentioned before" he murmured. "He has one division of investigators. It is called Surveillance also." I suppose they're the ones who wear the cloaks." As I took that all in, he continued. "You will have to meet him. He's arranging for a new security clearance for you and you'll have to be briefed about it. Won't be much different from the one you have now." "Like hell!" I thought. There were few clearances above Top Secret Restricted Data except for communicators and spooks. Talk time was over, though - at least for now. He was holding the O club door for me.

An hour later, I could see why he had a reputation with the ladies. He was the first man I'd met who actually devoted his entire attention to the woman he was with. People were constantly coming by the table to say hello and talk but he managed to never leave me out of the conversation and they seldom stayed longer than a few moments before he, somehow, managed to have them leave - usually with a speculative look that wondered if I belonged to him. I bristled a bit at that, at first, wondering if it was an acquired skill but it became obvious that, either he was the world's greatest liar or he really did enjoy listening to a woman. I found myself talking about things I'd never considered revealing to anyone other than, perhaps, my dearest friend, Margaret. Even when we were dancing - holding me so close, that I should have been uncomfortable - he talked but in a way that had me blabbing about my life like a school girl. Finally, again at the table sipping my third martini, I jacked him up about it. "Damn it, Hamlin! You've had me talking all night and haven't told me a thing about yourself." He grinned. "I thought we'd gotten past last names already." "It's your fault." I muttered, hating the stupid simper in my voice. "Your first word to me tonight was Squatter." He suddenly looked abashed. "Sorry about that" he grunted. Then after a moment, he said, "I, well, I still thought of you as the Chief of Fischbach Surveillance till - well - till I saw you in that dress. It was a hell of a shock." He lifted his eyes to mine and stared into them. "I guess, I was trying to hold onto the notion that you were just a - well - another inspector." I knew my face revealed my own shock at what he implied. "But -A I whispered. "But," he interrupted. "I wasn't prepared for a shock to my system hitting so suddenly." I knew I was gawking. To cover my embarrassment, I blurted, rather harshly, that I'd heard his system had been shocked twice before - then added that his seduction technique showed he didn't need any practice. It was obvious where his reputation came from. He leaned back in his chair, his eyes never leaving mine. "I admit that I've made some glaring mistakes. I hope I learned something from them. I screwed up my first marriage by letting my ego get in the
28

way of my good sense. As a result I ended up in a second one with a woman who was just like me. I hope I learned something from all that." A frown appeared on his face. "I want you, though, to - or would appreciate it if you would, tell me I'm wasting my time" he said softly. I started to do just that, but when I opened my mouth to tell him he was, I realized it'd be a lie. "For now at least." I muttered. Frowning deeper, he nodded.

Monday5 Dec 1966

      Monday morning at 1000 hours I was sitting in Montgomery's office at in the Admin building at Ramstein with a folder full of orders, mostly Temporary Duty papers. I had to keep jerking myself back to reality, as I remembered the good night kiss, I had gotten last night. It was a chaste enough kiss, barely a touching of our lips together - but it was enough to still send a little tingle through me, just remembering it. I forced myself back to the present as Montgomery started handing a badge across to me. "This one," he said, handing me the standard laminated access badge with a clip on it,Awill get you into anyplace in the area, including Zweibrucken, Kaiserslautern, and Ramstein. The main thing you'll need it for, right now, is the "Hot Pad" when you monitor the transfer of munitions shipments there. Your regular badge should suffice for anywhere else. We've got a new turn around shipment of Hercules warheads coming in. I'd like your take on the loading crew that Fischbach sends up. Might be a good idea to keep that" - motioning to the access badge – "tucked away till you need it." Then he handed me a black wallet. In it was an honest to God cop badge. "That's one you carry all the time and don't show it to anyone except for an emergency. If we need to use that one, it'll bring a lot more attention to you than is preferable. It, by the way, is a get out of jail free badge - almost as good as a black passport - so - careful with it. Never leave it unattended." He chuckled. "It's water proof but you don't have to shower with it."   "Where's your purse?" Surprised, I told him I never carried one at work. I used my pants pockets. "Well, you're going to have to start. You'll need a place to carry this" he said, solemnly as he opened a desk drawer and taking out an automatic, slid it across the desk along with two loaded magazines and both US military and German permits for it. I picked it up. It was a nine millimeter Baretta – a heavy one. Popping the magazine out I could see it was loaded. Pointing it at the floor, I wracked the slide. The chamber

29

was empty. When I looked up, he was watching me carefully. He nodded and said, "I don't think you have to carry all the time but, you'd better have it on you most of the time. Your records say you can shoot - Junior NRA champion for Texas with a pistol, and skeet gun. You, obviously, know how to handle a weapon. I don't suppose you've ever shot at anyone, though?" Flabbergasted, I shook my head. "Well, purses aren't the best place to carry - too hard to get the thing out. We can get you a shoulder rig but they're pretty uncomfortable - and, in the summer, kind of conspicuous. Might be a good idea to join the Post Gun Club - give you a chance to brush up on your skills without creating too much controversy. We can make sure your long time passion for weapons gets around. Any questions so far?"

"Yeah!" I grunted. "Just what the hell have I gotten into? I'm a damned Ammunition Inspector. I don't do Cloak and Dagger - also, why not one of the new light weight's? This thing would weigh down an elephant." He laughed out loud. "Welcome to the club, Miss Scarborough. I haven't worn my cloak or carried my dagger in years - only for dress up occasions." Turning serious, he continued. "If you'll check the rounds in those magazines, you'll find them unusual." I popped out one round and checked the head stamp. "British or Canadian." I muttered. "- and old as the hills." "Mark I British, circa 1940." he said. "Still, according to tests, good as new. Muzzle velocity of around twelve to thirteen hundred feet per second. Not as much stopping power as a good old .45 but a hell of a lot more than standard nine mil - also easier to carry and use. If you use that ammo in one of the new light weight automatics the slide'll blow off in your face. These have, at least, half again as much stopping power as the standard US load."

He shoved four boxes of Peters nine mil ammunition across at me. "Use these at the range. Some of those old gunners will recognize the difference in the sound those other ones make. You might have to fire a couple of rounds to get a feel for the difference in the recoil but try and do it when nobody is around too close.A He leaned back in his chair. "I don't really expect you to have to use that thing, but you've turned over an ant hill and the guys we're playing with, play rough. You're job will, for the most part, be nothing but what it appears. You're the only one we've got, though, that might notice little things that don't fit out there, when it comes to munitions situations. You should get to know the folks you work with, especially any odd habits. That shipment that got waylaid wasn't the first. We've lost a few

LAW's, Israeli Uzis and a bunch of grenades - that we know of and that nobody is willing to admit they are gone."

"Shit!" she muttered, her tone belying, the picture of her as I'd like her to be seen. Might as well get it over with. I knew what she was going to think of my ideas. "Probably wouldn't be a good idea to change your hair color but do you have any skirts? - preferably short ones?" I hadn't been wrong. She looked up, her eyes flashing fire. I held up my hand to stop the almost certain tirade. "There's a reason for my asking." I said. "Gorgeous blondes are expected to be dumb and that can be a real asset in your job. Since changing your hair doesn't seem a good idea, and I have it on good authority that you have great legs, a short skirt might just make up for the hair. Part of your job is to learn things that people don't tell to smart people. Besides, when dealing with a bunch of macho men, it's always a good idea to shock the hell out of them when you catch them screwing up and they find out you're not what they thought you were." I held my breath as the thunder cloud over her face grew darker and darker. After a long moment, though, it began to thin a bit.

"I've spent eight years trying to live down what I look like," she growled. "I don't like the idea of becoming a damned strumpet now - besides, a change like that at the depot would cause a hell of a stir." I managed to keep the grin off my face. She hadn't said she wouldn't." I took a deep breath. "You've played the part of a no nonsense field inspector as your job demanded for eight years - slacks at work and no purse. You've a reputation for cursing like a sailor and your nickname says it all. You've a new job now - a new part to play. As an upper level manager you might do well to try and become a bit more stylish. You don't have to - and you shouldn't change your habits when you're in the field. Could be, though, that, with your new job title, your off duty habits might also stand some modifications. The skirts could be a normal woman's response a promotion to an office or - to a man becoming interested in her. I could probably convince Hamlin to help out there. It was a suggestion to make your job easier - or, at least, more effective." "That reputation will be shot to hell if I agree to that. And what's this upper level manager bit?" she grunted. "Just think about it." I said. "It's not a job requirement. As for the other, Hamlin is going to need a deputy."

The blush that appeared made it appear that I hadn't been too wrong in my assessment of these two. When she continued to say nothing, I decided it was time to establish the truth. "OK Scarborough

31

there's one other thing. Our guys at home have been busy and they find a strong indication that you have had, what is best described, as - at least a fling - with homosexuality. The record says your lover was Margaret Connelly." I saw the color drain from her face and knew I'd struck home. Then she sat bolt upright and stared directly into my eyes. "I'm not a lesbian" she said coldly. "Not that I have a problem with that but Margaret is – and does. She is my best friend. I have not had an affair with her." Her back stiffened. "I'll admit to comforting her - twice - once when she was in pain over an affair gone bad I comforted her in the only way she needed it - and yes I didn't mind it at all. In fact, she comforted me the same way when I broke up with my fiancée. I needed it too. He had cursed me for being worthless sexually when I wouldn't sleep with him. He accused me of being Queer because of Margaret. If she needed me, though, I would do the same for her again if I had to. It's not my thing, though. I don't have much regard for men - most of them - but they're the only game in town." Her stare turned into a glare. "If that's going to screw up my security clearance then so be it. I'm damned though if I'll let you, or anyone else, put a dirty spin on it." Damn! I could really admire this woman. I hadn't missed her "most of them" remark, though. Could Hamlin be the lucky man? If so, neither of them seemed to recognize it yet. "Nothing you've told me goes in the record." I said, firmly. "As long as you don't go around telling others it's no business of mine or the organization - most of it. All the BI records show is a healthy relationship between you two. You do, though, have to be ready to explain yourself if it ever comes up. If you can't that leaves open the possibility of blackmail."

I thought about it, though, the rest of the afternoon as he filled me in on duties and briefed me on what he knew about the situation. I'd not been completely truthful with him. I'd be damned if I'd feel guilty about Margaret. We'd gone to a girl's school together and she gave me my first climax. I'd experimented with her lifestyle and had actually enjoyed her fondling and kisses. I learned how to please her and hadn't minded that. It just wasn't the way I was wired. Actually Montgomery pushing me to play at being a mindless bimbo bothered me more than my actions with Margaret. Hell! It was all I could do not to think about suffering the leering looks that a short dress always brought. I knew some girls liked those looks. I didn't. I'd gone out of my way, ever since junior high, to keep from drawing attention to my body - slacks, long skirts and bulky sweaters. I seldom had more than one decent dress for parties, a few sets of shorts and cropped tops for picnics and such and a damned bikini. I'd never have had those last things except for the fact that Ian had bought them for me. I'd always been embarrassed at how much he liked to show me off to his friends. He'd especially liked taking me to the beach so he could watch the other guys ogle me in that damned postage stamp bikini. I'd not worn the damned thing since we broke up. Now this SOB wanted me to again flaunt myself like a tramp. By sixteen hundred, though, my motivation had begun to overcome my scruples. Finally, Montgomery asked if I had any other questions or needed anything to help me settle in. I took a deep breath and muttered that if I had to get a new wardrobe I intended to consider it a uniform expense. He seemed surprised, leaning back to stare at me. "I'm impressed" he chuckled. "Let's see, a uniform allowance for your equivalent military pay grade would be - well - let's just say, put a thousand dollars on your expense voucher for - let's see - travel expenses. Send it directly to Hamlin under classified cover. I'll OK it." Irritated that I couldn't help blushing, I nodded and, gathering up all my newly acquired hardware, left.

I was bleary eyed the next morning. I'd not slept well, my mind wouldn't let go of the fact that I was to play a part that I'd spent my life trying to get away from. None the less, after a stop at American Express to buy a pocket full of Deutsche Marks, I drove into Kaiserslautern and headed for the biggest department store in town. In the ladies department, my college German earned me a young sales girl who couldn't be over thirteen years old - and who wanted to practice her English. After explaining that I needed some suits for work and remembering my problem with the O club last week, an evening gown and a "dressy" dress or two were needed. "Ones that wouldn't be out of place here in the city." I added, unable to actually say that the skirts should be short. The girl's eyes lit up. "Oh, but you're in the wrong department, Madam" she gushed, forgetting her English practice "Kommen Sie mit mir Fräulein bitte."

With that she led me to the "Junge Damen" department - at least that's what it sounded like she called it - adding "The Misses, department in the United States" she said. I wanted to protest that I was too old for "Misses" clothes, but held my tongue. I had to give the girl credit. Her eye for sizes was perfect. Too bad her taste ran to skirts that barely covered my butt. I was soon convinced that I should have been in the Frau department after all. Finally, though, she was convinced I was serious about covering my ass and, reluctantly, began to pull out

33

skirts that covered all but four or five inches of my thighs. I sighed, thinking that this probably wasn't what Montgomery had in mind but, it was what I could live with, so I let her sell me more damned girl clothes than I'd had in years - more clothes and less cloth, I thought, ruefully. I did manage to get a couple pair of nice slacks and jeans while she wasn't looking. In addition, she pulled out pairs of stockings that were now being produced for the "miniskirts" she'd shown me before. They were a lot longer than the ones I'd worn before. I decided on a half dozen pairs of them when I thought of those skirts I'd selected. I still thought of them as "mini" though the young sales girl assured me that they were much too long for the title. I also decided that for the new me, I needed a formal gown for O club parties. When it came to the evening gown, though, I put my foot down. I'd be damned if I'd wear something that left my back naked all the way to the crack of my ass. The one I finally, reluctantly, agreed on was not really one that I considered "decent." It was practically a second skin with a bodice that dipped alarmingly low in front. It, though, was only half backless and only to my waist. The skirt was slit and showed a lot more leg than I preferred but I could live with it - maybe, at home, I'd sew up a few inches of it. An errant thought flashed through my mind that Hamlin would like it. Shit that's all I needed - to let the thought of what a guy would like made my decision. Never the less, I took it.

Four hours later, I had made two trips to my car to stash my loot. Grimly, I hoped that Montgomery would be happy. I'd spent only a little over eight hundred dollars - a bit over thirty two hundred marks. I had to admit, though, to an unaccustomed - for me at least - pleasure at the thought of nice clothes. In the past, I had just thrown on whatever was easiest to grab before leaving home. I sighed as I drove back to Muenchweiler promising myself that I wasn't going to let myself get caught up in all that girly crap. Still musing on the changes in my life, I started to slow for the sharp downhill curve on the narrow road. When I touched the brake my foot went to the floor. The next few minutes were a frantic pulling of parking brake levers that didn't work, dodging oncoming cars that blared their horns at me as they dove for the side of the road and downshifting my two year old Porsche frantically. Amazingly, when I got the car to a stop in the weeds at the bottom of the hill, the car and I were still in one piece. As I sat shivering in reaction, one of the ever present German cops pulled up. He was frowning as he strolled up to my window, he asked, in German what was wrong. "I - Ich nich habe -" Shit what was the german for brakes.

My quirky school German was gone completely out the window. Bremse? Was that it? "Kine Bremse?" I got out. He frowned and opened the door. "Kommen bitta." I got out and he made a point of smelling my breath. Then he asked for my papers. I showed him my ID. Then he got in and pushed down on the brake pedal. He looked up at me. "You are very lucky" he said, haltingly. "I get - will get -A he paused then finished "tow wagon." He paused, on his way to his souped up VW and turned back with a smile. "vielleicht - Perhaps you - would – perhaps I call Americanish Kaserne?" I thanked him and told him that would be nice – I hoped.

An hour later I was riding in the cab of an Army wrecker on the way back to Ktown. I had thanked the German cop, profusely and when the wrecker arrived, he had, actually, saluted me before he left. I was surprised when we turned into the main gate. I had expected to have the car taken to the local Porsche Dealer. The driver, when I asked, about it, said, simply, "Orders, Ma'am." Hamlin was waiting at the motor pool when we got in. "You OK?" He asked, quietly. I told him that I was fine and he turned to the Motor Sergeant. "Tommy," he said, would you mind putting that up on the hoist and check out the brake\s for me?" I whispered to him that it wasn't imperative that we do this now. I could call Porsche. "Montgomery called as soon as the politizi reported the problem" he muttered back. "This'll get done here." Sure enough - a half hour later, the Motor Sergeant reported that the brake lines had been cut to both systems and the parking brake disconnected. He added that he had to call the CID. I sat there in shock as Hamlin turned to me, his face resembling a thunder cloud. "Looks like somebody had it in for you" he said.

"I hope there's a weapon in that purse." I was getting over the shock and hadn't heard Montgomery come up. I was damned, though, if I was going to break down and cry. Instead I was getting furious - at whoever did this but even more so at Montgomery's holier than thou attitude. I loved that little car. It had been my first real extravagance when I came in country. Even if it wasn't new, I'd grown really attached to its little growl when I downshifted. "I just got the damned thing yesterday and the purse today!" I growled. "I'll be damned if I was going to carry the fucking thing in my hand while I shopped. Also, it wouldn't have done any good to shoot the damned car! Now get off my back! I don't need a lecture right now!" I was surprised. He grinned. "Good. Then I won't give you one. I think a drink would be the best thing for you right now." He glanced, significantly at Isaac. "The O club won't open for an hour or so yet." I grumbled. "You got any at your place?" Isaac asked. I nodded, sullenly. He grinned wider. Then, why don't you get your packages out of that thing of yours and I'll take you home." I looked up at him. "You're taking a lot for granted." I growled. His damned grin remained in place. "Would you rather go to my place?"

An hour later we sat on her couch in Muenchweiller, our feet up on the coffee table. She was still frowning but when we'd come in the door, she'd gone to the fridge and gotten out a coke, dumped it in two glasses and added a respectable amount of Jamaican Rum and handed it to me. I noticed that her hands shook a little as she did. Finally, she said in a low voice, "Sorry to jump on you back there. I'm not used to - well this sort of thing." "You mean, somebody trying to kill you?" She nodded. "I just look at bullets and suffer through an occasional tongue lashing if I screw up." Then she added, defiantly "which I don't do very often." She took a deep breath and continued. "I guess I was also - well, a bit pissed at you to begin with." I chuckled at that. "What have I done now?" She looked up at me her eyes flashing angrily. She waved her arm at the pile of packages she'd thrown on the table."I don't like the idea of acting like a damned, prick tease to a bunch of Neanderthals - and if you laugh I'll kill you! Don't tell me you didn't put Montgomery up to that." I was a bit confused and told her so. "You didn't get him to push me to get a bunch of damned come leer at me' kind of clothes?" I managed to keep the laugh concealed. "No I didn't." I told her - but couldn't help adding "- You mean you don't like acting like a normal woman instead of the baddest gal on the block?" She looked, quickly, away but I detected a slight upturn of the corner of her mouth. "In this business, Hamlin, a woman has to be tougher than any of the men she works with or she doesn't get anywhere." I leaned over toward her. "On the other hand she'd better not forget she's a woman"

Damn it! I felt like I was pouting, of all the damned fool things to do. He was quiet a minute then said, "I assume Montgomery had a reason. As for being tough, you're, obviously, in a new business for a while at least - nodding to the packet I'd given him to store in his safe. In your new business, you have to be whatever the job calls for. You have to be tough - and at times, maybe even brutal. You also have to be, wary. Usually, your cover will give you some protection but you can never depend on it. Who, for instance, would think that a dumb blonde - or in your case, a red head, would be dangerous? I'll tell you who anybody who was a pro bad guy and valued his skin. In your case you are, obviously outed to somebody. Your cover will only help you with those who don't know. For the time being, you're going to have to get used to always be thinking about how somebody could kill you at this moment and what you would do if they tried?"

She sat frowning for a long time. Damn! Had I scared her so much she'd refuse to go along with Montgomery? Finally, though, she muttered. "You, apparently, have a lot more experience at this than you've let on. I'd better get some time over at the range." She looked up at me speculatively. "I suppose that shooting at a person is a lot different than shooting at a target." The slight shaking of her hands belied the calmness of her voice. "You don't shoot AT someone." I said, brutally. "You shoot them - not to wound them - to kill them. That means shooting for the center of mass – the chest. In critical situations even an expert marksman doesn't usually have time to be thinking about wounding. You only shoot when you have to but when you do it's almost always too late to worry about niceties." She shivered at the thought. I took a deep breath. "Look, Joanne. Chances are you'll never have to use that thing. I never have but I listened to an old Gunnery Sergeant scream that line at me over and over. I took it to heart. As for now, we've got another shipment coming in tomorrow at Ramstein. Montgomery's worried about it, though I can't see anybody crazy enough to try and hijack a shipment of Nukes. Why don't you take it? Then, afterwards you can slip over to the Ktown range." She looked over at me then nodded. I figured it was time for me to get out of there, so I got up and said so. If I'd only known how quickly my words would come back to haunt me I might have done something different.

I was surprised at how much I didn't want him to go. Surprised enough to realize it was a good idea. He hesitated at the door and I thought he was going to try and kiss me. I pulled back. He grinned then said "tomorrow might be a good day to begin playing the dumb redhead." Immediate anger! He laughed and held up his hands in surrender. I couldn't help a chuckle. "Get out of here you SOB!" I muttered, not quite able to work up a good frown.

STINGER
CHAPTER 3

Wednesday 7 Dec 1966

The next morning, I had an excuse not to cook - I'd get something at the Ramstein Air Force Base Snack Bar. It was pitch dark outside since I had an hour's drive to get there. I'd been surprised shortly after Hamlin left when a couple of GI's showed up with a jeep I could use until my Porsche was fixed. I studied my image in the mirror before I left and didn't much like what I saw. I looked like a tramp looking for a pickup. The skirt was too short. It left, what, to me, looked like, over a half foot of thigh showing above my knees. At least, it was sort of flowing, unlike most of the ones the sales girl foisted on me that were stretchy and tight. The blouse was too thin, hinting at the shadow of my bra beneath it - I should have bought some slips while I was at it - and I hated wearing makeup to work. At least, the suit coat would cover the blouse, except in the offices where they always kept the temperature too high. I grudgingly admitted, though, that, for an old broad of thirty three, I didn't look bad. The only saving grace today was that for the rest of the winter my long coat would cover me pretty well outside - except that today was unusual for a German winter. It was warm. Today, my job was monitoring the Hot Pad. We had a shipment of Nukes coming in. They would be replacing out of date Nike Hercules warhead sections that would be taken off their missiles this coming week. It was a periodic replacement operation as warhead sections components reached the end of their shelf life. A team from Fischback would be off loading these. That was going to be embarrassing since I, was going to know them all. I was going to have to take a lot of guff about my bare - well they might as well be bare with these sheer stockings - legs hanging out from beneath my skirt.

After suffering the looks from the airmen in the snack bar, I was disgusted with myself by the time I walked into the "Support Detachment" office and hung my coat on the coat rack. Peggy Kraditch, the receptionist, looked up as I came in and let her mouth drop open. "Heili - Shitzen!" Already fuming, I gave her my most disgusted look. "I am sorry Miss Scarborough," she said, almost as embarrassed as I felt. "I was - well - just surprised. "You look - well beautiful." "Like a tart, you mean." I muttered. She grinned. "Oh no - like I wish I looked when I was dressed for work." I couldn't decide if she was being sarcastic so I just asked if Montgomery was in. She nodded and told me to go on in.

"Well, Scarborough," he said as he looked up, a twinkle in his eye. "You clean up real nice." I wasn't sure I wanted to hear that remark again and frowned. "Ted told me you'd be coming up today. Sit down. We've got a few things to go over." "As if you didn't know." I thought to myself. I couldn't help a growl as I dropped into the upholstered chair - remembering, at the last minute I was going to have to be more careful how I sat in this skirt. "Can it, Sir!" I muttered as I tried, unobtrusively to pull the hem down. "Can I assume this is what you had in mind?" "You exceed my expectations," he said with a chuckle. Then he turned solemn. "I assume you hate it but at the risk being charged with sexual harassment, I've got to say that you're a hell of a good looking woman." The compliment almost wiped the frown off my face, but I managed to hold it. "Well, I never thought I'd see the day that I enjoyed cold weather but, I'd like to be wearing a coat on the Hot Pad today." "Come on, Squatter," he chuckled. "You don't have to flirt with those guys out there. Hell! I bet you don't even know how to bat your eyelashes. Let yourself go for a change. You might enjoy acting like a normal woman instead of a hard ass." Then he turned serious again looking, pointedly at my hand bag. "May I assume that your purse is heavy?" "Enough so that I'll set off any sensors I run across." I muttered. "That badge I gave you shows you as a member of the Security branch. It's not so different from a normal one that you have to keep it covered" he said. "If you have to go through a metal detector, simply let it show and hand your purse to the attendant. It won't go through with you."

"I hadn't realized that "Army Support" was considered part of the Security detail base." I said. He shrugged. "Normally, we aren't but here it's a little different." He pulled a folder out of his desk. "Now the plane isn't due in until zero 900. According to route control he's pretty much on time - maybe a half hour late. But you'll have plenty of time to get out to the pad because the tower will notify us when he contacts approach control. It shouldn't take more than a half hour to get there. The Fischbach crew is standing by in the Snack Bar so you'll be right behind them when they leave." I told him I'd seen them there. I didn't tell him what I thought of the looks they gave me. He grinned. "Dawson ordered Hamlin up here to keep an eye on that broad.' I suspect that the shit's rolling back uphill for a change. Probably be the last time he's able to get out of the office. I hear that Dawson is getting booted upstairs to COMZ"

I couldn't help grinning at that. "I don't suppose you knew anything about how that happened." I said. He laughed. "Come on Squatter. Big time transfers are way above my pay grade." It wasn't polite to ask what a Colonel's pay grade was but I was becoming convinced that, for him, manipulating transfers for GS14's wasn't much harder than for GS11's. I did have a question, though. "Before we go farther, I'd like to know who I'm working for, CIA, NSA - who?" He studied me a minute, frowning. "For now, let's just say you're not far off. I work for the army just like you do. My present boss is the DA Inspector General Brigadier Norman Morrison. Now, before you go out to the pad," he said, changing the subject while pulling out a folder from a desk drawer. "We've got some things to go over. First, your car wasn't just sabotaged. It was done expertly - if a bit stupidly. Whoever did it wasn't too worried about people finding out about it." They used parachute shroud cutters on the brake lines and activated them remotely. They probably followed you back and cut the lines just before you had came to that hill. Interestingly enough, they could have used a much more direct approach if they'd wanted to - one more likely to make certain of the result. The question is why didn't they?"

I had wondered about that all night, myself. I voiced the theory I'd come up with. "Maybe they didn't care if they actually killed me. Maybe they just wanted to send a message." He raised an eyebrow at that. "And just why would they do that?" "Because they thought I was just another silly woman who'd be easily intimidated. That might imply -" I added "that they were Neanderthals - some African and European thugs might still think that way. Arab or South American ones though, are more likely to think of women as little more than decoration. Either way, it doesn't suggest a pro did it." "Obviously, I'll have to stop thinking about you as decoration" he grinned. Then he added with a smirk "your appearance this morning not withstanding." Irritated, I growled "anything else? If not, I'm going to work." "Yeah" he chuckled, obviously enjoying baiting me. He passed the folder across the desk to me. It contained a report on my car plus fairly extensive dossiers on a second Lieutenant and ten enlisted men from Fischbach. It was titled "Load crew" with today's date. "I've been checking records and one of the guys on the loading detail has a secondary MOS as a parachute rigger. Be kind of stupid of him to call attention to himself by using a line cutter on your car, but maybe he's just that stupid. Anyway, watch him - might even make a point of it - maybe get him a little nervous. He's the crew chief, Staff Sergeant Sullivan." I knew Sullivan. He fits the category of Neanderthal. Lieutenant Meyers was a brand new shave tail Second Lieutenant, only a few months out of OCS. He was green as grass and it was inconceivable that he could be involved in munitions thefts - except, perhaps as a sacrificial lamb. I passed the folder back and got up. "Careful out there, Squatter." Montgomery muttered. "Don't let em drop a big bomb on you. Also, there's a practice alert today. Be sure you've got your badge where those Air Police can see it." I just nodded as I closed the office door.

It was an atypical December day at Ramstein Air Force Base. Of course, being warm near the ground meant above normal temperatures. Apparently it was cooler higher up because we had fog. It also meant, though that I had to leave my overcoat in the office or look stupid - or more stupid than I did in this damned "look at me" suit. The tower weather kept saying two mile visibility but it didn't look like it from where I stood watching the C123 move slowly off the taxiway onto the hot pad. Its approach had not been visible at all until it got to the end of the runway. Idly, I noticed that one engine was barely turning over. Off to the left about fifty feet was a fighter sitting, on another concrete hard stand. The pilot was in the cockpit and a power unit beside it had an airman sitting atop it reading a magazine. Obviously ready to fly, I assumed it was the alert aircraft. I, without thinking, nodded approval to no one in particular as the 123 came to a stop and one of the unloading crew attached a grounding strap to it. "With you here, Joanne, I could go home." I jumped at the sound of Hamlin's voice in my ear. Trying for nonchalance, I turned around. "I heard they were sending in the Big Guns for this shipment. Are congratulations in order?" I asked. He shrugged. "When my chief down at Fischbach caused such a stir, we got shorthanded in a hurry. Then, with other turnover's I was all that was left in more ways than one." With that we both turned to watch the elevator come down from the belly of the plane.

An hour later, the four old warhead sections were on the plane and the new replacements on the flat bed truck that would take them to Fischbach. The load master had spent the whole hour urging the crew to move faster. Must be in a hurry to go somewhere, I mused. Heavy wood framing was going down on the truck replacing that which had secured the old section containers for transit I had nothing to do until they finished and I had to sign the DD Form 626 Inspection Certificates

42

so they could go on the highway. So, while Hamlin watched over that operation, curiosity got the better of me. I strolled over to the F102 Interceptor and asked the airman on the power unit what was going down. "Well, Ma'am," he said with a grin, boldly looking down at the expanse of thighs exposed by my short skirt. I refused to acknowledge his attention. He shrugged. "When the horn sounds, this plane has to be in the air in less than one minute." That caught me by surprise. I looked back at the truck and the C123 whose pilot was already cranking the engines even though the Elevator still moving up into the plane. The airman beside me chuckled. "Don't look like that bird's got all its go power working. That flyboy doesn't want to get grounded here at Ramstein, I bet. Probably wants to get over to Frankfort to fix that engine." I asked him what he meant. He laughed again. "Didn't you notice, when he came in that one engine was barely ticking over. That model plane's notorious for shedding engines. Hell! We've got seven of them sitting on the tarmac now waiting for replacement motors to be flown over from the states. If he can get to Frankfort he can spend a month of R and R in a great town instead of being stuck here in Landstuhl. I had to chuckle at that and headed back to where Hamlin was standing talking to SFC Sullivan while the load crew tugged a fifty foot tarp over the warhead section containers. While I tried to act intimidating - with little result, I told them what I'd learned and he laughed.

Then I heard it - a raising whine of the base siren. "Oh Shit!" I muttered. Sullivan and Hamlin gaped at the Airman, jumping down off the power unit and beginning to start it. Sullivan took off at a dead run to the fighter. Hamlin turned to the load crew and screamed for them to get the tarp down and secured over the warheads on the truck. They began to scramble to get the huge tarp over the load as I turned back to the fighter. Sullivan was standing beside the plane screaming at a totally unimpressed pilot as the engine began to turn over. A second later the Airman grabbed him and hauled him bodily away from in front of the jet intake as the engine whine changed into a rising roar. Sullivan headed for the outside base phone booth while I, seeing the tail of the plane begin to turn in our direction, started running for the trailer. I heard Hamlin scream, "Let go of that damned tarp" as I dove behind the wheels of the Truck Cab. A second later, Hamlin dove in with me. Five other GI's piled in beside us. I wrenched my head around. Where were the other two? " A second after that, the roar of the jet engine rose to a crescendo as it seemed to fill the entire world. A blast of heated air poured around the truck. I was so busy trying to get those huge tires between me and that tornado I didn't have time to even be embarrassed by my skirt whirling up around my head.

As I tried, vainly, to grab my hat that flew off toward the open field and pull my skirt down, I cursed Montgomery and his ideas. Just then I caught a glimpse of something overhead. I looked up in time to see that tarp, billowing like a sail flying up into the air. The Jet exhaust was sending it like a parasail over the truck and into the air at least twenty feet high. Appalled, I watched two men hanging onto the tie down ropes flying with it. Forgetting my hat and skirt, I watched in horror as they flew out into the open field and dropped with the deflating tarp, into the mud. The roar of the fighter began to recede as his exhaust moved away from us and he began a fast taxi onto the runway. Seconds later his after burner sounded like a bomb going off and I got a glimpse of the plane rocketing down the runway. I and Hamlin headed, at a dead run, for the two men sprawled in the field, ignoring the fact that the clinging mud immediately jerked the new pumps off my feet. Stupidly, I thought to myself that I was going to ruin a brand new pair of nylons. By the time Hamlin and I had reached the men, both were sitting up staring, in shock at the tarp. The first one muttered in disgust, "Shit! It's gonna take all day to clean that fucking thing." Neither man seemed to be hurt so I couldn't help a hysterical laugh. The man looked up at me. "Sorry Ma'am, but that's a hell of a lot of work." Hamlin asked if they were alright. They looked at one another and nodded. Then they both broke out in a grin. "Bet they could make a fortune with a ride like that at Disneyland" the first one chuckled.

After the convoy had gotten on the road, and I had dug my shoes out of the mud, Hamlin and I headed for the Army Liaison office. An Air Policeman had showed up and told us that we were wanted there as soon as we could get there. I told him it'd have to wait. I'd taken time out to go to the bathroom, strip off my ripped nylons and clean my legs and shoes as best I could. As a result, I came in the middle of Hamlin's diatribe to the young Liaison officer. About that time, Montgomery came in introducing himself as if he'd never met either of us before. After the formalities, he said, "Ms. Scarborough, you and Mister Hamlin have to make a report on the incident at the Hot Pad." Better make it a detailed one. The commander of the squadron that plane belongs to is the son of a World War II fighter ace and he is

44

complaining that your crew got in the way of a quick response alert." Then with a grin, as the young lieutenant snuck out of the office, he added in an undertone, "Squatter, you don't have to include the fact that you showed off your underwear to half the base. The word is that you wore black bikinis today." "Screw you, Montgomery!" I muttered. He laughed. "Your cohort, here, also tells me you've got a terrific pair of legs. I never have any luck at all." I fumed as I felt the blush cover my face. Then he got serious. "Did you see anything in the operation that might help our problem?"

I took a deep breath. "Only that Sullivan is the dumbest ass hole I've ever seen. He damn near got himself sucked into a jet intake out there. That shit head's too dumb for anybody to trust him to steal for them. As for my report -" "Temper, Temper, Joanne" I thought to myself. "Well, I don't suppose you want me to say exactly what I'd like to do to that sky jockey. He deliberately turned that tail pipe on us when he didn't have to before he gunned that engine at a truck load of nukes. Those two dumb GI's could have been killed." Montgomery looked a little embarrassed. "The Air Force, Scarborough, is like any other outfit. They'll take up for their own. They'll explain how important it is to react to a war scenario and that mistakes may happen – and in this case it was an Army mistake." He held up a hand when I wanted to tell him what I thought of that." "We're not likely to get even a Letter of Admonition for the pilot. Colonel Schults though, is a hero's son. He's untouchable. Anything else?"

I thought about it a minute. "Well, they wouldn't be able to ignore a Nuclear Incident Report," I said. "Also, it's none of my business, but I'd also bet money that one of the engines on that 123 wasn't running when he left to take off." Montgomery chuckled. "You know an NIR might get you laughed out of the country." I shrugged. "It fits the criteria Gross negligence with a Nuclear Weapon. Not likely anything will come of it but it won't just be buried. It and the base commander's explanation will have to go to DC." He laughed. "You're a trouble maker, Scarborough." Then he added "you're right about the plane. The tower noticed, the engine, when the fog cleared a little. He got to the runway but then he was ordered back. He's now parked with the rest of those unflyables." Just then Hamlin spoke up. "Joanne, I think I remember a tasking for Fischbach to Palletize those Redeyes." I shrugged. "Yeah. We did that a few days after we got them." He frowned. "And how much do the things weigh?" I didn't know exactly, but gave him an estimate of twenty five pounds or so for two missiles and fifteen or so for the gripstock that was packaged with them. "So the empty containers would be forty odd pounds lighter than the others." I saw what he was getting at. "Son of a bitch! So they had to be stolen at Fischbach or by the crew who unloaded the plane and palletized the weapons." I muttered. "Whoa." Montgomery muttered. "You lost me." I explained. "After they were palletized, it'd be hard to open the containers without cutting the banding. That would be noticed. − it's one of the checks made when we pulled samples for inspection. And any boxes that were light by forty pounds should have been noted by somebody at the time they were put on the pallets. My crew noticed as soon as they lifted the box. They immediately checked to see that the seals had been intact - they had been. After the things are palletized, being light eighty or so pounds on a one ton pallet wouldn't be noticed and, from then on, only the Surveillance crew ever handles single containers until they're shipped. Even we wouldn't have, normally, pulled a sample out of the pallet if the samples we'd set aside had passed that test." "So," Montgomery mused. "You're saying that the things were deliberately stolen before they were put on a pallet and the seals replaced by the load crew, or your crew lied." I shrugged again, considering another problem.

"Come to think of it, I wonder who knew we were going to pull maintenance to remove the IFF on those things. If they didn't they might have thought that nobody would notice the problem until they were shipped out. You know," I muttered thinking on the problem. "Those things wouldn't fit in a small car - even a staff car. They're over five feet long - too long to fit in a trunk and the gates of the depot have lights that shine inside cars going through the gate. It's unlikely that somebody would have the balls to hope the guards wouldn't notice a bunch of rockets lying in the seat. A guard stands where he can see inside the cars as they leave post - even at quitting time. They're not the most alert guards in the world but they're there. The missiles had to go out in a truck between the time they arrived and the time they were palletized. If they'd been removed in storage the box seals wouldn't match." "Unless they're still on post - unlikely but possible." Hamlin said.

After we'd both filed Nuclear Incident Reports - the Liaison Officer had been horrified when we'd insisted on doing that, contending that the weapons were never in jeopardy. We insisted that they had been, though it was quite a stretch considering the steel containers they had been in. Probably, we'd get a blast for overreacting but not before half Ramstein AFB had gotten one too. As we left the office, Isaac asked what kind of wheels I had. I told him I'd checked out a jeep. My Porsche was supposed to be fixed today in Ktown motor pool. I was going to drop the jeep off and take it home. He nodded and, muttering to "Take Care," left me. I headed for the base pistol range.

December 8 Wednesday

As I slipped behind the wheel of my trusty Jeep, I reflected on the fact that it had been a pretty good day. The shipment and its aftermath had been scary but ended up - well, interesting to say the least. It had been scary because I'd never been up close and personal with the blast from a jet engine before, had never seen men thrown through the air like rag dolls, and had made a report that could come back to bite me in the ass just because I was mad - and interesting for all the same reasons. On the Ramstein pistol range, I found that I hadn't lost much of my ability with a pistol. By the time I'd burned the second box of shells, I was maybe half way back to my form of twenty years ago. I'd not win any new medals with today's effort but it was as good as it would get without daily practice. The first box of shells I burned was all over the place but most rounds were inside the first ring. I was finally able to impress the range NCO though with the second. I chuckled, remembering the way his face dropped when I put fourteen of fourteen rounds in the bull − barely in a couple of shots but in the bulls eye none the less, on my last set. Of course, it was obvious that he hadn't expected much out of the tart in the mini skirt so he was easy to impress. His head had jerked up, though when I fired those two rounds of Montgomery's ammunition. He was right. The damned things caused a noticeable increase in recoil and noise. Still it felt good to impress an old Top Sergeant. The last few days I'd felt as if I were in a different world from the nice comfortable one I was used to. It had been fun to enjoy the trip back to Ktown. I'd forgotten just how responsive - and, at the speed I was running - how dangerous the new jeeps were. The raw power of their little engine gave them a low speed acceleration that would probably leave my sports car in the dust for the first hundred or so yards. I was impressed by the fact that you could wind the speedometer needle off the dials eighty mile an hour top end. You just had to remember just how sensitive the new suspension could be, though. The slightest mistake could be dangerous and allowing a wheel to get off the pavement at high speed almost guaranteed a funeral.

Back at Ktown Motor Pool, Sgt McMann assured me that they'd kept close tabs on the Porsche but that I should watch myself. He suggested I always park where the thing could be watched. On the road back to Muenchweiler, I wondered how I was going to be able to do that. At the depot, I could park in front of Headquarters but at home, I had just another diagonal parking place in front of the building. I sighed, at the thought of having to remember every morning to check under the hood and pump the brakes.

9 December Thursday

The next morning after an uneventful trip over the mountain to Fischbach, I parked at the Admin Office and went in to check my mail. The Company Clerk told me there would be a staff meeting at 0900 so I hurried out to the Surveillance Office to make sure the day's work had begun properly and check on happenings here yesterday. My four inspectors assured me that nothing new had gone on except that more interest seemed to be building on the Redeye shortages. With a twinkle in her eye, Robin remarked that McLauren seemed to be "a bit upset about something." At that I guessed the reason for the staff meeting. I made sure to pack up my notes on the subject along with my revised draft of my report. On second thought, I added the original report to my folder. Then I headed back to the staff meeting, noting, as I did, that the sun was finally coming up. I wasn't sure I could spend my life in a place so far north that we got only six or seven hours of sunlight on a winter day.

Once begun, the staff meeting was uneventful - except for the glaring absence of McLauren and the equally glaring omission of any mention of the Redeye project. We had six truck loads of munitions coming in today from Bremerhaven and Christmas trees could be cut starting tomorrow, but, by order of the Forstmeister only from the tops of magazines. As we all got up to leave, the major added "by the way Ms. Scarborough, could you stay a few moment?" Uh Oh! I thought. Here it comes.

When all had left and I had resumed my seat, Compton looked me over a moment. "Scuttlebutt has it" he said with a straight face, "that you put on quite a show yesterday." Embarrassed and a little miffed as well as glad I had resumed my usual slacks and shirt today, I retorted, that it hadn't been as good as the one that fighter jockey had put on. He nodded then grinned. "None the less, I just wish I'd been there to see it all." His grin was infectious and I did really like Compton. A bit of a flirt but he was a straight shooter and his wife knew about his flirting and didn't mind. She was sure to know that he never went beyond a little fun. Of course, like any military officer, he was careful to keep his "fun" strictly for the civilian staff. "Well," I

50

grinned, "you wouldn't have seen it all but a lot more than I was happy with." He laughed - then turned serious. "Sorry. I didn't ask you to stay just to tease you. I'm interested in the Redeye project." I looked him over carefully, trying to gauge how much to tell him. Finally, with a sigh, I asked if he wanted the official version or the real one. "I presume I'll be able to read the official one" he said. "Just give me a rundown on the real one and why it won't be the official one." I just handed him the draft that was to be suppressed.

"Well," he said after reading the report, "I don't much like your conclusion that the weapons went missing here on post, but I can't fault your logic. Otherwise, MICOM's desires not withstanding I presume there is a reason, for not forwarding this report." I just nodded. He frowned. "One you're not willing to divulge," he said. "Not able to." I told him. He nodded and continued, "I also notice that you refer to the weapons as Man Portable Surface to Air Missiles. Knowing your style of writing, may I assume that you didn't give them their ordinary name for a reason?" Damn! I'd hoped he wouldn't notice that. Noting my hesitation, he said, "Perhaps that's another question you'd rather not answer?" I just thanked him. Then he asked for the draft of the "official" report. I handed it to him and sat back as he read it. When he looked up, he said, "Well, MICOM should be happy with this one. In fact, almost everybody in the chain of command should be - with the possible exception of the author." I kept my mouth shut. He chuckled. "Remember? I was there when you teed off on McLauren the other day. You can't be happy to submit this piece of shit." I couldn't help a blush. "Perhaps," he mused, leaning back in his chair and staring at the ceiling, "it has to do with the rumors of a couple of meetings at Kaiserslautern over the last couple of days and some unfortunate damage to a civilian automobile. Of course," he continued, not looking at me. "A simple Ordnance Company Commander wouldn't be expected to know about that sort of thing. Well, no matter" he said leaning back with his elbows on his desk. "I just want you to know, Ms. Scarborough, that, at the behest of a friend, I was asked, and will be happy, to help out in an emergency. If any further problems arise, feel free to call on me any time you think I can be of help - no questions asked."

What an extraordinary offer from a military officer, I thought as I went back to the office. I wondered just who the "friend" was. It had to be either Hamlin or Montgomery.

51

There was nobody in the Surveillance office when I got there. Probably, Robin was at the holding road. I'd heard the sounds of trucks arriving as I left the main post. George was, no doubt, back in the missile inspection bay and Howard, was, I hoped, out with the Magazine Inspection crew. I knew where Harry was. I'd seen him heading for the Weapons Assembly Building as I came back. No doubt he was in the middle of a receipt inspection on those warhead sections we'd received yesterday. I didn't envy him his job. Those Warrant's over at Assembly had no use for Civilians messing around with their big boomers. An Inspector was allowed in the building only on grudging sufferance - look but don't touch. Well, I guess I can't blame them. We don't much like Army Warrant Officers playing with our toys in the stateside depots either. Actually, I felt a bit sorry for them because of that. Nuclear Warrant Officers don't have much of any place to go except Korea and Germany because the work in the States is always done by civilians. As a result, they spend almost their entire careers rotating in or out of one or the other place - four years in Germany and one in Korea with a stateside staff job for a year or so sandwiched in between. Hell! One couple, in my building in Muenchweiler has twin girls who are more at home in Germany than the US. They were born here and have spent twelve of their seventeen years over here. They speak German like natives and are seriously talking, much to their parent's dismay, of staying here when they turn eighteen. It was probably just another case of teenagers pulling their parents chain but one guaranteed to be successful because, as far as the Germans were concerned, since they were born here they were citizens already - and always would be no matter that the US didn't exactly recognize the fact.

I spent the morning catching up on the never ending paperwork that didn't seem to have recognized that I had more important things to do. When the crew came in for lunch, I held an impromptu meeting to discuss the missing weapons. I wanted them all to be on the alert for anything strange that they noticed and to try and think of all the ways somebody could have swiped the weapons and or gotten them off post. I also warned them to keep their investigations low key since MICOM seemed unwilling to make a fuss. That afternoon, I made a swing around the depot looking for places that could be used to hide the things. It was a task unlikely to bear fruit since the whole depot, not used for military purposes was heavily wooded - actually part of a national forest. To complicate matters, the entire western fence actually ran along the French/German border. Even if we were willing to admit, publicly, the loss, it was unlikely that French cooperation would help much. For the same reason, I couldn't ask the local Forstmeister about anything suspicious he might have seen. I did manage to check out a couple of old WWII underground storage bunkers on the post but both were empty. I didn't bother with the large one near Headquarters. I knew it was full to within a couple of feet of the trapdoor with water.

I spent an hour in the inspection bay with George re-acquainting myself with the weapons in question. Idly, and I hoped, unobtrusively, I managed to get a measurement of the thing - an inch over five feet - and check over the operation to demount the IFF components. Finally, when George began to fidget I figured that he was fed up with direct supervision. I remembered how irritated I used to get when the boss stood over my shoulder. I left. On a hunch, before I left for the day, I stopped by the motor pool and had a look at the off post, trip ticket sign out logs for the last few days. If those things had gone off post, it almost had to be in an army truck. A panel truck, covered five quarter or deuce and a half probably. There were fifteen entries. How could I figure out which one might be one of interest? After all, they could have gone out in the mail truck - three entries, the mess truck - two entries or any of the other ten. I made notes of the entries and stopped by the guard shacks at the two depot entrances to determine the actual departure time for the vehicles. Then I left for home.

On the way, I considered the problem of the trucks. It didn't seem likely that if a thief was working here, he'd want too many others involved. If he were alone, he must have made sure he had a fool proof way to get the things off post. That meant he had to drive the truck. Of the fifteen entries, the mail and mess trucks and four others had only one name beside them. I pulled into my parking place at home, still mulling over the names. It seemed like a long shot, probably not worth a lot of effort - but something about that list seemed off to me. Inside, I kicked off my shoes and getting a beer out of the refrigerator, sat back on the couch to go over the lists again. With my feet up on the coffee table, I checked over what I knew about the men listed - Nothing. I wondered, idly, what I was going to fix for supper as I laid all three lists out on the table. Then it hit me. The departure lists! Fourteen of the trucks left post within a few minutes after being signed out. The longest time between checkout and departure was less than ten minutes.

One, however, A Ford Panel, number US1409, left the motor

pool on the day before palletizing of the Redeye's was to begin It was date stamped 1608 hours but departed, not from the gate nearest the motor pool but from the munitions area gate at 1715, an hour and seven minutes later. It had an overnight trip ticket and was driven by Sergeant First Class Ferguson, the Ammo Storage Sergeant. The purpose was to "pick up administrative supplies from Kaiserslautern." Under justification was a 0800 hour requirement for pickup the next morning. Why, I asked myself, was an SFC going to pick up paper and pencils and why was it so important that an army truck would be kept out overnight to make a 0800 hour date? I didn't have the return logs but when he came back wasn't as important, right now, as when he left. I picked up the phone to call Hamlin. Then stopped. Montgomery's warning came back to me. Could my phone be bugged? Also why was I calling Hamlin instead of Montgomery? Well, he'd told me to pass information through him.

I grinned, ruefully to myself. Face it Joanne. You keep on thinking about that man. I gave it some thought then dialed his number. When he answered, I said "where are you Hamlin? I thought we had a date for dinner tonight." I grinned at the likely confused look on his face. You Gotta give him credit though. After only a short pause, he cried, "My God! Is it that time already? Then he apologized profusely and promised to be here right away. "Better hurry up." I growled, trying for a disgusted voice as I grinned to myself - might as well get a decent meal out of this. "I didn't get myself in a damned cocktail dress for nothing." There was another pause. "Sorry, honey" he finally got out. "I'll be right there." I bristled a bit at the "honey" part but I'd started it all.

I wondered what the hell was going on. I didn't have any allusions that Joanne had just called me up for a real date - and what was that about a cocktail dress? Well, I'd find out in a few minutes as I pulled into the Hospital Compound at Muenchweiler. I glanced at my watch. Not too bad for having to jump out of my jogging suit and into a suit and tie - twenty minutes. Considering it was seven miles from my place to here, it was damned good. I finished straightening my tie as I climbed the stair to her second floor apartment and knocked on the door. I caught my breath when she opened the door. Damn! That black outfit she wore the other night was sexy as hell. This yellow one made it look like a maiden aunt's get up. The skirt was several inches shorter and the expanse of woman above the neckline was breathtaking.

"You've never seen a woman before, Hamlin?" she asked,

quietly. I raised my eyes from where I'd been staring. Her eyes were twinkling with laughter. "Never one with a nickname like squatter who looked like that" I got out. Then I added that I hoped she had a coat. She grinned and handed me a fancy black one. As she turned, I admired the expanse of naked back before I put it over her shoulders and let her slip her arms into it. One thing was for sure. There was no way to wear a bra under that thing. She picked up her purse and when she'd shut the door, I took her arm and we headed out. "I suppose you're going to tell me what this is all about." I muttered to her as we went down stairs. "You mean besides getting a handsome man to take me out to a fancy dinner, Hamlin?" Her voice had suppressed laughter in it. "You keep calling me Hamlin," I grunted, "and I'll go back to calling you Squatter." She looked up at me and laughed as I held the Mercedes's door for her. "OK, Isaac when we get someplace safe," she whispered.

When he'd gone around and gotten into the car, he told me that the car was safe. He'd had it debugged just today. Then he told me to "give." Feeling playful in this tart getup, I told him that if I told him now I might not get a free meal. He laughed at that. "Honey," he said, bringing another feeling of irritation from me, "the way you look tonight, I'm not about to pass up the opportunity to slobber over you like a dog in heat." The remark brought a surprising bit of warmth to me - along with a shiver of misgiving. Did I really want to get mixed up with another man so he could cause me so much grief again? There was no Margaret over here to run to. Well, it seemed my hormones had gotten over Ian, if my mind hadn't. I left that remark to dangle between us, like a snake ready to strike, and told him what I'd found. "I was afraid to call Montgomery from the apartment." I finished. "I hoped from what you said the other day, that you might have a more secure contact." Then curious, and noticing we'd left Pirmasens behind, I asked where he was taking me. Deep in thought, he murmured, "The Metropole over in Biche. I figured that a date with you in a cocktail dress warranted a first class meal." Impressed, and, I had to admit, a little pleased, I realized the French border was only a Klick or two away, I rummaged through my purse for my passport and ID card.

The pass through the French customs post was quick, only a cursory glance at our passports and we were waved on - surprising for the French. They'd always seemed to me as if they resented everything American. As Hamlin - Isaac - escorted me into the lobby of the Metropole Hotel, and to the entrance to the restaurant, I started to comment on the plush surroundings. "What came out almost caused me to gasp in embarrassment. "You always bring your women here when you're trying to get in their panties?" His eyebrows shot up in surprise, then with a chuckle, said, "only those whose panties are really hard to get into." I was already blushing from the stupid question and his answer only made it worse, especially since the Maître de had suddenly showed up right behind him. He gave no indication that he'd heard but simply asked us, in French of course, to please follow him. "Damn it! - Isaac," I muttered, as we followed him to a table. I was exasperated at myself that I had barely remembering not to call him Hamlin. "I don't know what made me say that." "Maybe our minds are both running in the same track," he whispered back. I decided that it was best to shut up before I embarrassed myself further. I ignored the remark. When I had been seated, and the Maitre de left, I whispered, "Back to - our problem" stopping short of naming the problem in a public place. "Is there any way to check on what he did with that truck? I'm sure the motor pool will have a record of the mileage." He looked thoughtful for a long time. "Well," he finally said as were led to a table, "It's a long shot but maybe - our friend will have an idea - should be a record of what came back the next day. It might be dicey, though, getting the information." He sighed. "Let's just drop it in his lap and see what he says. No matter what you might think, I'm, not really an expert in that business. Here comes the waiter. Why don't we just enjoy dinner?"

"Just shut up and eat?" I asked, managing to grin at him. He grinned back and, turning to the waiter, ordered for both of us - ignoring my frown. When the guy was gone, I told him that I was perfectly capable of ordering my own meal. He laughed. "Joanne, you are an amazing woman. You can be more macho than almost any man, but - in that dress - it'd be damned hard to be convincing. For once, can't you just let your hair down - so to speak - maybe pretend that you are just enjoying a date with a guy?" I could feel myself glowering at him - and knew it was really stupid - especially since I realized, that I was, actually, enjoying myself. I managed to work up a smile - a nervous, one since it'd been a long time since I'd let myself enjoy the company of a man. I ruthlessly stamped down the memory of Ian MacIntosh - two timing shit.

Shit! I was surprised to find out what that bitch had been up to. First that damned crew of hers and now this. Who'd ever expect them to pull a sample out of the bottom of a pallet? If I'd just known that they intended to run a maintenance operation on the things, I'd have waited till afterwards. Once in the field nobody would have ever figure out what happened. Then there was the truck. I'd never even thought about the departure logs at the gate. She still didn't have enough to worry me but I'd be damned if I'd let her screw up a sweet little racket like this. I knew damned good and well, what The Man would think about it. He'd have conniptions over it. He was still hopping mad about the mess with her brakes - called me an ass hole. That prissy bastard! "If you've got to try and kill somebody, at least you could do it right" he' shouted at me. Well, that uppity bitch had pissed on me twice already and now I had to listen to crap from The Man because of her. Next time, I'd do it right. The question was where. The how I'd already thought of. She was gonna just disappear. Maybe I'd make her wish she'd never heard of me before I off'ed her. I had to grin at that. Just the thought of having her to myself for a couple of days would make taking The Man's crap easier to deal with.

December 9 Friday

Her nervousness was apparent. Finally, she looked down and muttered, "Sorry. I'm just not used to dresses - well, not ones like this one - or dates - especially with men - a man - that - well, I really don't know you and you sure as hell don't know me very well. I couldn't help it. I had to laugh. "Hell, Honey - I know all about you - at least from the ground up above your navel." As her eyes blazed fire, I couldn't help add. "And a truly gorgeous navel it was too." "You! You!" She actually stammered she was so mad. "Please, darling." I was taking a real chance here but I thought I was right about her. "Ladies in nice restaurants don't use words like bastard and son of a bitch. They especially don't put the F word in front of anything." The fire in her eyes blazed hotter, then began to twinkle. Almost immediately, she looked away and her shoulders shook. When she looked back she was holding her napkin to her mouth and I definitely heard a very unSquatterlike giggle. "Consider them all said." She chuckled. "Damn it Ham - Isaac - I need to get as far away from you as I can." I grinned back at her. "Gonna be tough to do." I told her. "I've developed a liking for you - enough of one that, as soon as this is all over, I'm going to get you re-assigned to someplace where I can properly begin your seduction." She leaned back in her chair and laughed out loud. "Damn! I thought that was what you'd been doing all night." "Can't seduce a girl properly when you have to sneak her across a national border to do it - unless she'd be willing to spend the night in an upscale establishment like the one we're in." "Oh, man," she grinned broadly. "I heard you were a fast worker. I don't think, though, that I'm ready for what you seem to have in mind. When this is over we'll just go back to being what we are in the real world."

"What we were in the real world, changed the other night when I kissed you" he said quietly, A- and I think you knew it too." Thank god, the waiter showed up about then to see if we needed anything else. We both went back to eating, tension palpable now with what had been dropped on the table besides the food. I was frantically trying to forget that "darling" he'd dropped on me. Much as I'd like it to not be so, I knew he was right. I didn't know if the world had changed but something had. Not only that, I knew he knew that I knew it too.

59

Stuffing a fork full of Cordon Bleu, in my mouth, I raised my eyes. He was chewing and staring at me. I nodded and he smiled. The tension relaxed a bit after that, but our conversation was of mundane things - mostly work related. I realized that neither of us was really comfortable with the intensity of feelings between us - and neither was quite ready to confront it.

No matter what the sexy romance novels said, there had been no bomb exploding with that kiss, no swooning, knees getting weak or any of the subsequent guy-girl events the novelists touted. Never the less, there was no ignoring the heightened awareness that had arisen between us. The drive home was quiet. Even the good feeling I usually got when the German border guard said Guten Abend with a smile didn't give me the lift I usually got after dealing with the surly French guards. I debated all the way about inviting him up for "a nightcap." I grinned to myself in the darkened car at the absurdity of the phrase. Why did we always shy away from just saying "come on up and screw me" - or at least "come on up for some heavy petting." I couldn't help a sigh, knowing that an invitation to come up would have ended up one of those ways - and I wasn't ready for that right now.

Joanne was as quiet as I on the trip back to Muenchweiler. I felt foolish as hell, reaching over to take her hand in mine like a damned teenager on his first date. A comfortable squeeze from her, though, helped a lot. When I walked her up to her door, she turned to me and, without another thought I took her in my arms and kissed her. Her reaction caught me by surprise. She kissed me back - hard, lips partially open. I took up the invitation with my tongue, tightening my arms around her till she was plastered tightly against me. The kiss seemed to last forever and made me feel like I was breaking out in a sweat. Finally, she pulled her face back and stared, sadly, at me. "Oh shit, Isaac" she murmured. "Why don't you - well - say goodnight - before I - I don't dare let you come in". She dropped her head to my shoulder but not before I saw the blush. Only then, did I realize that she was pressed tightly against the hard evidence of my arousal. I loosened my hold on her. "Good idea." I muttered ruefully into her hair. "Not one I like much but still a good one." She lifted her head to look into my eyes. "I don't like it much either but - I'm not -" "Caught you by surprise too?" I said, softly. "Been a long time since I - Well, surprise wasn't the word I was looking for" she murmured. I had to chuckle at the thought of two teenagers dealing with their emotions. "Would torrid be a better word?"

60

With a rueful nod, her voice dropped to a whisper. "Yeah. A word though, that I've not dealt with lately." Taking a deep breath, I released her and bent to give her a soft kiss. Then, before I could change my mind, turned and went down the steps.

Monday Dec 12

By the time I got to the depot Monday morning, I had calmed. It had been a sleepless night and I sat at my desk staring at the damned baby shit green wall. I wondered who had talked the government into that particular color. Remembering Montgomery's suggestion, and wondering just what Isaac was thinking about, I wore a blouse hose and skirt, the longest one - though that wasn't saying much - I'd bought. Just thinking about that kiss, was enough to still make me catch my breath. Thinking about how close I came to calling him back made me shiver. How the hell could I have let myself get into a mess like this? When the thought surfaced as to whether or not he'd brought condoms with him last night, I shook myself and got up. I needed to get to work. I liked to make a swing around the depot to the various job sites just to keep everybody comfortable with my presence and let them know I was around if they needed anything. With the good crews, I always managed a few words with the crew chief at the site and, if possible, found something good to say about how the job was going. With the other crews, and normally, there were two or more working, I kept a smile on my face but kept a close eye on the activity. The chief of those crews tended to steer clear of me when I was on site - a condition that was fine with me. Sullivan was one of those crew chiefs.

Today, the storage crew was emptying a pair of semi trailers of small arms ammunition. A glance at the shipping documents showed that there were three different Federal Stock Numbers involved and a, half dozen manufacturers lots for each. Our receipt inspections were going to rise next week. There would be eighteen separate lots from this shipment alone. From the lot numbers, I could tell that they were all from North Dakota Army Ammunition Plant so they should be in good shape. The QA Specialists at the army plants were good and would have seen to that. The same couldn't be said from many civilian arsenals where production instead of quality was key.

I walked past the three pallets that the boxes were being stacked on, just to check the segregation then I turned to leave. As I was almost to my truck, I realized there was a nagging question about that shipment. I turned back to look at them again. As I came back, Sullivan frowned at me. I paid no attention. It wasn't as if he and I were bosom buddies. I stood there a long several minutes, studying the pallets. What the hell was I missing? Finally, I shrugged and turned back to my truck. I knew that my strange memory would come up with the answer in time. I also knew that until then, nothing I could do would push the answer to the surface. I did make a mental note to have the crew put a priority on pulling samples from those lots for inspection. On the way back to the office, I remembered one more job I had planned on doing. I'd wracked my brain to try and come up with a good reason for returning to the motor pool but hadn't managed it yet. I was going to just have to ask the question and accept the fact that a lot of people would wonder what I was up to.

Sergeant Metcalf, the motor sergeant, raised an eyebrow at my request for the trip ticket for panel 1409. "Problem Ma'am?" I shook my head. "Just need to clear up some paper work on its load." I said, trying for indifference. He didn't look entirely convinced but pulled the Trip Ticket from a file and handed it to me. I copied down all the information from the form even though I was only interested in times, and distances. I noticed the times matched pretty well with the departure and return logs from the guard shacks. The distance, however, was a bit of a surprise. Metcalf, looking over my shoulder, grunted. "Must have had a lot of running around to do in Ktown." he muttered. He'd seen the same thing I had. There had been over a hundred forty miles put on the truck between the time it left here and returned. Ktown was only fifty or so miles away. It would take a lot of "running around" to make up a forty odd miles - possible but unlikely to have been on government business. Of course, Sullivan might just have a girl up around Ktown but that would be Montgomery's problem. He was the spook, not me. I put in a quick call to Isaac to meet me at home, that I had something for him. "I hope it's the same thing I've got for you." he laughed. I told him to get serious. "OK," he said with a chuckle. "I've got to make a quick trip to Speyer right now but I'll be back before you get off, probably - or shortly thereafter at least. I'll just stop at your place."

I hung up and went back to checking "Administrative receipts" for the day Ferguson got back. In the midst of checking the stock and lot numbers it dawned on me - Lot Numbers! That was what was wrong with that new shipment. I'd never seen lot numbers like those on those boxes. There was no AND" plant that I knew of now and no depot consolidating or renovating material had that for an identifier. North

Dakota? There's no North Dakota plant, stupid! The only depot in the Dakotas, Black Hills had been shut down for years. I didn't remember the prefix for the Black Hills lot numbers but was pretty sure it wasn't ND. I sat back to think about that - one more odd thing to check out. Then a second realization struck. Ferguson had checked the truck out but it was Sullivan's name on the sign in sheet. When had he switched with Ferguson?

When the rest of the crew left at four, I still had another half hour's work before I put it all away and left. It was an empty road over the mountain - a dark empty road. When I got to the highway, though, there was a German Politzi stopping traffic. A Mercedes was parked beside the road and one was checking papers while two others directed the cars around the scene. Odd for Polizi to have a Mercedes but I pulled up to, the cop. He said, "Papers, Bitta." It was unusual for them to stop a car with Army plates but I pulled open my bag and handed him my ID. "Fraulein Scarborough," he said, "would you please step out of the car?" A German with an, almost American accent? None the less, I got out of the car. He led me around to the side away from the highway then, said, calmly, "Hold out your hands." "What?" I gasped, though the reason was obvious. He'd pulled out a set of handcuffs. "Just be calm, Ms. Scarborough and you might live a little longer" his other hand held a pistol. "Put them on." He no longer pretended to sound German. I debated about my purse but took the cuffs and snapped them loosely on my wrists. He grinned and, with his free hand, grasped first one then the other wrist and squeezed. The cuffs bit tightly into my flesh. "Now get in the car" he growled. I looked around to see if I could yell for help but could see that they were now letting the cars whiz on by. To the drivers, it was just another German traffic stop. I got in the car, pulling my purse into my lap as I did.

Moments later, the other two climbed in the car. The one who got in back with me, gave me a nasty leer. "Mayhaps, I should search her, chief" he said, grinning eyes never leaving me - actually my chest. My heart dropped. Surely he was going to find my pistol. "Go ahead" the driver said with a laugh. "You might find something interesting." With that, my "partner" reached over and ripped my blouse open. A second later he tore open my bra and grabbing my breast, squeezed hard. I gasped in pain. At the same time a little voice in my head said to be thankful that he was more interested in sex than in search. "Like that, do ya," he chuckled grasping the other one and doing the same

63

thing. This time I managed to not make a sound. I just got my terror under control and taking a couple of deep breaths concentrated on getting mad - and getting into my purse. At least, while the SOB was slobbering over my body he wasn't thinking about my purse. I caught my breath, though, when he forced his hand up between my legs and into my panties. "Ah," he grunted, pulling my panties aside and shoving a finger roughly inside me. "A finger in the cunt's what turns you on." I tried for calm as he bent down and bit my right nipple. Just then, the car slowed. "What the hell?" "Better stop and see what's going on. We don't need any suspicious witnesses," the other one said." The guy chewing on my breast never even raised his head. Looking through the windshield, I could see a car pulled over beside the road and a man standing in the middle. I heard the driver say. "Karl, when I pull over you get out and get rid of that guy. Waste him only if you have to." Just then, I realized that the car was a Mercedes and the man was Isaac. Frantically, I jerked my purse closer to my hands and opened it. "Just be still, bitch." my attacker said, barely lifting his head from my breast. "Make any noise and I'll bite the damned thing off fore I skewer you." As Karl, got out, the driver said. "If he gives you any trouble wait for a break in the traffic before you shoot him and get him off the road quick?"

I fumbled around in the depths of my bag and got my hand around the grip of my pistol. With the man practically laying on me it was a struggle to get it clear enough to jack the slide. The noise got the guy's attention. "What the hell," he cried and grabbed for my arm. It was too late, I pulled the trigger. Unable to get a really good angle, I must have hit him in the belly. He jerked back screaming. That cleared my lap enough to get the gun up on the driver. He was already spinning around with a gun in his hand. I shot him between the eyes. Jerking open the door, I practically fell out of the car. Isaac and the other guy were wrestling in the road but as I squirmed around onto my knees - no small feat with my hands cuffed - the guy kicked Isaac in the stomach and threw him to the ground. Then he pulled his weapon and fired. I threw my weapon up and started pulling the trigger. When the hammer clicked on an empty chamber, I caught my breath. Frantic, I scrabbled in my purse for another magazine. "It's alright, honey. It's alright." The terror leached out of me as I looked up and Isaac was kneeling beside me.

Oh God! I couldn't believe it. She was alive. Her clothes were ripped to pieces and her eyes were wild but she was still trying to reload that damned nine mil. Finally, though, her eyes cleared and she tried to grab me. "OH, God, Isaac!" she cried. "I thought he'd killed you." Clinging to me like a leech, she began to cry. With her arms together between us, I could feel the gun beside me but I held her till her body stopped shaking. About then, a voice behind me said, quietly, "Miss, would you put your weapon down?" Joanne looked up and I looked around. An MP stood there with his weapon drawn. A second later I heard Jo's weapon clatter onto the pavement. "Now would you both get up slowly?" the man said. "I think she's - he's shot" our voices joined together making a muddle of it all. The release of tension brought out laugh. A second later, Joanne joined me. The MP stood there with a weapon in his hand staring at two laughing lunatics. I helped Joanne to her feet and, only then noticed her naked breasts with vivid red tooth marks around her nipples. "Shit!" I muttered pulling her shirt closed. Then I realized her hands were cuffed. Then I saw the blood on her face. "God!" I cried. "You're bleeding." Still laughing she said "Not me. You."

As soon as I got the call, that a "Special ID" had been used, I called the OD and got the duty chopper warmed up. It still took me almost an hour to get to the scene. Traffic was still blocked in both directions so the pilot set the chopper down in the middle of the road. There were, at least, a dozen German cops and as many MP's milling around. All were taking pictures or measuring things. The MP Captain met me as soon as I jumped down. "How is she?" I asked. "A bit bunged up sir but nothing major. The guy's been shot but it missed anything vital, may have broken his shoulder blade. They were lucky. The bad guys weren't. That girl shot one in the balls. He bled to death before the ambulance arrived. She got another between the eyes and the third she filled with enough lead to make Swiss cheese out of him. As far as I can tell she all told, capped off fourteen rounds and got fourteen hits, twelve of them from almost fifty feet away sprawled on the ground in handcuffs." "OK." I said. "Everything about this incident is classified TS. I'll talk to the Politzi." After explaining the security position to Deutsche Inspektor Hoffman, promising to have him in tomorrow to take the official statements from Isaac and Joanne, I, finally, got time for them. They were, in an ambulance and, as the Captain said, "- in pretty good shape". The medics were in a snit to not be allowed to take them in to the hospital but otherwise agreed that they weren't in immediate danger. Isaac's arm was in a sling and Joanne's shirt was taped together with surgical tape so, aside from asking them how they were and getting the answer I expected - "Fine" - I told them I'd see them in the morning. I told the medic that I'd take them to Landstuhl in the chopper, and for the MP's to get their cars and bring them there. The Lady's is a few miles back up the road the captain said "but we'll take care of it. As I was getting ready to have them taken to the chopper, Joanne, spoke up. "Could we have a minute alone with you?" I frowned. What now? I wondered.

The damned Darvon the medics had given me was making me woozy but, when Montgomery managed to get the others away from us, I told him what I'd found about the panel truck. He just nodded and motioned for the medics to return. Each of them took one of us and helped us to the chopper. I started to protest that I didn't need help but as soon as I stood up I realized that I did. My legs were like rubber. When the helicopter took off, I was strapped in beside Isaac. I leaned over and asked, having to shout over the noise of the engine, if he was alright. He laughed. "My pride's taken more of a hit than my shoulder," he shouted back. "Here I came to save you and it ended up the other way around."

It was almost midnight before I got in to see Isaac. The damned doctor had insisted we both stay in overnight, "for observation." By then I was tired of being poked and prodded. Irritated, I told him that I thought he was just looking for an excuse to play with my tits again. He just laughed. "Don't you know doctors don't even notice things like that - even when they're as pretty as yours?" Mollified, if hugely embarrassed, I let him finish giving me a Tetanus shot and putting little bandages on my bite marks then, gratefully donned the hospital gown he handed me. My skirt was still intact so I didn't have to worry about anybody ogling my ass as I hurried down the hall to Isaac's room. "Hi babe," he said as I came in "you look pretty damned good to have gone ten rounds with an octopus." "Too bad I can't say the same about you." I grunted. "You look like hell." He grinned. "I'll show you my scars if you'll show me yours." "Dream on, Boyo." I muttered, blushing. Then being more honest, I looked back at him. I remembered the fear I'd felt when that thug had shot him. "At least not here" I whispered. Perhaps he felt the same way for his face clouded and he said, "Well there's nobody here maybe I could, at least get a kiss." I moved quickly to his bed and bending over kissed him. As my breathing quickened, and without thinking further about it, I lifted his hand up to my left breast.

"That one's not too sore." I whispered into his mouth.

STINGER
CHAPTER 6

Tuesday 13 Dec 1966, Landstuhl Army Hospital Germany

It had been a very pleasant few minutes - our time curtailed by the fear that we would be interrupted by a nurse at any time - and the fact that we both were covered with bruises. I spent the night in the lounger in Isaac's room. I was too tired to go back to Pirmasens especially, with only a green hospital gown for a blouse. I also didn't know where my car was. I was surprised to find that I actually slept - surprised at the sound of Montgomery's voice sneering, "Now ain't that a homey scene." Opening one eye, I muttered, "Go screw yourself Montgomery." He laughed. "Now is that any way to talk to a guy who went out of his way to bring you both some decent clothes to wear? Hell! I even arranged to have your cars brought up here so you wouldn't be without wheels." By now, I was awake and sat up. He was leaning comfortably against the door he'd come through. "OK." I muttered. "Now we know you're a saint. What do you want?"

"First, to congratulate you," he said smiling. "You saved lover boy's ass out there - as well as your own - course with him standing in the middle of the road like an ass, to stop your friends, he was some help. Second, I've got to say that was the neatest bunch of shooting I ever saw - if you did go somewhat toward over kill. The CID has decided that you shot off one guys balls, plugged a second between the eyes and dumped twelve rounds into the third before he hit the ground - all on a dark night while, mostly laying on the ground with your shirt torn off and wrists hog tied. Impressive as hell. You should review the report sometime. You killed that third guy with your first shot though the heart then put two more in his chest. As he spun around you put the next two in his lungs from the side. All the rest except one went in his back as he was falling. The last one, hit him in the ass." "You just came over to give me a critique on my shooting." I asked, sarcastically. "You hit it on the head," he replied, his face changing to a frown. "Any critique, to be complete, has to include the fuck ups. First, you let yourself get fooled by something as simple as a badge and uniform. Next, with a gun in your purse, you let yourself be put in a strange car and man handled. Now some of that can be explained by the circumstances and your inexperience. Giving up your gun when you had a get out of jail free card isn't. With an MP pistol in your face that wasn't so bad but you didn't just give it up. You dropped it on the ground had a girlish bout of hysterics and left it there. Course the damned thing wasn't much good to you anyway. You didn't bother to see the results of your first shots. You just kept on till you'd emptied the magazine. Don't you know that an empty magazine makes a weapon not much better than a high tech club?"

I'd had enough of this! "Damn it Montgomery!" I shouted. "What do you expect of her? She's not one of your damned trained assassins! I defy you to find another woman around here that could have done what she did." He'd been staring at Joanne. Now he looked over at me. "You're right," he said his voice a low rumble. "The trouble is she's not just any other woman around here. She's the woman around here that somebody is trying hard to kill. She's been lucky, so far. They all thought they had a patsy - a little girl they could terrorize and she'd pee in her panties. Next time, they'll know better and the last damned thing I want to do is to have to go identify her in the morgue." I knew he was right but I was still mad - until he turned his attention on me. His eyes glistened with fire. "As for you, you stupid ass hole - what do you think you were doing standing out in the middle of the road like a damned deer. What if they'd done what they should have and just run over you? She would maybe, have ended up killing all three of them anyway from the looks of what she did. You, on the other hand wouldn't ever get a chance to get in those panties of hers you're so hot for." I glanced over at Joanne. Her anger had changed to embarrassment as a blush crept over her face. That made me mad again. "Just what, the hell, would you have done last night?" He grinned. "I'm glad you asked. First, I'd have had a piece on me, something that you didn't think you'd need when I offered, remember? Second, I'd have pulled out that piece and had it handy. Third, I'd have followed them till I was sure they weren't going to a cop shack. Then, I'd have run them off the road or something till I could blow them away. Finally, unlike her, you should have known better. We trained you better than that."

Isaac and I were now both embarrassed. We sat there, trying to think of something to say. I, especially! "They'd trained him better?" What the hell was he my keeper? Finally, Montgomery's grin widened. "OK. Enough of the after action critique. Both of you did a credible job last night - for civilians, an excellent job. Just remember the mistakes. More lives are saved by brains than by guns. Next, you have another

70

ordeal to go through. I'm told that you are well enough to give your statement on the events of last night. We have the Base Commander, the AWSCOM commander, Chief of CID, And the Feebie SAIC in the base conference room. You'll brief them on the entire operation, including what you found, AND REPORTED, at Fischbach, Scarborough." I noted the qualification. "I don't like that, but I've been overruled. The Chief Investigator for the Deutsche Politizi will be here at 1100 hours. At that time you'll go through the entire sequence of events of yesterday. Neither of you will mention, at that meeting, anything about why you might be a target. He is aware that he is not to question you about that. He has been told that you, Scarborough, are the target of an assassin, for reasons unknown. I'll let you two get dressed and pick you up in fifteen minutes. Hamlin, you've already been checked out of this place." He opened the door and paused. With a sneer in his voice, he said over his shoulder. "Oh I forgot. Scarborough, if you'd be embarrassed to undress in front of Hamlin, you can use the room next door." The door closed.

Joanne looked at me, her face a bright pink. Trying for flip, she gave a nervous chuckle and asked if I was really hot to get into her underwear. I was in no mood for flip. I simply said, "Of course. I have been since I first saw you." She caught her breath and her eyes widened. She stood still a moment, then, reaching behind her, untied the gown. She shrugged it off her shoulders and let it drop to the floor. I guess, I wasn't too bad off after all because that got an immediate reaction. She stood still a long moment to let me survey her torso then reached behind her and unzipped her skirt. All I could do was stare. Damn she was gorgeous. Bare footed and wearing nothing but lacy bikini panties and a few band aids on her breast I hoped I wasn't drooling. A smile quivered on her lips but as she took in my reaction, it bloomed. Then she turned and went to the chair containing our clothes. It was obvious she had decided to put on a show for me. Casually, she tossed a bra aside. "Won't be wearing one of these for awhile." she muttered. Then picking up a blouse, she turned to face me and slipped it on. I watched, openly lusting for her body as she, very deliberately held the blouse open for a long moment before she slowly buttoned it and wriggled sexily into a short skirt. When she finally sat down and began to slide long stockings up her legs. She looked up at me, with a wicked grin. "You need help dressing?" she murmured.

71

We came out of the room exactly fifteen minutes after Montgomery left. We'd had to rip Isaac's shirt sleeve all the way to the shoulder to get his cast through it. With his sport coat thrown over one sleeve and buttoned, it didn't show too much. We were now finishing up the second briefing. In the first, we had both been congratulated, in the Base Commander's words, "on a damned fine job" The CID chief had returned my automatic, newly cleaned and reloaded. I remembered that I'd have to remember to exchange the rounds in it when I got home. This second one had gone easier - not nearly as many questions we couldn't answer. The German had just wanted the facts of the shootout. When he was gone I asked Montgomery to stay a minute. He sat back down. I wasn't too sure how to start without sounding like a fool. Not looking at him, I finally, said, "I didn't get too much sleep last night." He chuckled. "I'm not surprised, though impressed considering the condition Hamlin was in." I looked up in surprise. He was pretending a Groucho Marx leer. My temper flared, increased by the realization that I was blushing. Damn it! I couldn't remember the last time I blushed before a few days ago. "Screw you Montgomery!" I practically shouted. "Just shut your damned mouth till it's time to answer questions!" I was surprised to see that he actually, looked embarrassed. I started to apologize and thought better of it. I was still mad.

After I got over the shock, it was all I could do to stifle a laugh. Then I realized that Montgomery only pretended surprise. Son of a bitch, he'd been baiting her all day, trying to give her something to think about besides what happened last night. It was still funny but my opinion of him went up. "I spent a lot of time thinking." Joanne growled, glaring at him as if daring him to make something out of that. He didn't. "This isn't just a local ring of thieves. It takes money to put on an operation like last night. At first, I thought, Soviets but I think I read where they already have a SAM that's, that's more or less, the equivalent of those that were stolen. Also, those thugs didn't seem professional enough for them. Why didn't they just shoot me? Also, they spoke good English - though they didn't sound American or British. One used the word mayhaps. Strange for an American. Finally would a professional spy like an NKVD agent forget all about searching or guarding me so he could - well - do what he did to me - or is my idea of their methods from too many movies?"

"Can I answer, that" he asked. She frowned, then sarcasm dripping, said, "Please." First, you're mostly right about their SAM 7.

It's very similar to ours, though not nearly as effective. They don't have nearly as good manufacturing techniques to produce the seeker. It is, though, good enough to use on an airliner. Having one of our missiles wouldn't solve that problem, though. They do have one thing going for them, though. They're available on the clandestine market. Second. You're right about the thugs. That's exactly what they were - British - actually Irish. CID already has the names of two of them. Any more questions or observations? You're doing fine so far." She looked at him suspiciously - and, apparently, decided he wasn't being snide. "Yeah" she said. "In that case, they probably planned to use them. That means a terrorist organization." She paused and frowned. "Why, though, Redeye II's?"

He grinned and nodded. "Damn, Scarborough. You'd make a good analyst back home. Want a new job?" She just looked at him. He chuckled. "OK. They were low level IRA muscle, and you're right. They probably intend to use those things around some airport." She sat back, thoughtfully. "IRA? Don't they - what if they had some sort of official backing? Backing that wouldn't want the things identified as US weapons?" Her frown deepened. "MICOM won't admit the things are even here. The fact that they even exist is not well known. Maybe they don't mind giving the things away but don't want the US directly involved?" She was quiet a second then looked back at him. "You didn't answer one question" she said softly. "You mean, why didn't they just shoot you?" She nodded. "Well, one possibility was that they didn't want to be so brazen about it." "Yet they left my car alongside the road." She was still looking hard at him. "What are the other possibilities?" "You know what they are" he said quietly. She shivered. "Yeah" she whispered. "They wanted me somewhere they could - well - do whatever was necessary to find out what all I really knew – or fix some problem with the weapons they've got." She hugged herself. "That wouldn't have been much fun for me." She groaned. "I'd have told them whatever they wanted to know too. The trouble is they probably wouldn't have believed that I know so little." Then she paused, and added. "I don't suppose that would have mattered after they'd finished - using me, though." Now I shivered. Somehow I'd known that all along but hadn't let it surface in my mind until I heard the bleakness in her voice.

I had to admit I was shook up. I don't think I'd ever been so scared in my life. "Joanne," Montgomery's voice was very soft. "I'm going to try and keep anything from happening to you. I want you to move up here so we can protect you. You can actually be what your title says you are." I looked up. I'd have to give up what I did best just to - for what? "I can't do that." I said, fearfully. "It'd be giving in." He smiled. I assumed you were going to say that. OK. I spent most of the night arranging for three agents to be assigned to Fischbach. One will be a new GI Ammunition Inspector." I couldn't believe it. That Military Operating Specialty was so new that there were very few in the field. I think he read my mind. "This one's gonna be real green needing training the worst way. You'll have to spend a lot of time doing that. He'll have to ride around with you on the job a lot. He and the other two are being transferred in to the depot tomorrow. You'll hear about it from the Depot Commander at his Commander's call. He'll insist that you bring the Inspector up to speed because he's going to be deployed to Nam within a few months." All I could say was "Thank you." "Now, for tonight -" he continued. I'd like you to spend the night here." There was a pause. "The only alternative I'll consider is, at the risk of having you scream at me again, you and Hamlin stay together where the limited resources I have today can protect you both." The thought gave me pause. It had its good points. Unwilling to concede that, though, I growled, "What in hell are you up to, Montgomery?" He grinned. "Hamlin's already given me shit for not protecting you before. He explained that if I couldn't do it he'd do it himself." He grinned at Isaac. "Of course, recent history would indicate, that it's likely to be the other way around." He held up a hand as I started to protest. "Think of the advantages. He has a house on the economy - so gossip will be at a minimum. He has a bum wing so needs a protector. Mostly, though, I've a feeling that he doesn't intend to leave your side anyway." When neither of us said anything, he laughed. "Besides, your reputations shot to hell anyway as soon as word gets around that you spent the night with him last night in his room."

Joanne apparently was going to let that pass because the look on her face showed that another thought had struck. "If they were going to shoot down an airliner, Montgomery, why not buy an SA7? Why would they need something better?" Her eyes glazed over as she went into, what looked like a trance. I was surprised to see Montgomery give a start. This time he had gotten a shock. Finally, she muttered.

"MICOM is desperate to cover it all up. Why? Just to cover their ass? What if - who would our government, or someone in it, want to give some advanced anti aircraft missiles to? Surely not the IRA! Then why's the IRA involved?" I was watching both of them now. Montgomery was stunned. Joanne's eyes unglazed. They focused on him with an intent stare. "Do you know?" It was almost an accusation. He shook his head then looked, sharply, at her. "No, I don't. I told you that before. I think, though, I'd better try a bit harder to find out." He shook himself. "Your questions, though, raise some scary possibilities. Why don't you two go home and get some rest while I try and find some answers."

There had been no teasing in Montgomery's last remarks. His whole manner had gone deadly serious. After a few seconds, Isaac had taken my arm and urged me out of the room. He'd insisted we take his car to "go home." We argued, but I finally agreed since he, obviously couldn't drive. Montgomery said he'd have mine brought down later. On the autobahn, we had little to say to one another. I don't know why I was so damned mad. I was going to spend the night with a guy that I had, but would damned sure never admit to having, the "hots" for. Oh yeah. I had them. Last night, I wanted nothing more than to climb his bones in that bed. Finally, he broke the silence. "Is it going to be a totally quiet night? Is it really so bad being with me?" I couldn't look at him. I couldn't help a sigh. "It's not you." I muttered. "I - well, hell! I'm not sure I'm up to a - clandestine affair." He chuckled. "Don't you dare laugh," I cried! "I'm not laughing at you," he murmured. "I'm just not sure I'm up to one either." I looked over at him in surprise. "Joanne, it's taking all my willpower to keep my hands - well, hand - off you - and after last night, I think you feel the same as I do." Ruefully, I had to admit he was right - but I didn't say so out loud. "I think we're both too - well, conventional - for this sort of thing. I don't know exactly what to do about it, though." I looked over at him. He was staring fixedly at me. "I think we both know, though, that we're going to end up in bed together tonight - don't we? I took a deep breath and nodded. "But I don't feel comfortable with it at all." I whispered. He grinned broadly. "I'm not surprised," he said. "I'm not used to waking up with a woman in my bed anymore, either. We'll probably both, act like jerks in the morning."

I hoped I didn't appear as nervous as I felt. She was quiet a minute, concentrating on exiting the 'bahn to pick up the road to Pirmasens. "Well," she said, finally looking back at me, with a chagrined chuckle. "I should be able to defend my honor against a man who has only one arm." I laughed. "Who's going to protect mine?" She grinned broadly. "Didn't you hear Montgomery? That's my job." "I didn't say me. I said mine." She laughed aloud. "Come on Isaac. Everybody knows a man doesn't have any honor when he's dragging an innocent girl off to his lair - especially one who's - well, has the reputation you do." I winced. "Reputation and facts aren't always the same thing." I muttered, desperate to lighten the mood. "Are you an innocent girl, Joanne?" I teased. It surprised me when she looked over at me. It was a very serious look. "Not exactly a girl, but a lot more innocent than MY reputation purports," she said quietly. She turned back to watching the road. "My last - well - the last man I dated seriously, couldn't accept that." She shrugged, dispiritedly. "I don't suppose I should blame him - but I have - for a long time." Well, I thought. There goes any chance of scoring tonight. Oh well. "You don't have to be afraid of me, Jo." I said. "Nothing will happen that you're not comfortable with."

I shook my head with a rueful chuckle. "Isaac," I muttered "what I'm comfortable with and what I want may be two different things." Then, reluctantly, I took a deep breath and added, "and what I want is - well, as a new experience, it's a little scary." He said nothing and I steadfastly kept my eyes on the road. I grew more and more fidgety as the silence lengthened. Finally, I could stand it no longer. "Well say something, damn it!" I snapped. "It's not often you get to discuss the defloration of an almost thirty year old virgin, Hamlin." He chuckled. "I don't recall ever discussing defloration of a virgin of any age - especially with the virgin herself. You'll have to bear with me. It's a new experience for me too - and a hell of a challenge." "Damn it!" I muttered. "What?" "Well, we're a hell of a pair. You want in my panties and are afraid you'll make me mad and I want you in them and am afraid to let you." That brought a deep sigh as he leaned his head back in the seat. Finally, he said "well, why don't we just play it by ear. When we get home, we'll just pretend we're teenagers on our first date. I'll grope you and you decide when to turn me off - or on." I had to laugh. "So it's all on my back, figuratively or literally, huh?" He chuckled. "Well, I know exactly what I want - so it has to be up to you to decide whether or not you want to give it to me. I'm prepared either way." Curious, I looked over at him. "Prepared? How?" He grinned, "an unopened box of rubbers in the night stand and a cold shower next to the bedroom." We both had to laugh at that.

As I turned into his street and shifted into low to climb the hill, I saw a tan Opel parked. Montgomery had given us a description of his MP guard and told us if we saw any other suspicious car, to call him at home. We'd stopped at the Commissary at Ramstein and had three bags of groceries. Isaac took one and I the other two. He didn't know it but I had made a quick detour through the PX and gotten him a new watch. I didn't know if he needed one but how can you buy a Christmas present for a guy you barely knew when you were planning on - well, hell - face it Joanne. You're gonna give yourself to him as soon as he's able. Anyway, he had waited in the car - protesting he was fine - while I shopped. Now a half hour later we were at his place. When we reached his door, I shuffled the bags around to get the key in the lock and opened the door. When Isaac sat his bag down on the counter, I noticed he was pale with a bead of sweat on his forehead. "Go sit down and I'll bring you a pill." I told him. He insisted he was OK but I insisted and pretended not to hear the groan when he dropped onto the couch.

I brought him a glass of water and a Darvon then went back to the car to get the suitcase Montgomery had packed for me. Finally I returned to the kitchen to put the groceries away. It took a while to find the proper places for the stuff. When I came back to the living room, he had his eyes closed. I looked around and decided the couch was big enough for both of us to get a nap. When I sat down, though, he opened one eye."You're too far away." The soft, slurred, mutter caused a tiny flutter in my belly. I scooted over next to him. He put his good arm around me and pulled me closer. "Hell of a time to take a damned pill.' he whispered. "Looks like an assault on your virtue'll have to wait a bit longer." I sighed, with either pleasure or relief - I wasn't sure which, and, kicking my shoes off, curled my feet up on the couch and laid my head on his shoulder. In only seconds, I was asleep too.

Wednesday Dec 14

Isaac had run a fever and was barely conscious. I was still sore too but managed to get some cereal for breakfast and make us soup for lunch. His fever broke around mid afternoon but he still wasn't hungry so it was more soup for supper. I wasn't feeling so good that I was willing to start a marathon yet either. I spent most of the day curled up against him in bed - napping off and on and letting him fondle me in between - while we listened to Christmas music on the radio. That evening, we made out, somewhat chastely. He had asked me to take off my clothes and I did, somewhat nervously. I was now enjoying a bit of love making as he kissed me and, lovingly, fondled me. I caressed him as I enjoyed the feel of his tongue twining with mine. "Lower," he mumbled. It took a moment to realize what he wanted and I blushed when I did. Never the less, I, slowly, slid my hand down his naked body - unable to prevent the little twitch at what I found. "You sure," I muttered. " chuckle. "Oh yes." I raised my head and told him he was a pervert. He just grinned and a moment later, I curled my fingers around his large erection. Leaning up on one elbow, I slowly, began to move my hand, unable to prevent my eyes from dropping to watch. When he groaned, I asked if I was hurting him. He gasped, softly, and shook his head. As his heart began to pound and his breathing come in great gasping breaths, I was a little worried about the effect on him. When I started to remove my hand, though, he groaned, "Not yet!" I returned to stroking the self imposed task. Probably not very expertly but with a wicked instinct, I forced the inevitable response.

When his shudders had ended, I stared, thoughtfully, at his wet chest. "One of my - hundreds of other women -A he murmured, "would have been - neater. She wouldn't have wasted it." I looked up at him a moment before I realized what he meant. I couldn't help the heat of the blush that spread over me. I took a deep breath and deliberately dipped a finger in the white puddle. "Maybe I'll do better next time." I murmured then bent to kiss him.

He was much better the next day and got up on his own, this time, to go to the bathroom. I lay nervously on the sheet, having been ordered not to move till he got back. When he came out of the bath, he was, again, aroused. I stared at the thing as he crossed the room, debating whether or not I was up to what he, obviously had in mind. As if he could read my mind, he said, "No your turn now." Ten minutes later, I was writhing with passion as he crouched between my legs, my body a raging furnace and I was out of my mind with the need for him. Moments later he gave himself to me as, like a slut, I thought, I screamed in delight. When it was over he lay beside me, panting almost as hard as I was. My seduction had taken more out of him than he'd been willing to admit. As my body calmed, I snuggled up against him and in moments was asleep.

78

The next day, passed with mostly resting. Isaac was still weak but, against his pleading, I had gotten dressed and cleaned the house in between making meals. Now it was evening and I was once again curled up against him on the couch. I hadn't realized I'd fallen asleep until I was startled awake, my heart pounding in terror. "Oh God! I didn't mean to hurt you." a soft voice said. I gasped and dropped my head back on the couch realizing it was Isaac's hands fondling me. As I tried to catch my breath, I gasped "NO! I mean, you didn't. Hurt me, that is." "Then what - Oh" he murmured. "Sorry." I twisted around to look at him. "It's OK. Just - uh - surprised." "Not a good surprise - considering the other night." I gave him a quick kiss and grabbed his hand to keep him from taking it off me, and reached up to unbutton my blouse. I pulled it open and tugged the tails out of my waist band to bare myself to the waist. He covered my breast with his hand and squeezed, gently. "Sure it doesn't hurt?" I'd squealed a bit when he'd squeezed my sore breast yesterday. I grinned up at him. "You can use that one anyway you like. The other one's kinda iffy."

"Well, maybe a quick inspection of the equipment" he chuckled. "I thought you had inspected it all intimately yesterday mister Senior Quality Assurance Inspector. Don't tell me you missed something." I whispered looking down. In the light given off by the little night light on the other wall, I watched his fingers gently squeeze my breast mound into a round shape before his finger caressed my slowly hardening nipple. "Nice job." I whispered, leaning my head back on the couch to enjoy the sensation. "Find any defects?" "A couple of minor ones - not enough to reject the merchandise though. Hard to do a proper inspection though with only one hand" he chuckled. I thought about it a moment then said, "Maybe you can find more from a different perspective." With that, I squirmed around until I could lay across his lap, careful to not jar his shoulder. Then, not giving myself a chance to chicken out, lifted my butt enough to wriggle my skirt up around my waist. "Well, that provides a lot better view of the merchandise - still too much packaging on it though." He slipped his fingers in the hip band of my bikini and tugged down, suggestively. I took the hint and, lifting my butt again, helped him remove the offending packaging. "Better" I asked my voice a bit shaky. "Much" he replied, lifting his hand to lick his middle finger. I watched, fascinated, but still couldn't help a gasp when the inevitable happened. Taking a deep breath, I decided to give him more room.

I'd been staring at the thatch of red curls, when her thighs slowly opened. I tore my eyes away to look at her. Jo raised her face to stare into mine, her chest beginning to heave a bit as a slow smile appeared on her lips. "It's brand new" she said, the look on her face becoming serious. "I haven't - it hasn't really been - broken in yet." I bent my head and kissed her. I was quickly getting to a point of no return when I pressed my tongue against her lips. She opened hers invitingly meeting me with a fervor of her own. Sucking it as far into her as she could she licked it from tip to base then let me return the favor. Sometime in the midst of it all, as my inevitable reaction took over. She moaned slightly, but, never taking her tongue out of my mouth, opened herself wider – then still wider to give me room.

I hadn't let anyone make such a move on me. Well, I guess a little with Margaret when she was consoling me two years ago but that was very different. I became very aware that it was a lot different with a man. Up until that moment, I'd been slightly afraid that I preferred girls. Obviously I didn't for, my juices were flowing copiously. Wantonly, I wanted his mouth on my breast. I squirmed upward and pulled his mouth from mine. It didn't take long for him to get the idea. I sighed, in delight when his lips settled over my mound and his tongue rasped across the nipple. I lay back against his shoulder, in thrall to his questing tongue and caressing hand. Running my own hand through his hair, I nibbled the lobe of his ear and whispered that I hadn't made out on a couch since high school. He raised his mouth up from my breast enough to murmur. "The bedroom would be more comfortable but if we go there your - equipment - is almost sure to get broken in." I shivered at the thought as he returned his lips and tongue to my breast - but I'd known when I came here what was going to happen. "Maybe we should - do that before - well - my warrantee expires." He lifted his head and with a long survey of my nakedness, said, "I've wanted to carry you off to my bed for days." I grinned. "Fat chance, in your condition. Guess I'll just have to go to my doom on my own feet." I gave him a quick kiss and chuckled, "Hell I'll probably have to ravish myself." "Not a very macho image, for me" he laughed. Then he added, "but, certainly, a provocative one. If you'd get off me we could go." I laughed back. "If you'd get your hands off of me, I could get my gorgeous body off you." He leered. "Come on, Miss - whoever you are, I'm the invalid here. I thought about it then told him he was a blackmailer.

Together we went into the bedroom. Once inside, she slipped out of my grasp and walking, purposefully to the bed then laid down and spread her legs wide. I told her, I thought a bit more petting was in order first. She smiled and said, she didn't - that she was ready as she'd ever be. When I still hesitated, she held out her arms to me. "Please, Isaac. Do it quickly before I chicken out." I went to her. Before getting into bed, though, I slipped my arm out of the sling and flexed it. Carefully, I didn't flinch at the stab of pain. It was bearable, though and, in this case I needed both my arms. Still a little worried about taking her like this, I, never the less, crawled atop her and leaned forward. I reached between those legs. Glancing up, I could see her eyes were focused nervously on mine. "Relax honey!" I whispered. I heard her catch her breath. She gave a tiny squeal as with a sharp thrust I made her mine. At that moment, I decided that I'd never let her go. There was no easy way to do this so I was quick. A small scream announced success of our endeavor.

Bottling up my need to ravish her, I paused and asked if she was alright. "Conflicted," she gasped a pained look on her face. I raised an eyebrow at that. She caught her breath a bit. "It hurt and I was wondering what I was thinking about - letting you do this to me." Another breath, "Then wanting you more than I - thought I possibly could." Her eyes grew big as an amazed look replaced the frown. "I just realized - I think I'm falling in love with you." I felt my heart pound. "It's a good thing." I muttered "considering that you've got half of a very important part of my anatomy stuck inside you." I wasn't prepared for the burst of laughter. Apparently she wasn't either. She squealed sharply as her vaginal muscles contracted tightly. "Oh God," she gasped. "Don't make me laugh." I bent and kissed her, assuring her that was the last thing on my agenda. "Just - oh shit, honey – don't waste the other half." Without thinking more about it, I did as ordered

I lay back as the pain began to slowly diminish. I tried to relax I could see the sweat appearing on his brow as he tried to control himself. His breath was coming in gasps now. Suddenly I felt his whole body tremble and his arms begin to shake. Still barely able to breathe, he started to raise himself up. Instinctively, I threw my legs around his hips to stop him. "No!" I gasped. "I'm about - to crush - you, Jo! I can't - hold myself -" "OK!" I ordered, releasing my legs. "Roll us over!"

81

With, seemingly, the last of his strength he did. Carefully, I adjusted my body atop him to get into a less stressful position. When I was semi-comfortable, I lay my head down on his shoulder and let my breasts flatten out on his chest. I was fully aware of his, upset but was comfortably lazing when he apologized because I hadn't -. I covered his mouth with my hand. "Next time." I murmured.

December 17 Saturday morning early

Thomas Mendenhall acknowledged the Rhine Main tower's clearance for takeoff and glanced over at Charlie Conklin. He was just finishing up his checklist and in a formal voice said, "Check list complete Captain. We're ready to go." Tom grinned at his friend. "I'm surprised you didn't find a reason to stay over here another night Charlie," he teased. "That was a delectable young fraulein you were working on last night. Get lucky?" "A gentleman never tells," his co-pilot shot back. The grin on his face, though, made plain that he had. Thomas turned back to the windshield. He'd already advanced the throttles on the Boeing 707 and was standing hard on the brakes as the engines rose rapidly to a roar. He clicked the throat mike as he released the brakes. "BOAC one niner four six eight, rolling." he announced as the plane started to move. "You know, Thomas, I'd think that after six years in this bundle of bolts, you'd no longer have that shit eating grin on your face every time you start a takeoff run." Charlie was talking from the side of his mouth as he watched the instruments. A moment later, he said "V1". Mendenhall released a bit of pressure on the wheel to let the nose wheel come up off the runway. He waited for that feeling he always got when the plane was ready to fly. He really didn't need Charlie's notification of the necessary flying speed to take off but he waited for it anyway. When it came he added a little pressure to the wheel and got that euphoric feeling when the wheels stopped rumbling and the plane returned to its natural element, the air. "I just wish we'd get the Comet back." Thomas muttered. "This thing flies like a truck compared to it." Both were busy cleaning the plane up for flight and getting up the gear as he steadied the craft on a smooth climb out attitude. The tower came back on the air to give departure instructions, even though he knew them by heart. The flow of information, unintelligible to a non pilot was interrupted by "Shizen! Vas -." Thomas frowned and started to ask what the problem was when it became apparent with a loud explosion on the right wing. The plane shuddered violently as Charlie cried, "the right outboard engine! It's on fire!" "Extinguishers!" Thomas cried as he fought to correct the sudden pronounced yaw to the right. As the plane struggled to maintain altitude with a full load of fuel and passengers, Charlie announced the fire dying some. Then, with an awed voice, he said, "Tom, the whole aft end of the engine is gone - along with a big chunk of the wing over it.

There was pandemonium in the tower. The Air Traffic Controller was responding to a Mayday from the crippled aircraft and the tower supervisor was screaming into the phone for the security personnel to get to the forest beyond the end of the runway where a flash was seen on the ground followed by what, the old Luftwaffe pilot readily recognized as a rocket trail. The plane had been attacked. Could the pilots control the aircraft? If they did, could they get back on the runway, safely? If not would the crash occur in an inhabited area? Was the attacker still out there ready for a second try? As he barked his questions and instructions, he listened to the controller radio traffic. He had declared an emergency and was putting all inbound traffic in a holding pattern. All planes on the taxiways were on hold. The stricken 707 was still holding altitude though its path was erratic. In answer to the controller's question, the co-pilot said that they were dumping fuel and thought they could maintain enough control to re-enter the pattern and land. He asked for emergency equipment and clearance. The supervisor had to give the Limey credit. His voice sounded calm despite what the supervisor knew must be going on in the cockpit of that plane.

"Charlie," Tom grunted as he struggled to stabilize the yaw of the plane brought on by having half the right wing ripped to pieces. "If the fire's out, see if you can dump the fuel from that wing." I checked the instruments. There was no fire light. I looked outside to scan the wing. "I don't see any." I told him. "But there's a stream of vapor outboard of the engine. We're probably already losing fuel. Thank God it didn't start before the fire died." I reached for the small switch and flipped it on. A red light came on now. "Right tank open." I muttered, staring out at the increasing stream of vapor. "Can you get us around for an approach to the runway?" "Turning won't be a problem." Tom grunted. "Straightening out will be a bitch. That wing feels like it's made out of lead. Better get ready to give me a hand. We're not much above stall speed - whatever that is in these conditions." I took the wheel, holding it lightly, as Tom eased pressure on it. The plane jerked hard right. We fought to keep control. In a series of jerks and responses, we eased it around until we were on a reverse course. "How far off the line?" Tom grunted. "Miles." I replied staring out at the runway off in the distance. "We'll never get back to that end. Better go

84

completely around." I called ground to announce out intentions. "What ever you can do, six eight?" they came back. "The field is shut down until you are on the ground."

It was almost oh three hundred before we finally got to sleep. As I lay, curled up, naked against his chest, I couldn't get over what he still wanted to do to me - after having already done it to me twice - out of my mind. I smothered a silent chuckle. That "twice" had taken almost four hours. Both times he did it we'd rolled over so I could hold him for an hour or so each time. I probably wouldn't have let him up even then if we hadn't both had to go pee. Could I let him "do it" again?" I wasn't sure. I was, sore and exhausted, but still willing, I decided just as the phone rang. "Shit!" Isaac grunted. "Don't answer." I muttered. "Maybe they'll go away." They didn't. After the third ring, Isaac reached across me and answered with a growled, "What?" A second later, he sat up straighter in the bed and muttered "Shit" - then "OK!" "What?" It was my turn now. "Montgomery" he grunted starting to get up. "We've got to leave in five minutes." "No way!" I cried. "It'd take me longer than that to get out of this bed." "An airliner took a rocket up the tailpipe at Rhine Main" he said, pulling on his pants. "He wants you there to identify the launcher."

I came out of the bathroom in only my skirt and panties - my already damp panties. I really needed a bath and a douche. I had to settle for a wad of toilet paper that had turned pink and soaked through almost before I left the bathroom. I'd combed my hair and put on lipstick but nothing would help the dark circles under my eyes. I'd grabbed my wrinkled skirt, because I knew that I'd never be able to pull a pair of tight pants on. I started to jerk a sweater over my head and changed my mind. I pulled it off and rummaged in my overnight bag for my silk blouse. Without a bra, which I couldn't wear, the wool sweater had felt like sandpaper rasping over me. The blouse helped a lot. Grabbing my coat, I headed for the door that Isaac was holding for me. "Hell of a knack you have for ending an evening." I grumbled as we went out the door. There was our shadow, sitting in the Tan Opel in Isaac's driveway. There were two of them now so Isaac and I got in the backseat.

Once in the car, the driver - his name was Jonathan Logan - headed for Ktown. Almost as soon as we got on the highway, a German Polizei pulled around us and, siren screaming led us to the Autobahn.

He left us there and Logan put the hammer down. It was pitch black and there wasn't another car in sight. Isaac asked what they knew about the situation. The passenger - no name given - turned around and told us that a Brit airliner had been attacked on take-off but had managed to get back on the runway without killing anybody. A number of people had some bruises and some with minor sprains and a couple of busted legs from the evacuation of the plane. The plane was damaged pretty badly when it veered off the concrete but was still intact. Airport security had found where the missile was launched from and found the launcher. The shooter, though, was long gone. While he was talking, curiosity got the better of me. I leaned forward enough to see the instrument panel - and set back, silently saying a prayer. The speedometer needle was pegged on the right side - the last number on it was one sixty KPH. That damned Opel had something under the hood the factory didn't know about.

It still took almost an hour to reach Rhine Main, and get into the security office. Montgomery met us at the car. "Be careful what you say in there. I only needed you, Joanne, to make it official. I didn't want to seem too knowledgeable on the subject," he said. "They don't need a detailed explanation just an identification." When we entered the office, there were two air force generals, one US and the other German - a dozen civilians, both male and female, and several politizi. Lying on the desk was a very familiar sight, the empty launch tube of a Redeye II missile. I identified it as a "US Man Portable Anti Aircraft Missile" - carefully avoiding calling it a Redeye or by its still unapproved name – Stinger. I added that it came with a second part that contained the launch sequence. "You probably won't find that though. No doubt the shooter took that with him." Then I stepped back to listen to the cacophony of a dozen voices all trying to speak at once. Occasionally, I had to answer a question - generally with respect to the missiles capabilities, of which I could only make an educated guess. I kept in mind Montgomery's warning and didn't mention where it came from. When all the questions and implied recriminations were over Isaac and I were driven back home - at a more sedate pace this time. Logan held the speed down to a careful one twenty klicks.

I was bleary eyed as I drove into work Sunday my trusty tail behind me. I hoped Jo felt better than I did on her trip over the mountain to Fischbach. We hadn't gotten back to the house until almost six, so aside from a little half hearted love play in my big shower, we'd simply gotten dressed, ate breakfast and left for work. This Sunday wasn't going to be a day off. Both the AWSCOM and Fischbach staff had been called in. Simply getting dressed hadn't been, perhaps, very descriptive of what happened. She had mentioned, coyly - a stretch I thought for her, that she didn't think she "could wear pants today." As a result, I was treated to the sight of her seductively wriggling another of those short skirts up over her hips. Then she sat down on the bed and, with, first one, then the other, leg, stretched high in the air, slid on a pair of stockings with all the aplomb of a seasoned stripper. Almost the instant she'd finished, she stepped into her heels and gave me a quick kiss. "Just wanted to give you something to remember," she whispered as she grabbed her purse and went out the door.

At the office, I faced a mountain of paper that had accumulated during the last few days of my absence – all the while waiting for the inevitable staff meeting. After two cups of coffee, I attacked the stack. By nine hundred, I had established a pattern. Those things I could handle right away went into one stack and anything that required a lot of research or staffing, that I had no capability right now to handle, especially with just one hand - since I'd put my sling back on, went into another. Just before noon, I got a call from the CO's office. His clerk asked if I could come to the office now. In army talk that meant "Get your ass down here right now." Colonel Richmond was a pretty good guy so, when I was shown into his office, I wasn't surprised to have him tell me that he didn't mean I had to drop everything and come down. I was surprised that none of the rest of the staff was there. Apparently the meeting wasn't about the airliner and he'd just wanted me to come when I could. "Then, sir, you should instruct your clerk about what - at your convenience - means." I chuckled. He laughed. "Yeah, I tend to forget what a simple question from me means to her. Anyway, since you're here, I had a thought yesterday." He leaned back in his chair. "I needed a question answered and didn't have an inspector to answer. With Dawson gone, it would appear your office is too short handed to be effective. I've queried your career office and they tell me that the only person in our command that is, presently, on the best qualified list for promotion is the one at Fischbach. If you brought him up here would it hurt their operations too much?" I tried to pretend to think about it knowing, full well, that he knew the chief, at Fischbach wasn't a "him". While I did, my suspicions began to rise. Choosing my words carefully, I asked if It were possible that "the Colonel had an ulterior motive." His eyes twinkled, belying his disclaimer that he only had "the efficiency of his Surveillance Division in mind."

87

I was irritated at his blatant manipulating but said I would talk to the career office Monday. "I understand that they have promotion papers on the way now," he said with a grin. "You might see about getting him on the list for field grade quarters, though. I understand he's in company grade now." I just nodded and turned to leave. "Oh, by the way," he called after me. "What's this fellow's name?" When I turned back there was a large shit eating grin on his face. "Scarborough, Sir." I grunted, "Joanne Scarborough." "A female?" he muttered. "Imagine that! Doris will be so happy to have another woman for her coffee group." It was my turn to laugh. "Joanne - Miss Scarborough sir is an unlikely candidate for a coffee klatch. You should remember that her nickname is Squatter." "Oh yes" he laughed. "I remember now. That teletype caused quite a stir around here. I thought Mister Dawson was going to have an aneurism." He was still laughing when I left. I wondered if our affair had already spread all over the headquarters staff. Damn! Jo was going to hate that.

I'd made another useless swing around the depot looking for missiles that I was sure were long gone. There was a message from Isaac waiting for me. Robin had taken it. I called him back. "Miss Scarborough," he said, very formally, "I need you up here for a meeting this afternoon. Would fourteen hundred be OK?" "What now?" I wondered but didn't ask. I simply agreed to be there.

I had been careful to make sure I was on time so sat down in front of Isaac's desk at exactly fourteen hundred hours. His face was expressionless as he pushed a folder across the desk to me. "It seems, Miss Scarborough, that the Colonel thinks I need a deputy. He has queried the Career Office and found you are eligible for promotion. The message confirming the promotion to GS 12 is on top there. Next is a personnel memo reassigning you as the Deputy to the AWSCOM Chief of Surveillance. The rest of the file is a list of GS 9 eligible's to replace you at Fischbach. As you can see, since Byrnes has gone home, the only one in this command is Robin Laurence. There are several senior to her in the European command that could be transferred in if you don't think she's ready to take over your branch." Elated to be promoted and concerned at the effect it will have on relationships, I started reading the file. Robin was the only female on the list. The other three were men. All were, certainly, senior to her. Two I knew and the other had been an inspector for eleven years. I suspected that his abilities were no better than I knew the others were - sorely lacking. I folded the file and simply told Isaac that "Robin will do."

I nodded and pointed out that the promotions and transfers would become effective on Monday, the beginning of the pay period - that she should use whatever time she needed cleaning up at Fischbach and settling Laurence in. Playing indifferent boss was wearing but I continued describing her duties and ended up remarking that the Colonel had pointed out that we'd arrange to get her on the Field Grade Quarters List. Housing had told me it would probably take a month. I hesitated, then added, "Are your present living arrangements satisfactory that you can wait a month or so?" As I watched her, I could tell she'd gotten over her surprise and was, now, laughing behind her calm demeanor. I knew I was right when she, very deliberately, crossed her right leg over her left - leaving a tantalizing length of silken thigh almost to her butt.

I had a lot of trouble suppressing a grin at the somewhat, worried look on his face with that last question. I managed to look very businesslike and told him that my present situation seemed fine - that I really didn't need to change it. I couldn't help a tiny grin when I added, mischievously, "Of course, my sleep has been disturbed a lot lately but the perpetrator will probably get tired of harassing me soon. If not, I'll get my boss to make him stop." I plastered a solemn, innocent, look on my face as I watched him try to stifle a guffaw.

Enough damned flirting, I thought, wondering at the same time how the hell I had gone from never even looking at men I met to flirting, and outrageously - sleeping - with one. I couldn't help a rueful grin. Let's face it Joanne, sleeping is not what you're doing with him. You're letting him screw your ass off. Anyway, I'd thought of something else today - other than wanting to spread my legs for him - we needed to discuss. I got up and closed the door. "I was thinking." I said as I sat back down. "Why should anybody steal a non type classified missile for shooting at airliners if the Russian SA7's are available on the black market? That was a big risk they took getting the Redeye II's. Surely they know that they'd be watched like hawks - though recent experience doesn't bear that out." I paused to let him think about that then I went on. "What could they want to do that requires a new, undeniable, US missile? As far as I know it's never been officially released yet to any other country - not even the Dutch. Technically it doesn't even have a name yet. Stinger is not officially recognized." He leaned back a thoughtful frown on his face. He flicked his eyes past my shoulder and muttered, "you know -A glancing back I saw his secretary had left the office. As I turned back he was grinningA- you've got a lot more unexplored depths to you than I realized." Affecting a haughtiness to cover the unexpected tightening of my nipples, I said that I didn't think I had any depths at all that hadn't been explored - pausing before adding, "thoroughly." "Oh, for an office without windows and a door I could lock so I could prove you wrong," he murmured with a fake hang dog look on his face. "I think we need to get back to business." I said, nervous at the flirtatious tack the meeting had taken. He sighed and said, "Yeah. I wonder if Montgomery has had that thought."

Damn! Was I going to have to spend the rest of the day behind the desk to hide my reaction to Jo? How was I going to live with her in the same office? Hoping that real business would help, I picked up the phone and dialed Montgomery.

As I listened to the G4's voice on the scratchy secure phone, I was thinking hard. "But sir! It's gotta be a put up job by somebody over there. Somebody's gotta know who's setting it all up. It's gotta be one of the spook outfits and, surely they'll have a presidential finding to back them up."

"I know, Mac. I don't like the sound of it either - and right now I've got no idea just what they're planning." I listened some more.

"I can't take credit for the idea. It was those two civilians we're dealing with." I grinned at his curse. "Ok. I'll give them both the briefings on Monday - and yes, I'll make sure he starts carrying. Not sure how much good it'll do, though, with his wing out of commission." My grin widened.

"Yes sir. Too bad our analysts at home are so concerned with covering their asses. It's irritating to have novices outperform pros." I couldn't help the dig. "Of course, he might as well be a novice. That last job didn't begin to fall in the same league with this." More cursing!

"I'm stretched pretty thin here. I can't protect them like it should be done. My MP's aren't trained for this sort of thing." No comment.

"Yeah. I've got that itch not so much about him but they've already made two tries at her. I can't figure out why, either. She's no real threat to them. She's already brought it out in the open. What more can she do? There's got to be something I've not thought of."

"Well, they're pretty thick. That helps some. She's spending nights, so far, at his place so the shadows aren't spread too thin. I don't expect that to last, though. She's damned independent. She'll, sooner or later, get antsy about reputation."

"Yes sir. She's scared. She's already getting over her fright though and has gotten mad."

"Yeah. She's gonna want to do that pretty soon. She's not one to wait for trouble to come to her."

After I'd hung up, I shook my head and sat back to try and come up with a plan of action. It was useless. I needed a drink. Still worrying the problem, I got up and fixed me one - a stiff scotch with a cube of ice. What the hell did they want with those particular missiles? They had gone to a lot of trouble and danger to get them when others were available. It had to be an attack of some kind - one that would point at the US - one that would cause an international problem? Was the shot at the Brit's airplane just a test? With the damned IRA involved? It had to be considering the attack on the Brits airplane. Why target Scarborough, though? Once the cat was out of the bag, she meant nothing to them - or did she? She killed three of their troops but that information was pretty close hold. Could they know that? Probably. Could they simply want revenge? Back home if a Brit whacked one of theirs, he became a target just to uphold their image. They didn't usually operate that way outside the country, though - except against traitors - especially not against Americans. It caused problems with fund raising in the US.

Hell! Lots of questions but damned few answers. What was the purpose of swiping those particular missiles. Of course, they could be made to appear Dutch but why bother? Could they have some exotic plot to create an intelligence scandal? How the hell was the Missile Command involved? They obviously were considering the blatant cover up. They didn't have the chops to pull such a thing off, but they could have been convinced to go along. Only the spooks would actually try such a thing. It was unlikely that the FBI would dare try and expand their mandate overseas. NSA? The National Security Agency was usually a lot more competent that this seemed to be. CIA? Central Intelligence seemed more likely. They were more decentralized with their agents operating like cowboys some of the time. If it were Military Intelligence Brigadier Morrison would likely have at least an inkling of it and he denied any knowledge. I didn't want to even consider that he'd lied to me.

Could individuals have done it? If so they would have to have had a lot of conspirators in high places. I couldn't even imagine how high it would have to be to arrange the theft of a super secret missile system. We had to be missing something. What?

CHAPTER 8

21 December Wednesday

At the O club, Tuesday night, between my cast and Joanne being on my arm, we got a lot of looks. That was inevitable in a small close knit group such as this. There wasn't much doubt that the word on Joanne's exploits were all over the community. Combine that with her promotion and the speculation as to what she had to do to get it and the result was probably inevitable. Out in public with me now just added to the speculation. Not much to do about that, though. I'd be damned if I was going to sneak around like a thief in the night and the Christmas party was as good a place as any to start. We ignored the buzz and had a pair of steaks for dinner. I hadn't thought about my sling until it came time to cut the meat. To hell with it,. I thought. I slid my arm out of the sling and picked up the knife. It still hurt a little but I could live with it. Gritting my teeth I started cutting. I noticed Jo frowning at me. I frowned back and she didn't say anything. "How can you eat all that and still keep a figure like yours?" I asked, a few minutes later, as I watched, in amazement, as she practically gulped down an entire large Porterhouse. "It's a secret diet I've just started," she whispered, grinning and leaning across the table. "I have sex all night - and think about having sex all day." "Well," I replied, Amaybe I can help with your diet. You need to go home and get something to wear tomorrow? If not we can spend the night at my place, dieting." She giggled a sound that I was still surprised to hear from "Squatter Scarborough." "Why do you think I brought that big purse? Everything I need is in it."

Dec 25

It had been a hectic couple of days since the party. Now back at Isaac's. Christmas morning he was running a little fever. I'd wanted to call the hospital again but he'd insisted on just an Aspirin. "Hell of a Christmas present," he muttered. "I've got one on lay away at the PX but you'll have to wait for it." I slipped his new watch on his arm and kissed him a Merry Christmas. I followed up with a quick, and totally wanton, display of my newly acquired - and diligently working to improve - erotic skills. After that we just lazed the rest of the day. We, actually, got to sleep fairly early.

Dec 26

Monday morning, after my shower - Isaac was limited to a

sponge bath by his big bandages - we'd, again, gotten in a little more practice. It was a holiday for most folks but not us. We got dressed and went our separate ways. Isaac to the office but I had to go to Ktown-shadowed by my, now familiar bodyguard, to handle my transfer from Fischbach to AWSCOM. With my temporary promotion, I was informed that I had been put on the list for "field grade quarters" as soon as they were available. The housing officer was, obviously put out a bit that a Colonel had insisted on him coming in on a Holiday to handle a Damn DAC, (Damned Army Civilian) housing request. It was almost noon by the time I got back to Pirmasens and was taken in to, formally, meet Colonel Richmond. He got up from his desk and shook my hand before waving me to the chair in his office. "I understand that congratulations are in order, Ms. Scarborough. That was, truly, an amazing performance you gave the other night. I understand you were injured slightly. Are you sure you want to go back to work so soon?" I told him that my injuries sounded a lot worse than they were. After that, he chatted a little, ending up saying that he recognized my "unique position in the command" and if I needed anything from him to just ask. He then became very solemn. "That's not just a phrase from your commanding officer. I know you've become involved in a situation that's very much out of the out of your 'other duties as assigned' category. If there's any way this command can help don't be shy in asking for it."

When I got to the office, it was almost two. Isaac was already in a meeting with the Facilities Engineer. I moved into Isaac's old desk in the office, Fraulein Kohl brought Amy messages". When she hesitated a moment, I asked her if there was something else. "Well, Miss Scarborough," she said, nervously, "I hope you - well, the whole headquarters is talking about what you did the other night and I just wanted to say how impressed we all are with you." Shit! I thought, questing for something to say. "Well, you just do what you have to do. I guess." I finally got out. Then, remembering something else, I said, "By the way, everyone I've worked with in the past has called me Joanne.A Then, unable to hide a grin, I added, "or, lately, Squatter." A wide grin spread over Miss Kohl's face. "Oh, I know," she laughed. "The whole headquarters is aware of that teletype too." "Take your pick, then." I said with a smile "Well," she said, frowning, "Perhaps I could do that, if you would call me Signe." Then she added, "I hope you won't think me rude but - well - would you like to borrow some of my perfume?" What the hell was that all about? I wondered, looking up at her. She had a really worried look on her face. She gulped and said "the scent you're wearing is - well - very distinctive" I was really confused. I never wear perfume. Then it struck me. Shit! This morning! No! I'd been very careful about that. Did just thinking about what Isaac and I had done - Damn! I had forgotten the lovely day dream I'd had coming back from Ktown. I must have, as the old Victorians used to say, "spilled some of my essence." Oh double damn! Had the Colonel? Oh Shit! Embarrassed, I thanked her and said "yes. I'd like some." I was glad she didn't smile. She handed me the little bottle. After that was done, she straightened up and, once again, became Fraulein Kohl. "One of those messages was marked urgent," she said. "Would you like me to get the Ramstein Support Detachment on the phone?" I picked up the top message and looked at it. "Important you get in touch with this office, soonest. Chief Ramstein Support Detachment." "He wouldn't leave a name." Signe said, huffily. "Not very -?" "Polite?" I finished for her. She nodded. Still embarrassed, I nodded back, staring down at the second message. "She was very polite." Signe said. I frowned. Robin had left a similar message. I told Signe to call her first.

"Hi Boss." Robin's voice, as usual, was cheerful. "We've got a problem - actually several more. You know your old problem from last week? We've finished counting today and found six more." All I could say was, "Oh Shit!" When I'd had time to think, I asked if the packages were palletized the same way. "Sure enough," she said. I told her to report it to the Major and that I'd be down as soon as I could. Then I told Signe to get Ramstein on the phone. When Montgomery's voice answered, I asked if this was the "Ramstein Support Detachment - the "Impolite" chief. "Miss Scarborough, I need you and Mister Hamlin up here right away" he said with no prologue - and no comment. "Sorry." I said with a grin. "He's in a meeting and I've got to go see my inspector down south." "This is important" he shot back. "So are six more problems." I told him. He was quiet a long time. "Well, as soon as you get back." There was a click on the phone. I put it down and told Signe I had to go to Fischbach and to tell "Mister Hamlin" that "the finished inventory at Fischbach, was bad and that, as soon as I got back, we had to go to Ramstein." She frowned. "He'll know what you mean?" I just nodded. With that I got my coat and left.

We'd had sleet today - apparently Indian summer was over -

95

and as I passed through Pirmasens and I knew the mountain road to the depot would be treacherous so I opted for the long way around. As a result, it was almost fourteen hundred by the time I got to the Surveillance Office. Robin got up from my old desk as I came in and we headed directly for the Magazine in her truck. "How you like being the boss?" I asked. "It's not as much fun as I thought it would be" she muttered. "Are all inspectors so thick headed?" I laughed. "Most actually, you've got some pretty good ones. They've got, though, a thing about working for a woman - especially one that's just gotten promoted over them. All of them think they should have had the job. No doubt, they all think you got it because I was a woman and influenced the action." She glanced over at me. "Did you?" "Of course, I'd be a lousy supervisor if I didn't have feelings about the quality of the hired help.

In your case, though, none of the ones here were on the list I was presented, and, of the other ones that were, you were significantly above the rest in qualifications." As an afterthought, lest she let her ego get too big, I added, with a grin, that, "Besides, I knew you and you were already here." Then I decided to give her some advice based on my lofty new rank. I told her that she had one thing she had to watch out for. "Any inspector that's worth a damn wants to get his hands dirty. They also have an opinion as to how something should be done. A branch chief, though, needs to lead - not do. They have to let their crew do their job, giving an opinion on how to do it only when asked - or when it looks like it's gonna get screwed up. In the last case, you have to explain why you gave an unsolicited opinion – and you should do it in private. It's the one most common situation that makes or breaks a first level supervisor and one that women, especially, have a problem with. Women are, by nature, inclined to express their opinions more than men. In a crisis, you can lead by doing. The rest of the time you lead by managing what others do." Robin thought about that a minute as she drove. "Supervisors don't get to have much fun, do they?" I had to chuckle at that. "Well, the problems are just a little different. They have to deal with people problems, not hardware. It's a lot more frustrating but, once you get used to it, it's fun in its own way."

Once we got to the magazine, it was obvious that it had been a wasted trip - except to show that the crew had done their job well. The empty containers had been taken to the shop and the rest didn't give a clue to what had gone down. The Magazine Data Card, though, did confirm that these weapons had been stored and palletized on the same days as the others - and by the same crew. How the hell could one man get ten missiles out of the magazine without anyone else knowing? And, how the hell could a crew palletize empty boxes and not know it? I told them all that they'd done well and, while Robin drove back to the office, I pondered that question. Back at the office, as I got out of Robin's truck and into my car to head back to Pirmasens, I gave the problem to her.

Isaac must have seen me pull into the parking lot because, by the time I got to the door, he met me, blurting, "Montgomery's having a coniption. Let's take my car." He'd hustled me into the Mercedes and, if the Germans had speed laws, he'd have broken half them on the way to Kaiserslautern. Thus, we were in Montgomery's office in less than a half hour after leaving Pirmasens. He wasn't alone. Deutsche Inspector Hoffman was sitting on his couch. "Shit!" I thought. I wasn't ever going to be rid of the investigation of my "incident." I decided I'd best be civil though. I held out my hand and told him it was good to see him again - then added "did I forget to complete some form?" His eyes twinkled a moment as he surprised me by lifting my hand and kissing it. "I wish I had thought of that stratagem," he murmured. "I enjoy taking statements from beautiful women." I barely held back a cutting remark as, embarrassed, I blushed. His eyes, though, had lost their twinkle. "Unfortunately, I'm here on more serious business."

I was surprised to see the blush. Scarborough seemed to have mellowed in the last few days. I wondered if that was Hamlin's doing. My security detail was reporting that only one bedroom light was being used. Oh well - "Inspector Hoffman is here on business related to our problem." I said, before she could say anything. Then turning to him, I remarked that he had met Mister Hamlin. "Yes, indeed." He said, dropping Scarborough's hand and extending his to Hamlin "Miss, Scarborough's rescuer." Taking the proffered hand, Hamlin grunted that, "it was more the other way around." Hoffman raised an eyebrow and simply remarked that the two of them made a formidable team. Then he turned to business. "I have encountered a problem in Kaiserslautern - one that I thought Mister Montgomery might be able to help with. He, in turn, contacted you, telling me that you two would also be interested and, perhaps of some use. You see, my office has been monitoring a group of local men, believed to be working for an arms dealer - or, at least, involved in activities not sanctioned by my government.

97

Yesterday, one of my men intercepted a telephone conversation, indicating that the group had probably been exposed and that they should take immediate steps to "move the merchandise." As a result, we tightened our surveillance and, when they loaded a truck at a warehouse, raided the installation. They resisted, violently - unusual in our country. One of my men and one of them was wounded. Two of them were killed. We captured two more. The truck was loaded with arms and ammunition and the warehouse contained more of the same plus other supplies. We are, presently, in the process of inventorying the contents and would like Colonel Montgomery's help in evaluating the material we have found. He, then, called you two as being his experts in arms and ammunition - and said that there is a possibility that he has a problem that might be related to mine." It was time I chimed in. "I've explained to Inspector Hoffman," I said, "that the classified nature of our problem might prevent our full cooperation but that, to the limit of our law, we will cooperate as fully as possible. You both know the dilemma I face. I've worked with the inspector for many years and trust him implicitly. Still, without obtaining clearance from Washington, I'm in a bind."

Isaac and I had not been surprised at Montgomery's silence, when Inspector Hoffman had asked if there was a problem in obtaining the clearance. After a moment, the inspector had simply nodded and suggested that we forget he'd asked that question. It was obvious that Montgomery had a question of trust - but that it probably didn't extend to Hoffman. After a moment, Montgomery told Hoffman that he'd appreciate it if he would keep our involvement in the matter "Low Key - preferably secret." Hoffman frowned. "I have a crew working in the warehouse," he said. "They have been carefully - in your words - vetted. Still, there is no need to introduce your people to them." Turning to us, he asked if we would mind riding with him, that he could return us to here afterwards. We agreed. On the way to the site, Hoffman turned to the rear window and commented that we were being followed. Isaac told him that we knew that and he asked no more questions.

By the time we got to the large warehouse on the outskirts of Ktown, it was dark. Jo and I both wore black leather jackets with the word POLIZEI on the back. When he led us into the warehouse, I was astounded at the sight. Weapon and ammunition crates were piled high on one side with crates of other material on the other. Walking down the aisle I could read the Deutsch labels for everything from army rations to all sorts of clothing. The weapons crates were stenciled in the same language. Just a quick check of the inventory Hoffman carried revealed everything from mortars and antitank weapons to automatic rifles and pistols. Jo had been very quiet on our tour. Finally, looking into a crate of RPG 7 launchers, she frowned and muttered. "Brand new and Too many." "Depends on how many men you want to equip – and the RPG has been around forever." I chuckled. She glanced up at me, obviously ignoring my quip. "I don't know about European armies but US units used to have around two hundred men to a company and eight hundred to a battalion. As for the weapon, the RPG 2 has been around a long time but this is the new seven variant. It just came out in the last couple of years." Hoffman caught her drift before I did. "And there are small arms here for equipping eight hundred men" he growled. "I'll bet that if you check, you'll find the heavier weapons match up to those of an American battalion also" she said. Turning to me, she asked "How many times have you looked at the inventory for an infantry battalion basic load?" She was right, of course but I pointed out that these weren't US weapons. "No" she agreed. "They're all eastern block or European. Why would an arms dealer stock this specific number of foreign weapons - especially since, even on the black market, it has to be cheaper to simply buy US ones?"

I wasn't surprised when Hoffman asked if I'd care to speculate on that question. I was sorely tempted, but instead, I looked up at him and, smiling, said that I wouldn't. He grinned back at me. "In that case, perhaps you'd like to see something else we found in a locked room," he said. Turning, he led us to a hallway and, at the end, through a small door. Stacked against one wall were a pile of crates that I immediately recognized as those that Russian SA 7 missiles were shipped in. One was open and contained an SA 7. Looking around the room, I spotted three different crates. One of them was open and two of our missing Redeye II's lay in it. I couldn't help a gasp. "Care to comment on the contents in this room," he asked, this time frowning. I took a very deep breath and told him that I would very much like to but that, perhaps, he should talk to Mister Montgomery.

Hoffman frowned at me. "Miss Scarborough, I'm no expert but that looks like a variant of your US Redeye missile - the same as the missile that damaged an airliner just recently. Can you comment on that? I thought quickly. "Yes," I said. "I can verify that it LOOKS LIKE a variant of the Redeye, and APPEARS to be similar that missile." I studied him carefully. Montgomery trusted him. I took a deep breath and said very carefully, "It would seem that nine should be a more likely number to find. People who steal multiple things seem to do it in groups of ten." A slow smile crept over his face. I hurried to add that I wouldn't like to see speculations like that, spread around, though. "As we say back home, it's sort of a WAG - Wild Ass Guess." Hoffman grinned widely. "Our literal translation is Wilde Esel Vurmutung. We have a similar phrase in our language. I would never pass on something like that to anyone I didn't know very well." He grinned wider. "It so happens that we have nine here. I smiled back at him and thanked him.

I couldn't help a grin but I hid it behind my hand as Joanne talked to Hoffman. I suspected that Montgomery would, officially, blanch at what she'd said but, privately, he'd applaud. Then Hoffman asked her if she had any other speculations, "Wilde Esel or otherwise." She frowned again. Oh shit! I thought. She's going to do it again. "Well," she said, her face screwed up in thought. "I've wondered about those Irish thugs that attacked me. Surely, all this is connected somehow. The problem is that I can't see the IRA actually mustering a US type battalion for an operation. Unless they're hiring their muscle, a lot more than I'd have thought they had, out to others, there must be something else going on." I tried to let out my breath slowly. There was nothing too worrisome in that statement. It should be enough to make Hoffman think, though. I'd been quietly worrying about the Irish element for several days. It didn't seem to fit then and even less so now - unless those missing missiles were significant.

We picked over the piles of equipment all night, taking samples from each pile. More and more, it looked like a standard TO&E for a light infantry battalion - one that intended to fight in the desert – assuming that they intended to use Eastern Bloc weapons. Also, there was that nagging question again, the one I remembered having at Fischbach on that ammunition we'd received. The damned thing just wouldn't come through and, I knew was going to drive me nuts until it did. Also, I was sure none of this had come through Fischbach since I'd been there. All the clothing was new, tropical weight Olive Drab US Army uniforms. "I wonder if the troops in Nam have equipment this good" Isaac mused? I had a thought of my own on the subject. "I wonder who'll step up to claim the stuff," I asked "Whoever does will have to admit that their security is lousy."

After watching our MICOM rep at work, it should be an interesting situation." Hoffman, who had been standing nearby, laughed. "Perhaps the Wehrmacht will acquire much new equipment. It is, after all, in our hands. Do not you "mericans have a saying that having something is like owning it?" I had to laugh, myself. "The expression is that possession is nine tenths of the law." "Ja!" he chuckled. "And, at present, we possess this equipment. Of course, as good allies, we would, naturally, return anything that your country might have lost - or misplaced - if asked."

It was almost 0800 hours, and still dark, when Hoffman dropped us off back at Ramstein. Montgomery was still at his office and his staff was arriving to start the work day. We briefed him, quickly, on what we'd seen and our speculations, then told him we were going go get some sleep. I napped as Isaac drove back to Pirmasens and we both checked in at the office. There were several messages on our desks for action but none that couldn't wait so we checked out and went home - well, to Isaac's place. At the sight of the tan sedan pulling in behind us, I wondered if our bird dogs had been up all night too.

Man! I was beat. Even, though, the sight of Joanne coming out of the bathroom in that practically, transparent baby doll outfit, had brought out a lustful reaction, I could still, barely drag myself into the bathroom to shower. Somewhat more awake after a cold shower, I wondered if I was up to taking advantage of that outfit she wore. Perhaps I should come to her fully aroused but, unfortunately, my body seemed too, tired to oblige me. I sighed and put on a pair of shorts. Steeling myself to become the lover she deserved, I opened the door - to see her lying atop the sheet, gorgeously displayed for my view - but dead to the world. I chuckled to myself as my body reacted sluggishly to the sight but I ignored it and crawled into bed beside her. Slipping my arm under her head, and sliding up against her, I lost consciousness myself.

When I awoke, I was half draped over Isaac's body as he snored lightly. His arms lay outstretched on the bed. I looked down, ruefully considering the fact that the sexiest outfit I owned hadn't been enough to get me laid. Then I realized it wasn't yet dark. Glancing at the clock I saw it was not quite 1500 hours. I wondered how the world had gotten on without us all day. Carefully, I slipped out of bed and padded into the living room. I called the office and Signe told me that there were no really important things going on and that she had handled all the routine stuff. With that, I hung up and went to the kitchen to make coffee. After I got the pot to perking, I checked the refrigerator. It appeared that, unless we went out, supper was going to be eggs, bacon and toast. I took them out of the refrigerator and was carrying them to the counter when a half naked man appeared in the doorway. I caught my breath at the tingle in my body when I caught sight of him. Even with bandages covering his shoulder, he was sexy as hell. When, the hell, had I become so aroused by a man, I wondered for the millionth time in the last week. I wasn't the only one aroused, I noted as I watched, fascinated by the slowly rising bulge in his shorts. "What more could a man ask for when he wakes up?" he muttered, adding, "Coffee perking, food, and a gorgeous, practically naked, girl waiting for his pleasure." I shook my head to clear my mind a bit. "The same practically naked girl who didn't even rate a kiss a few hours ago." I said, trying to look angry. "Coffee's ready." He laughed. "Unconscious girls don't remember kisses when they get them. As for coffee, it can wait." With that, he came to me and, scooping me into his arms took my mouth in a passionate kiss that I greedily returned.

Stretching up on tiptoes, her arms circling my neck she kissed me back, out tongues, frantically, seeking each others. Ignoring a stab of pain, I slid one hand - the weak one - down inside the back of her bikini panties to grasp her soft buttocks and the other up under her top to fondle her taut breast. "You've got too many clothes on." I muttered around her tongue. Her breath quickened but one hand snaked down to tug at her panties. Between our two hands we managed to get them down off her hips. I pushed them down until they fell at her feet. Pushing my hand between her legs I determined that she was already ready. While I did that, her hand was fumbling at the opening of my shorts. "Better" she murmured as her fingers took a very important part of me in hand. In answer, I grasped both her buttocks and, ignoring a twinge of pain in my shoulder, lifted her up until I felt her fitting the object of her attention in the place where it belonged. "There" she whispered as she settled herself firmly, in place. I took the hint and did my part in this play. With a gasp and a groan, she lifted her legs and threw them around my waist. I loosened my grip to let her body drop before lowering her onto the table.

I reveled in the wanton feeling of sitting on a surface meant for eating and using it for something entirely different. My mind was saying, "Joanne Scarborough, you're acting like a slut, fornicating like that standing in the middle of the kitchen." "Shut up!" I muttered to myself. "We're not fornicating. He's fucking me like a damned rabbit and I'm not standing at all. Besides, I'm loving every bit of it" - and I was! Panting like a man who hadn't had sex in years, he seemed bent on making sure that my body would never again accept anyone other than him. As for myself, I was concentrating on helping him, tightening my legs to the rhythm of his body. I screamed into his mouth as I felt my body convulse. He continued the assault long after my shaking body quieted. I clung to him still quivering, my head now on his shoulder as he continued to pleasure me. I sighed with delight as I felt my body beginning to react for a second time. This time, I couldn't help a very unladylike squeal as this reaction turned my belly to mush. My squeal turned into a satisfied groan at his gasp as his body stilled. I was just catching my breath when he gasped "we're going to have to shower again before we get dressed." It slid into my fuzzy brain that tonight was the party.

Damn! I couldn't believe it! Three men dead trying to kidnap a single damned girl. If - no when - the word got out we'd look like a lot of fools. I rounded on Liam so angry I could have, willingly, killed him then and there. "And what were you doing when this was happening?" I shouted. "I was at the cabin guarding the weapons, Sean" he said, quietly. "They were supposed to bring the lass there and we were to terrify her into getting out of the picture - all because that arrogant son of a bitch told you to?" I growled. "Just how were you going to do that?" "Well he didn't want any outside marks on her but he said we could all use her. He was sure she'd become so hysterical, maybe even go mad, so nobody would pay much more attention to whatever she said." "Yes! She sounds like the hysterical type." I sneered. "That type always manages to make Swiss cheese out of three grown men. Stupid men that didn't even bother to see if she had a weapon when they captured her! And another thing, what were you doing listening to an idiot when you were to simply take out a plane and move the rest of those weapons from there to here? Hell! You couldn't even do the plane job right." When he hung his head, I knew why. "Shite!" I muttered. "You took the job on your own, didn't you? How much? How much to

103

kidnap an American woman who works for the government, rape her and hope she won't tell anyone? Didn't you realize that after all that you'd have to kill her?" It was all I could do to keep from pulling out my pistol and killing him on the spot. The SOB started to lie then thought better of it. "A thousand Quid apiece" he muttered. "He said, it was to be an extra requirement for letting us have the missiles." "You stupid -!" I caught my anger and stopped short of telling him what I really thought. "We paid twenty thousand pounds for those missiles. They were ours. He knew he couldn't hold out on us. If he had, we'd have blown his whole operation. He was bluffing and you should have known it."

I really thought Liam was gonna kill me. Instead he took a deep breath and turned away. Finally, over his shoulder, he said, "you know what you've done, don't you?" I decided not to answer that - I wasn't sure what to say anyway. He turned back to me. "You've let one girl make us the laughingstock of Europe. There's only one way to make up for that even if it brings the whole American army down on us. She has to be taken out or no one will ever trust us again. You think if I give you three more men, you can keep from getting them all killed too?" All I could think of, was, "Yes Sir." He pointed a finger at my face. "You'd better! If another of my men gets killed it had better be you!"

STINGER
CHAPTER 9

Jan 16 1967 Monday

It had been two weeks since our visit to the contraband warehouse and the State Department and the Germans were negotiating over the contents. Aside from evaluating the condition of the weapons for State, we hadn't been required to do anything more. This morning, we had come in as usual and were going through the mail and messages on our desks. Signe had, as usual, done a good job of sorting it before we had gotten in. Isaac's dealt mostly with policy and the normal traffic from above. As usual, I could tell from the scowl on his face, there was another query, usually a note, from Dawson at COMZ HQ. He seldom let more than a few days go by without asking for some piddling information on our activities - usually with a note of implied complaint in the question. I had gotten down to a report from Robin at Fischbach and was frowning myself. Howard Marcum had made his quarterly visit to Siegelsbach to check the 259th Ordnance Company magazines and had passed on a request from the Commander for a permanently assigned inspector. It had been a year since we'd had an inspector over there.

The last one, Oliver Werner, was one of the old school guys who thought he could bully his way to anything he wanted. The result had been a message to Colonel Richmond, from, the major commanding, at the time, demanding that he "get rid of either him or me!" We'd moved Oliver to Fischbach until he rotated home last month. The new commander seemed to have a different attitude. That was both good and bad news. The good news was that we would probably be able to justify a new personnel space - one that we'd lost when Oliver went home. The bad news was that before we could do that, and get a replacement we'd be even more short-handed at Fischbach than we are. We'd yet to get a replacement for Robin when she was promoted to chief. At best her replacement would take a couple of months. More curious than that was the last line of the report that suggested that she and I should discuss this situation. Did she want me to try and get a temporary replacement from Miesau? It might not be a bad idea. Homer Hill over there had a much larger staff and could probably spare one, with a lot of complaining about his work load, better than Fischbach.

I turned to Isaac and, while I waited for him to finish whatever was causing his frown, told Signe to call Fischbach and ask Robin to come up whenever she could get away. Signe, smiled, benignly, at me and suggested I look at my last phone con. Digging down to the bottom of the stack of paper, I found it. Robin had called and said that, if I was going to be in today, she'd be here at 1100 hours. "Getting a little aggressive, are you girl?" I thought to myself but had to grin. "Good for you."

      "Call her and tell her that would be fine." I told Signe. Just then, Isaac slapped the offending message down on his desk and growled. "What's he want now?" I asked, grinning. "You reading my mind?" he grunted. "Just your face," I laughed. "Weather report Storms with freezing rain." He couldn't help a laugh. "It was attached to a series of messages from the supply section. That stupid - twit - wants to know how much materiel we can store at our depots." I chuckled at what he'd almost called Dawson. "What kind of materiel? And why doesn't he ask the supply people?" I asked, still chuckling.

      "I'll read it verbatim," was his reply. "How much stuff can you store at the AWSCOM depots including outside pads?" "Stuff?" I laughed. "Sounds like Dawson." "He's not the only one" he growled. "Our supply sent back a message asking what kind of "stuff" and the reply was -" he lifted the clipped messages and, turning to the back, read, "Re: Stuff". Need tonnage quantities of large, medium and small." He slapped the messages back down on his desk. "What kind of shit heads we got working up there?" he asked, rhetorically. Barely able to keep a straight face, I asked "you mean the ones that have been praising Dawson's brains ever since he got there?" Hearing the chuckle from behind me, I growled, without looking around, "Negative thinking about your superiors is bad for your performance report, Fraulein Kohl." "Oh, I'm so sorry, Miss Squatter. I was just remembering a Der Spiegel Joke." She murmured behind me, not sounding too contrite.

      Well, at least the office was less oppressive now. I thought. I wondered how I was going to be able to keep it like this and have Jo too. At least we'd, finally, been able to bring ourselves to act in a professional manner in the office - even with the occasional prurient thought when I'd look up and catch her looking at me. Her solemn gaze seldom failed to bring on an immediate erection. Thank god for my desk, for I suspected what her gaze entailed. I'd been surprised to realize the other day that she was wearing perfume. When I'd asked about it, she'd grinned, impishly and said that Signe had let her know that certain day dreams tended to leave embarrassing results in the air. It was with difficulty that I brought my thoughts back to business. When she told me about the Fischbach situation I agreed that she should call Homer and see what she could do. When she suggested it would be better coming from the chief, I told her that I thought it was women who were supposed to be able to get men to do anything they wanted them to do. With a quick look back, she stuck her tongue out at me - then turned back to pick up the phone. "Oh and I'd like to sit in on your meeting with Robin. I'm curious." I told her. She waved a hand at me as she spoke into the phone, obviously telling Homer's secretary that she'd like to speak to him.

When Robin came in, I waved her to a chair. She gave a minute shake of her head. We had worked together long enough to know what she wanted. Puzzled, I asked, if she would rather we found some place more comfortable. "You look like it's been a long day already." She grinned and said she'd like that. I told Signe we'd be in the conference room and, nodding to Isaac, got up. A few moments later we sat down side by side at the conference table and she plopped down in the chair opposite us. "You were, actually, right," she said. "It's been a stressful morning. I got the damnedest call from the Ops officer at the 259th. He wanted to know what I knew about a message asking about how much "stuff" he could store. Isaac and I both laughed. "We've been puzzling over the same message" he said. "Well, he's new over there and I didn't know what to tell him. Also, and I'm suspicious of coincidences, he had asked Howard if we could get an inspector over there on short notice. Then, right after he, Howard, had made his report on the irregularities in one of the magazines, Major Plumb, told him he'd look into it' and asked him about a permanently assigned inspector. Considering the flap when Oliver got thrown out over there, it was an amazing request. Is there something going on that I don't know about?" I looked at Isaac and could see the light dawn on his face. Then it hit me. I remembered what month it was and the articles I'd read in the Stars and Stripes. Isaac leaned forward. "What were the irregularities in the magazines," he asked. Robin frowned. "Dunnage." she replied. "They had stored pre cut blocking and bracing in one of the weapons magazines and, of course, that's not allowed. Still both the Depot Commander and the Ops officer blew him off when he reported it." "What kind of blocking and bracing, Robin?" I asked. She leaned back. "The kind you'd use to secure warhead containers to a truck bed - six truck beds."

Damn! So it was real. We were actually, going to do it. Six 32 foot trucks, assuming the standard army flat beds meant twenty four weapons. I wondered if Colonel Richmond had been told yet. I'd better have a talk with him. In the meantime, our perceptive new Fischbach chief was going to have to be mollified. I could tell she was pissed. "OK, Miss Laurence." I said. "First, as far as stuff is concerned, you might suggest that the Ops officer at the 259th do what we have always done to fools. Lie to them. So many tons of big little and medium stuff. Have him make up some figure. It won't really matter. I doubt that the people who get it will know enough to call him on it anyway. Second, we'll put in a request for a new position and Jo - Miss Scarborough has already gotten Homer Hill to lend you a body for ninety days. After that we can hope that your vacancies will be filled and he can take up the slack till we can fill the positions, permanently. Third, tell the Ops officer that you'll manage to take care of short notice staffing if it becomes necessary. If you get in a real bind, Miss Scarborough or I will take up the slack. Finally, leave the dunnage issue for the time being. Hopefully, it'll sort itself out."

Robin frowned at me. "You mean ignore a safety manual requirement? Howard is expecting us to slap those folks." I nodded then grinned. "Tell Mister Marcum that you told us but think there hasn't been much change at Headquarters. We're still afraid to rock the boat." "Hah!" Robin grunted. "Boss, most of us don't know you too well, but we know Squatter is up here. You really think anybody down at Fischbach will believe something like that?" I had to chuckle. "And just what do you think Marcum will do if you tell him that?" I asked. "He'll think you're a liar," she said, angrily. Then her forehead creased. "But he'll shut up about it till he finds out what's going on." I grinned at her. "Who could ask for anything more?" She frowned at me. "You know, Squatter once told me you were devious SOB. I should have believed her." I glanced over at Jo and caught the tail end of a blush. Robin must have caught it too, for she muttered, "you're a bad influence on, what used to be a really great bitch of a boss. Well, if there's nothing else, maybe I'd better go." When I didn't respond, she got up and left.

"Well, now we know what you think of me," he said looking straight at me, "a devious Son of a bitch." Embarrassed, I shot back "well she thinks I was a bitch." He chuckled. "No" he said, "she called you a great bitch." Then his grin widened. "I guess I don't mind, though, as long as you agree to be my great bitch." Resisting the urge to get maudlin, I told him I'd remind him of that the next time I had my period. He took my hand and squeezed it. "I'm sure I'll hear about it" he murmured. In the meantime, how 'bout holding down the fort I need to talk to the Colonel. I asked if he thought the Colonel didn't know. He frowned. If he does, he should know that the secret's unraveling.

When Isaac came back, he called me into his office and shut the door. "He knew" he started off. "And he told me I wasn't to talk to anyone about it. When I pointed out it was you who brought the information to me, he said you had a higher clearance than he did but neither of us had the need to know. He approved of how we handled it with Robin, though, and said he'd put in an emergency request for a new replacement at Fischbach to fill the 64th and 259th requirements. He said to make sure Robin and Marcum kept their mouths shut." "Well," I said, "I've been checking the NATO requirements list. Six trucks are only half enough. Sure, as hell, Fischbach's gonna get the same tasking." "Shit that'll take every inspector they've got." "More than they've got if it happens when we think it will." I told him. "Harry Trent's down with the flu."

19 Jan Thursday

Sure enough, Thursday morning, the phone rang and Signe, nodded to me. "Squatter," an agitated, Robin was on the other end. "I've got a problem. "One too few inspectors" I asked trying for calm. There was quiet a moment. I could hear her take a deep breath before she replied. "You knew!" she growled. "You could have, at least, warned me. They won't tell me a thing." "No, I couldn't." I said, trying for a sympathetic voice. "You go ahead and take Marcum east. I'll come down and fill the hole for your local requirement. You go home and pack for a week's TDY. Tell Howard and George to do the same. You take Howard - no better have Howard take his own car - on east today and have George report to me here by 1400. If you rush, you can probably get a briefing as soon as you get over there." "There's a briefing here at 1400" she said. "OK, then, have George get home, get packed and meet me back there then." There was a pause before she said, "Yes ma'am." I chuckled. "It's too late to remember your manners now girl. Just be careful on the road. While you're at it, why don't you have a talk with that major over there? Let him know we won't send him another dud." That got a chuckling, "Thanks" out of her before she hung up.

Isaac had been listening. "I'll see if the Colonel has anything you need to know now" he said, getting up and heading for the door. Turning before he went out, he said, "By the way, I called Montgomery. He swore a bit but you'll have another bird dog to tag along with you. Better tell the 64th MP's. They might get nervous otherwise."

I pulled in to Isaac's house to get packed and was surprised to see Jonathan get out of his sedan with another man. He'd been our unacknowledged daytime companion so long we'd gotten to know him well - though, he had been reticent about his last name. "Miss, Scarborough, this is Allen. He's to be with me on your - well to be with you on your trip." The boss insisted I introduce you so you'd know who he was." I shook his hand, with the usual glad to meet you sort of thing "He's already aware of the limits on his job." Jonathan said. "I don't suppose you want to tell me your last name either." I said, only half irritated. He smiled. "Just call me Allen." I couldn't help a grin and went on inside.

An hour later, I pulled into the gate at Fischbach depot and the guard told me I was expected at the conference room. Glancing in my rearview mirror, I saw "Allen's" tan sedan pull up across from the gate and the guard reach for the telephone. As soon as I entered the conference room, Captain, Buckholtz, the depot Security chief, button holed me. "You have a new bird dog, Miss Scarborough?" It was only half a question. "His name's Allen." I told him. "He'll be going with us." He just nodded. Just then, Major Compton came into the room, accompanied by the usual call to attention so the other military could jump to their feet. I slid into the chair next to George Pettigrew.

Jan 20 1967

It was a relief, and near dark the day after our briefing, when I was, finally, able to get out of the car at the gate to the French Missile Site. It had been a long five hours trailing along behind the convoy. On Highway 10 and after we'd gotten off the Autobahn it had been a mere

110

thirty miles an hour except when maneuvering through the innumerable German villages on the way through the mountains. It had been all narrow back roads, especially after we'd gotten into the southern end of the Black Forest. Our speed through most of those roads had been no more than twenty, often closer to ten. My little Porsche complained all the way. Even a quick stop at a gasthaus on the road, to get beer for myself and my two bird dogs, hadn't helped much. Finally, though, the MP Lieutenant at the last rest stop came back and suggested I go ahead and give them a heads up, at the site, that we were coming. I'd resisted the urge to kiss him and, with my trailing tan ford behind me, passed around the convoy and had made tracks to the site. I had a terrible urge to let the little Porsche out on the twisting road but held myself in check. The Opel behind me would never have kept up.

I walked up to the front gate of the site and was confronted by the biggest man I had ever seen. He must have been seven feet tall, black as the ace of spades and wearing a French Foreign Legion uniform. When I told him I needed to see the American Detachment Commander, he just looked down at me, a look of disdain on his face. Insolently, he looked me up and down as if he were thinking of buying me. I started to get mad. I was hot and tired, frustrated at a long slow drive and in no mood for male chauvinism. Without thinking, I thrust my finger in his face and shouted, "Listen to me you -." Just as I was about to blow up, he turned and called out, in French, to the guard shack. Looking over, I saw the other guard was already on the phone. Without another word, the giant turned and left me fuming at the gate.

It was five of the longest minutes of my life before I saw an American officer coming toward the gate. When he got near, I saw he was a very young captain. Arriving at the gate, he frowned and asked what I "Needed." Barely managing to cover my irritation at his surly attitude, I told him that I "needed" to tell him that a platoon of assembly personnel, a company of MP's and an Infantry company would be arriving in less than a half hour with plans to remove the Nuclear Warheads from this site and pack them for shipment back to the depot on Monday. I wanted to give him a "heads up" so -A He interrupted me by filling the air with expletives. When he'd, apparently, exhausted his supply, he growled, "those sons of bitches! The plans were for us to decommission those missiles at the end of the month. Damn it! They haven't even been taken off the launchers. This is Friday. There's no way they can be ready for shipment by Monday. The French will never stand for it! They're all Catholic and not about to work on Sunday."

When he paused for breath, I told him that the orders came from NATO headquarters and that we had personnel able to handle the removal from launchers or anything else that might be needed. I also added, that the convoy route orders had already been published and that the Infantry Company with us was only the lead element of a regiment, assigned to this operation and that the Warheads would be on the trucks by Monday.

After a furious phone call from the Captain, a French officer showed up. I wasn't much up on French rank but he was introduced as Capitaine DeMoyer. He immediately ordered the gate opened and invited me into the guardhouse. He, actually, kissed my hand when I introduced myself and, again, went over the situation. "Mademoiselle Scarborough," he purred. "I'm sure we will do our best to accommodate our allies, though we have limited facilities here for billeting". I told him that our people had come equipped to live in the field and that, I was sure that the open field beside his compound would suffice for their needs. Since he was being so polite, I also, apologized for the "apparent mix up" in orders relating to dates of this transfer. He waved my apology aside with a smile and said, "The US has more than made up for that by sending the most beautiful woman in Europe to make up for their lack of courtesy." As I gaped, and blushed at his blatant flirting, he took my hand again and kissing it, said, "Much as I hate to leave such charming company, I must get back to start preparations for this operation. If you need anything more at any time, come to the gate and ask for me. I will be happy to accommodate your merest desire at any time." With that and a sharp command to the Sergeant of the guard, he turned and left. The sergeant came to me and asked if I would like a cup of tea.

An hour later, I was standing with Lieutenant Grayson and CWO Martin watching the very efficient establishment of an army camp in the field beside the missile site, when a young French officer strode up. Hitting a brace, British style, he saluted the Lieutenant. "Capitaine DeMoyer has sent me to invite you, your officers and Mademoiselle, Scarborough to the Dining In tonight at the Officers Mess." His words were in carefully enunciated and obviously practiced, English. Grayson looked a little flustered. It was obvious that he wasn't sure just what a "Dining In" entailed in a European Army. Using my barely remembered French from high school, I spoke up and asked if the "Capitaine" was aware that none of us had brought dress clothes with us. Turning to me, he smiled and said that the Capitaine had waived the normal attire for tonight. "In that case," I said I'm sure I'd be happy to attend" and looked, significantly at Grayson, I translated. He spoke up and agreed that he, Lieutenant Fitzgerald and CWO Martin would attend also.

I'd attended a Dining In with the AWSCOM headquarters group once. With the influx of female officers it was no longer a stag affair. I wasn't sure about the French but wasn't surprised that theirs wasn't much different, though there were no female officers on their post. The officers were scrupulously careful to conduct almost all conversations in English even the ones involving traditional army matters. The toasts began, of course, one to the President of the Republique and to the President of the United States. They, then continued down the chains of command of both armies, and, finally, to "The Gallant Allies of the Republique, gathered with us today."

Grayson, was, I was pleased to note, able to hold up his end of the toasts, alternating with his hosts in his sentiments on the French. Finally, Capitaine DeMoyer, stood and, to my surprise, toasted "The beautiful lady who, this day, like a lion, faced both the Foreign Legion and it's allied command and conquered it." What could I say to that? I knew I had to say something. Grasping for straws, I stood and, simply said, "To the Legion!" Wide grins and a loud grunt that must mean something to the locals, greeted this along with the usual round of polite applause.

By the time it was over, the three of us headed back to the camp, much the worse for drink. Never let it be said that an American could drink with a Frenchman. The same giant who had met me this afternoon was the guard and he hit a stiff brace as he saluted in the French style. When I nodded to him, a wide grin spread over his face, revealing a huge set of white teeth set in the midst of his black face. As I passed by, he muttered, softly, "Mademoiselle, Coeur Du Lion." Impulsively, I reached out and patted his upraised arm. I stopped at my car to pull out my back pack with my work clothes in it. As we walked, a bit unsteadily, away, Grayson, muttered with a chuckle, "I don't think you're supposed to pet a soldier when he's at attention." Martin chuckled. "Son, when you've just been named Lady Lion Heart, you're allowed a little petting." I couldn't help a half drunken giggle and turned to, mockingly, bow to him.

Just then, I was thrown off balance by my pack jerking sideways, and fell on my ass. Grayson, started to laugh but before he could finish, Martin knocked him into me and we all fell in a pile.

113

"What the -A was all I got out before, there was a damned war going on. Squirming around, I tried to sit up. Martin dragged me back down. "Get your butt down ma'am" he growled. "Somebody's shooting at us. Where'd he hit you?" Then I saw it just before my face piled into the ground. My shadow was outside his car across the street, emptying his pistol into the trees on the other side of the road. I tried to tell him I was alright but with my mouth in the grass, it was hard to do. Suddenly a whole squad of MP's were surrounding us and had their weapons pointed in the same direction.

The next half hour was a period of bedlam in the camp. I was hauled off and pushed down behind a truck while a platoon of infantry and MP's charged off across the road and into the forest. Martin called for the medic and wouldn't be satisfied until he was told I had no bullet hole in me. "Damn it! He muttered, I saw you knocked down." Then I remembered my pack. Hauling it around in front of me, I felt around. Sure enough there was a hole in it. A few minutes later, a platoon of French Legionnaires rushed into the camp, led by DeMoyer himself, they conferred with CWO Martin and joined the rush to the woods. Finally, I was allowed to get up and brush myself off as the troops began to filter back into camp. Capitaine DeMoyer came over and said that they had followed his trail to a side road where a car had been parked. It was no longer there. He held up a clear plastic bag in front of his flash light. "We did find this" he said. I took the bag. The rimmed cartridge case told the story. 7.62 – 54 millimeters. I said. "Sniper rifle cartridge. Probably Russian Maybe a Dragonov - probably equipped with a night scope to have hit me in the dark like that."

So much for my plan to spend the nights in a local gasthaus. I ended up in a tent of my own, sharing a trench latrine with the rest of the guys - with a guard to fend off any other users when I was "in residence." All of us were allowed, in shifts, to use the French showers to clean up. The men and Martin, though, along with the French assembly crew, spent about eighteen hours a day at the site inspecting and packaging the warheads as fast as the French crew downloaded the missiles. When I got up on Sunday morning, my tent sported a hand lettered sign that read, "The Lioness's Lair." The whole weekend infantry patrols moved through the woods looking for intruders and wherever I went, I was accompanied by either Jonathan or Allen and four or five MP's. In camp they were American and in the Missile site, French Legionnaires. It was embarrassing but comforting.

It was with some regret that we met our Monday route schedule

114

and by nightfall, we were back at Fischbach. Robin and Isaac were there to meet us. She took over the job of monitoring the unloading and storing of the weapons while Isaac followed me like a shadow as I made a report on my attack to the CO. We left for Pirmasens and he followed me all the way home. It looked like a convoy crossing the mountain, with my Porsche, his Mercedes and the tan Opel all in tandem. As soon as we got into the living room of his house, he swept me into his arms and grunted, "Damn it Jo! I was scared to death. Our first word was that you'd been shot. I've been out of my mind ever since." I shut him up by kissing him. "I'm here now, darling." I whispered. "Only my pack was wounded and I've been a bit antsy too. I think, though, that if you take me to bed I'll let you explore me enough to satisfy yourself that I'm still in one piece."

By morning, I had been thoroughly explored and both of us, I think were satisfied.

CHAPTER 10

Jan 27, 1967 Thursday night

It had been three days since Jo's return. Three days of meetings and after action reports. Montgomery was frustrated and becoming a real pain in the ass - at least he would have been if it weren't Jo's life he was trying to protect. She was taking it all calmly, though, the signs of strain were there if you looked hard enough. We had settled into a routine at work. George Pettigrew was spending one week at the 259th and one at the 64th. No further progress was made on the problem of the Redeye II's and Montgomery vacillated between wanting to bring Sullivan in and use a rubber hose on him and leaving him free in hopes of leading him to the man behind the whole affair. Our love life too, had settled down a bit from the almost frantic passion of the days after Jo's near assassination. Tonight had been a wonderful loving melding of bodies and going to sleep in each other's arms. The pounding sense of dread that brought me awake and catapulting out of bed, came as a distinct shock. The pain of something crashing against my head was the last thing I remembered until I came awake tied to a chair in our bedroom, blood running down over my ear. No. It wasn't our bedroom. It was a small room with rock walls and an overhead bulb. It was the sound of Jo's scream that woke me.

I stared at the man sitting on the mattress beside me. He was leering down at me as I continued to struggle against the ropes that held my ankles and wrists to the frame of what passed for a bed. I knew it was useless. I'd struggled as they'd dragged me, naked from the bed but was quickly tied hand and foot and thrown into a van. I tried again as they'd dragged me in here and held me down to tie me spread eagled in this position. Never the less, I had to try. He grinned. "Go ahead and struggle, bitch," he growled. "It's fun when they struggle - even more fun when they scream. "I don't suppose you want to tell me what you and that asshole were doing messing in our business?" I didn't even know what he was talking about, but supposed it had to do with the arms cache or the Redeye II's. I glared at him. He grinned again and reaching over, gripped my left nipple and squeezed - hard. I yelped in surprise at the pain. "Even better" he chuckled "gives me an excuse to be creative." With that he hit me in the stomach - hard. Then he drew back and slugged me on the cheek. He then took out a thick belt and began, methodically, beating me on my breasts, stomach and thighs. Much as I hated myself for doing it, I screamed until I lost consciousness.

I awoke, sputtering, as a bucket of water splashed in my face. The grinning man was, now standing but, quickly returned to the bed. "My collogues have reminded me that beating you to death wouldn't get the information I need from your lover." His grin widened. "So we'll just have to get a little more creative when your fuck buddy wakes up. I twisted my head to see Isaac, tied, tightly in a chair beside the bed. His head was just rising off his chest.

"Well, the sleeping beauty is back with us" a rasping voice said with a malevolent laugh. Blinking to clear my vision, the first thing I saw was Jo. She was spread eagled naked on a thin mattress, her hands and ankles tied to the corners of an iron bed frame. "We've been playing with your woman while we waited for you to wake up, lover boy. Now we can get serious," the man in the black hood standing over her said. "Didn't want you to miss seeing everything what happens to a bitch who fucks with the brotherhood." He laughed again. "That's a good one! She fucks with us and we fuck her to death. You could probably save her a lot of pain, though by telling us what the hell you two are doing screwing around in our business. She killed three of ours. We don't forget. We might though just kill her instead of cutting her up one piece at a time." I looked back at Jo. She lay motionless, her eyes, one swollen almost shut, blazing fire. I cringed, though, as I saw the tear streaks on her cheeks. The man followed my gaze. "She was crying just a few minutes ago. She's mad now," he laughed. "Not as feisty, though as she was when I started working her over. I started to beat her to death but decided letting you watch us raping her would be more fun. Not many guys get to see their broads gang banged. We can finish the beating later. "fter that, unless I get some cooperation from you I've promised to see how much skin I can peel off her before she gives up the ghost." He thumped a cord stretched up from her nipples to the light fixture, and bringing a gasp from her. He nodded to another man sitting beside a black box. There was a high pitched hum and Jo's body jumped off the bed. "Electricity makes her come alive. She don't scream much anymore but just wait till she's been raped a half dozen times and had chunks of skin tore off her. A We've taken bets on how much she'll howl when we start humping her and her tits start to

118

bounce.

After we split her from from neck to crotch I'm gonna leave you alive to watch her bleed to death." He paused then grinned "on the other hand, I'd be willing to just use the garrote on her if you want to tell us all you know about screwing up our nice little game here. By the way, there won't be any cavalry coming. You're watchdog back at your apartment is dead." I panicked at that and struggled to get loose from the tight ropes. "Don't sweat it, boyo," he laughed. "We're not going to hurt you any. It'll be more fun to think of you crying over your late piece of ass." With that, he turned, gave Jo a few more vicious licks with what looked like a heavy willow switch. Then he unzipped his pants and crawled atop Jo.

As I cursed and tried to get loose, the first guy was back. He grinned at me as he crawled into the bed. She squeezed her eyes shut again. I couldn't help the start as multiple explosions shattered the room.

CHAPTER 11

Jan 27 Thursday

I woke up to the ringing of the phone. I could feel myself blanch at what Jonathan said. "OK." I grunted. "Seal off the house and tell - who's on Sullivan?" He told me, Mac. "Yeah. Tell Mac to pick him up immediately and bring him over to the house. I'll be there as soon as I can." I hung up the phone and ordered a chopper. Five minutes later I was dressed and on my way to the helipad. Twenty minutes later, I had the pilot sit the chopper down in the street between the two flashlights held by Jon and Mac. I ignored all the lights that began to come on at the sound of the helicopter landing and sprinted for the house. Mac joined me and, while we ran, filled me in on Sullivan. I threw open the door and stomped inside. Sullivan was cuffed to a chair in the dining room. "Scarborough and Hamlin have been taken." I growled. "Where would your friends take them?"

His eyes flashed anger as he said he didn't know what I was talking about. I pulled out my old forty five and pulled back the slide. "In that case I have no use for you and we'll take you out of here in a body bag! I'll go find them myself!" "You wouldn't dare" he shouted. His eyes, though, registered a lot less anger now. It was fear. "Listen to me, shit head!" I growled. "I've got you dead to rights on theft of US Government weapons for use by your Irish friends. If I don't find those two before they kill them, you've already been tried and convicted by me. Nobody will ever find the body with its knees and elbows blown out and its balls shot away." "If you don't help me right now that's exactly what's gonna happen. I won't lose a minutes sleep over the fact that, maybe you didn't know." Now he was shivering.   When I pointed the forty five at his left knee, he began to blubber. "They've got - a - an old house in the woods just south of Muenchweiller." I turned to Mac. "Bring him." As I headed for the door, I told him over my shoulder, that if he were lying he'd be taking a fall, broken limbs and all from a thousand feet over the forest". I turned to Mac. "Get the AWSCOM guard detachment on the road to Muenchweiler on the double. We'll give them instructions on the way. Use the guard channel."

As the chopper headed east down highway 10 with Sullivan handcuffed to a cargo ring, I kept badgering him and drew back my fist. I wanted to hit him so bad I could taste it. He cringed. "Which way?"

"A little north." The pilot veered in that direction. "Look for a road leaving the intersection where the Fischbach road goes south." We found the road. "It's about a mile up that road." I asked the pilot how far we could we could go without making too much noise. "Maybe a half mile." he told me. "OK set us down in the road there." I told him "It's awful narrow," he said. "We could lose the blades." I told him I'd buy him a new chopper. Just set us down. We held our breath as the machine settled to the sound of tree limbs being brushed aside by the blades. We settled on the ground with a thump. "Ever used a pistol?" I asked the pilot. "Some." "Good." I said as I threw open the door. "You follow us and shoot anybody, that's not one of us or a girl that runs out the door of that place once we get inside." I set off, at a fast trot, down the road, wishing my leg was in good enough shape to run.

As the house came into view, I could see lights in the rear window. I refused to massage my aching leg. "I'm going through the front door. Come in behind me and shoot anybody who I haven't shot." I muttered over my shoulder to Mac. "We'll head for that back room."

I was panting heavily as I got to the old wooden door and, stifling the urge to throw it open, motioned Mac to one side and Jon to the other. Then I eased it open and jumped inside. Nobody there. I heard the sound of a whipping, followed by a feminine cry of pain, coming from behind a door at the end of a short hall. I hurried down the hall and, again, motioning Mac and Jon into position threw open the door and jumped inside. I took in the scene of Hamlin tied to a chair on the left and Joanne spread eagled on a bed with red whelps all over her. A naked man was bent over her with a knife grinning like a devil. I shot him three times in the chest, fast as I could pull the trigger before I could stop myself. The force of the forty five slug knocking him off Joanne and across the room. Whirling, I covered the other three, equally naked, men in the room as Mac and Jon jumped inside with me. "Give me an excuse to blow your fucking heads off."I shouted. All three threw up their hands.

CHAPTER 12

Jan 28 Friday morning early

The chaos in the room had started with the door flying open with a bang. The man atop Jo whirled his head around to see what I did – Arthur Montgomery standing in the doorway holding a forty five pointed at his chest. Fire flashed from the muzzle and the man flew across the room smashing into the wall."Give me an excuse to blow your God Damned heads off!" he shouted at the other three. They didn't, just held up their hands. He moved inside the room and two more men rushed in to confront the other rapists. In seconds all three were on the floor with their hands cuffed behind them. Montgomery, then rushed to the bed and released, the lines holding Jo down. Only then did I realize she'd fainted. "You OK," he asked over his shoulder as he worked on her. "Yeah." I told him, my anger flaring. "You're about an hour too late for her though. They've been raping and beating her for, I don't know how long and they were about to get serious." Then he slipped a sheet loose from the bed and over her and turned to me.

"Sorry," he growled. "It took that long for my other man to make his rounds and find agent Allen." As my hands came free, I told him I wanted some time with that big guy. "You take care of Scarborough" he grunted. "I have first dibs on him." I realized, Jo needed me more than I needed revenge - at least for now - so I did as I was told. I moved to the bed and gathered her into my arms, being careful not to touch her striped body and breasts and to keep the sheet covering her. As I stroked her hair, I heard Montgomery tell one of his men, "I want that one." They hauled one of the men up and dragged him after Montgomery out of the room. All was quiet for several minutes. Then there was a shot fired in the other room. An anguished scream followed, along with a loud babble that I couldn't quite catch. A minute or two later, Montgomery came back. His hand was bloody and his eyes shot fire. Pointing to the leader, he growled. "He's next."

His man hauled him up and headed for the door. "You can't hurt me!" he screamed. "You're not allowed." Montgomery turned back, with an awful grin on his face. "Not allowed," he said, malevolence dripping from his mouth. "After what you did - and planned to do? If you're lucky, all I'll do is kill you trying to escape. Otherwise, I'm gonna blow your kneecaps off then your balls. Granted it's gonna be hard to explain how your cock got stuck in your mouth but I'll manage somehow. Maybe you'll just disappear off the face of the earth. The only question is how long it's gonna take before you spill your guts to me?" I hadn't realized Jo was awake until she moaned, "Arthur, NO!" "Shut up Scarborough," he growled. "You've done your part. You stayed alive. I couldn't protect you like I promised but I can, damn sure take revenge on a nest of snakes." With that, he left dragging the leader by the shirt collar, after him.

"Hush, darling." I murmured as Jo began to cry. I held her rocking her softly as Montgomery's furious shouting echoed through the house. The equally loud expletives of the gang leader echoed back. Suddenly quiet descended then the thug's voice. "You stupid pig! You don't dare!" It ended in a scream of pain that brought a shudder from Jo. Montgomery growled something so softly I couldn't make it out and the man started babbling. It went on for a long time as, in the distance, the rising and falling wobble of a German ambulance got louder. Finally, in the other room, Montgomery spoke up louder. "Go get the chopper out of the road so the ambulance can get here." There was a return to the furious voice." Now listen to me, you shit head! It's too bad about you cutting yourself -A "Cutting myself" the man screamed. "I didn't cut my balls!" Montgomery's voice continued in the same calm tone "knifing yourself when you attacked me. It'll be a lot worse if you decide to clam up and not tell the Germans everything you told me. If you do that, I guarantee you'll never live through the first month in jail." Then raising his voice, he said, "get this pile of shit out of here before I do what I'd love to do. After the medic treats Scarborough, he can tend to his scratches."

A moment later he came through the door and knelt beside the bed. "The medics are coming, honey," he murmured. "Just hang in there." Jo looked up at him, tears sliding down her cheeks. "What did you do to him, Arthur?" Montgomery dropped his head, then after a pause, lifted it and looked into her eyes. The fury was still evident in that look Amore important, was what I intended to do. I intended to kill him," he growled. "- but I didn't." She stared at him. "God help me but I wanted you to." His look softened. "I know, but a year from now you'll hate yourself for wanting that." "I won't!" I muttered. "Give me a gun and I'll be happy to go to jail for using it." He scowled at me. "Joanne would love to see that, I'm sure" he said, the sarcasm dripping. "Don't worry. His life's not worth a plugged nickel now. He gave up the man who ordered the job, Liam McPhearson. He's been like Teflon for years - no more. There's even a good chance we'll be able to find those remaining missiles."

Saturday Jan 30th Monday, Three days later

   I breathed a sigh of relief as I pushed Jo down the hall toward the front door of Landstule Army Hospital. Aside from dark bruises on her cheek and chin, mostly covered by makeup and a black eye that wasn't, she looked gorgeous. She was, obviously, feeling better too, complaining that she could walk and didn't needAa damned wheelchair." I wasn't sure she was so certain of that, though. I'd been sitting in the hospital room with her for three days and, even having been kicked out when the nurses and doctors came in to treat her. I had still, seen the bruises over most of h er torso. Even the deep angry circles around her wrists and ankles were still evident due to her struggles to free herself during her ordeal. I still got angry at the sight of her puffy violet flesh around her nipples the one time she had raised her gown to look at them. The doctors had assured me that no permanent physical damage had been done her but I still relived the helpless rage I had felt as I watched her violated. As if she could read my thoughts, she reached back and patted my hand.
   "It's alright, darling," she murmured. Then she looked up at me and grinned. "I told the doctor I had to get back to work because you'd never be able to take care of the office without me." "The hell you say!" I grunted. "He told me you should take, at least, a couple of weeks. Besides you've got counseling sessions scheduled." "Go ahead and say it," she chuckled. "Rape Counseling - hell! That's all I need, some quack telling me what I should feel and how it's alright to feel sorry for myself. No thank you! I just need a man who'll hold me if I need to cry and screw me if I need that." She dropped her head and, hiccupped. "And won't be too put off by how I look." The last came out in a whisper. I wanted to shove my fist through a wall. Instead, I stopped and knelt down beside her. "I know a guy who'll hold you and adore everything about you and love you however you need it." I whispered. Then I leaned over, and in the midst of the lobby of the hospital, kissed her. When I pulled back, she touched my cheek with a finger. "Better hurry and find that guy and bring him to the car. I hate to cry in public," she mumbled.
Feb 2 Thursday morning

Sure enough, two days later, she insisted on going to the office. Most of the swelling had gone down around her bloodshot eye and face and skillful application of makeup had mostly covered up everything but it. She'd agreed to a counseling session this morning, though. Two nights of waking up fighting against unseen attackers had convinced her. As we hung up our coats, she muttered that she felt like a freak with everybody staring at her. I tried to tell her they weren't but she laughed. "Of course they are. They don't know whether to commiserate with me or congratulate me." "Probably just admiring you, I said. You look particularly fetching today." We were both dressed in black. The ceremony to return Allen Mabry's body to the US was to take place at noon at Ramstein and we intended to attend. It had been held up in order for the coroner to do the autopsy here and to prepare the body for the parents and family back home. His wife was to fly with the coffin. "It's sad that we only learned his name after he was dead," she said.

It had been an eventful day. I'd no more than sat down at my desk than Signe brought me a cup of coffee, said she was glad to see me back and handed me a phone con from Robin. I sipped the coffee as I dialed Fischbach Surveillance Office. Robin answered and hearing my voice, blurted, "Joanne - Ma'am - how are - Shit! That's a stupid question. Just pretend I said I was happy to hear from you." I had to laugh. "OK. I've pretended. Now is that what you wanted to talk about?" There was a pause, then, "No, but I hate to ruin your day so early." I waited. "George just called from the Siegelsbach. Have you seen the plans for the 259th's new assembly building they're getting ready to build over there?" I told her I hadn't and that I was sure they hadn't come through here since I've been here. "Not surprised." She said. "I understand they've been approved for over a year. Anyway, they've included a window in the western substantial dividing wall." I frowned calling up a picture of the depot in my mind. "Oh Shit!" I muttered. "Yeah," she said. I turned around and called for Isaac to get on the line. "Tell Isaac - Mister Hamlin what you told me, Robin." She did. Isaac was silent for a moment. Then he told Robin to have George bundle up those plans and bring them over here. We'll send a chopper for him. When Robin agreed, he hung up. "Problems," she asked? "I can't believe anyone would approve that plan." I agreed with her but added that someone did. Privately I was uncertain about how big it was. Surely the plans had come through this office. How could we have missed a mistake like that?

Hanging up, I went into Isaac's office. He was just getting off the phone to the helicopter pad. "Didn't we get a copy of those plans?" I asked. "Hell no! I told Dawson last year they were being staffed but he ignored me. He and Major Phelps were feuding and I knew Surety was insisting that Surveillance didn't need to sign off on them. I warned him he should go to the Colonel over it but he didn't. Now the shit's going to hit the fan. It takes years to get NATO to approve changes to already approved plans." Turning to look, apologetically, up at me, he said the helicopter wouldn't be able to get over there and back until 1400 hours and he was going to have to be here to meet it and tell the Colonel. "I'll have to drop you off at the hospital and get Montgomery to send you back," he said. I told him it was OK, that we might as well get some use out of our bird dogs.

"I could always put off that appointment." He grinned, half sorrowfully at me. "And keep on beating me over the head every night?" he said, eyebrow raised."You keep it." I surprised myself at being able to laugh at his jibe. I told him that if someone would go ahead and do his duty by me, maybe I'd sleep better at night. I fought hard to keep the grin on my face but it slipped off. Angrily, I brushed away the tear that popped out of my right eye. His face grew serious. "You sure Jo?" he asked, softly. "I can wait till you're ready." "I'm sure." I muttered. "And, I think, I'm ready as I'll ever be, now! I refuse to let those bastards affect my life." The absurdity of that caught me. I had to laugh or cry I forced a chuckle. "Well, maybe not right this minute." I took a deep breath and added that his desk was too damned cluttered. He laughed out loud and squeezed my hand.

We'd met Gloria Mabry, Allen's wife at the Ramstein terminal and had expressed our sorrow. She'd been gracious enough not to point out that it had been my fault that he'd been killed. I suppose it was just my feeling of responsibility for his death that made me think of that but I couldn't help it. Montgomery had arranged for the base band and an honor guard for a full blown ceremony. I think she appreciated it. After the plane had left, Isaac dropped me off at the clinic and left. It was, now, almost 1500 as I got back in the office. Coming down the hall, I could hear the shouting coming from the Colonel's office. I checked Isaac's office first. Sure enough, he was studiously pouring over a set of building plans. I walked in and stood beside him. Immediately I saw the rendering of the west wall of the 259th's new assembly building. As reported, there was two foot high glass block window extended across the entire length of the wall. With that window, the wall could no longer be considered "barricaded". Explosive safety for buildings is calculated based upon two factors, the amount of explosives and the distance from other important places. This is expressed in the term Quantity of explosives and Distance – shortened to QD. The QD for an unbarricaded quantity of explosive would be at least twice that for an unbarricaded quantity. Any explosives operations inside an unbarricaded building would create an impossible on post Quantity Distance problem between it and any ammunition magazines. Siegelsbach is a small depot and half the magazines facing that wall, would be unusable for storing anything other than inert materials or small arms ammunition. Conversely, any high explosive munitions stored in those magazines would preclude any weapons assembly operations in the building. The separation distance between two un-barricaded high explosive locations would be so great that there wouldn't be room on the whole depot for them.

Those plans had just rendered the 259th useless as an active weapons company. The depot could still be used for storage of weapons but any maintenance operations would have to be done at Fischbach. The alternative would be to conduct weapons maintenance there but store the weapons at Fischbach. Either way meant a round trip of almost two hundred miles for a high security convoy. It would be useless to apply for a safety waiver for a building that had been approved but wasn't even built yet. It would never fly. Chances were that if that building was built, the installation would be useless to any ammunition operations at all – not even the helipad could be used.

It was almost 1600 hours when Signe, her coat half on, picked up the ringing phone. "Yes ma'am," she said hanging up. Looking over at me, she said that the Colonel wanted to see both of us "at our convenience." I sighed and called for Isaac. Colonel Richmond stood up when his secretary showed us through the door. "Miss Scarborough," he smiled. "I hope - well, you're looking well. I hope things are - well - at least improving." I had to smile at his, surprising nervousness. "Much improved." I told him. He motioned to chairs and Isaac and I moved to stand by them. "Oh," he muttered as he realized why we weren't sitting. He dropped back into his chair, with a chuckle. "Sorry. I was raised in the south. I still forget how to be a Colonel sometimes. Where I come from, ladies always sit before a man - even a - well always." When we were seated he seemed to relax. I suspected he'd expected some indication of discomfort when I sat down. His look

128

became serious.

"Miss -A he paused a moment watching me. "Would you think it condescending if I used your given name? My wife tells me some women do. I much prefer it, though, among members of my immediate staff." Well, I wasn't part of that staff but I assured him I'd like that. "Good," he smiled. "I'm sorry to keep you two after hours like this but we have a problem - more than one, actually. I'm running into a shortage of personnel." He paused again. "Major Phelps has been recalled to the states on rather short notice." Translation, I thought - "I've fired the ass who single handedly had crushed a major NATO political agreement, and sent him home." I simply nodded and noticed from the corner of my eye that Isaac followed suit. "It seems," he continued, staring hard at me, "that Nuclear Security and Safety Officers are in short supply and I need a replacement immediately. In review of personnel records for the command, I find that people in your career field are fully qualified in the field and, can be replaced in a much more expeditious manner than an Army Officer. So, I'd like for you to take the job until a suitable replacement can be found - if you feel up to it, that is."

That was a surprise. I looked over at Jo and could see that she was as surprised as I was. She was quiet a moment, then said that she'd be happy to help out in any way she could The Colonel, leaned back in his chair, visibly relieved. "Good. I'll start by having personnel rewrite the position immediately. It'll probably take a few weeks but I'd like for you to sit in the office till then - get familiar with everything. Unfortunately, Major Phelps won't be able to help much. He's - unavailable until his transfer is complete. Translation - "Confined to quarters." It was all I could do to keep from grinning. At the same time, I knew our office had a bit of dirty linen with respect to his downfall too. I was still mulling that over when Jo remarked that the Colonel had said he had more than one problem. I glanced up in time to see him blush slightly. I frowned at that. "Well, yes," he said, "but your taking the Surety job can solve both at one time."

"Sounds very intriguing," Jo said with a laugh. "Should I know how I accomplished that?" Richmond frowned then leaned forward onto his desk. "Perhaps you should," he said, quietly. "Please don't take this wrong but Major Phelps house will be available within a week and you're at the head of the list for field grade quarters." Jo's grin faded.

"In other words," she said, quietly, "I'd no longer have to live with Mister Hamlin." When the Colonel didn't reply, her face took on the look of a thundercloud. "Can I assume that there have been complaints along that line? If so, you should know that I'm not ashamed of my actions. Also, is that the reason for the job change?" The Colonel sat back.

Very seriously, he said "to answer your questions, I'm sure you expected some talk about your living conditions, especially since you two haven't gone to any trouble to hide your feelings for each other. Second - it's obvious that you aren't ashamed and I didn't expect you to be. Third - I am impressed with the way you've handled yourself under trying circumstances and believe you're the proper person for the job. Your love life, being so open and above board, has nothing to do with it." He grinned. "It does, though, have an effect on me personally. My wife has taken a liking to you." "But I've only met her once." Jo blurted. "Never the less," he continued, "she has been after me to - as she put it - arrange it so that you no longer have to, as she put it, " live in sin". I explained to her the problem of a husband and wife working together and she simply told me to fix that." He chuckled. "My wife has much greater faith in my abilities than I do. Anyway, as I said, your transfer to Surety will solve two problems at once - assuming you're willing to do the right thing." This last was directed at me.

I was about to get mad at Mrs. Richmond when Isaac spoke up. "Sir, it won't be a great burden on me to alleviate you wife's worries. I can't speak for Miss Scarborough, though." I twisted my head to frown at him. That was a hell of a way to put it. Me a burden? He was grinning at me. My snit faded. Turning back to the Colonel, I told him that I'd try to relieve Mister Hansen's burden as much as I could, but I wasn't sure just what that entailed. Richmond's eyes were twinkling. "Perhaps we should get clarification," he laughed. Turning to Isaac, he said, "Mister Hamlin, will you take this, very prickly woman for your wife?" Isaac laughed out loud. "I will, sir," he replied. The Colonel leaned back again. Miss. Scarborough, will you take Mister Hamlin for your husband?" To say I was surprised by a third party proposal would be an understatement. Then it plucked at my funny bone. I couldn't help that damned giggle so I just nodded. "Well, why don't you two go somewhere else to work out the details of all that? In the meantime you are dismissed."

130

Saturday 4 Feb 1967

It was Saturday and I stretched, luxuriously in the morning sun - the morning sun that meant we were still in bed when most others were out and about their weekend activities. Isaac had proposed to me, himself, last night - even going so far as to get down on one knee to do it. The formality of the event was lessened somewhat by the sardonic grin on his face but I had accepted his proposal anyway. I lay there, fully aware that we hadn't screwed since my - incident. The thought had been repugnant to me, even though I'd blatantly asked him to in the office, and he seemed to know that. The nightmares were still tearing at me every night but I was determined to ignore them. I'd even asked him last night if he was sure about his proposal. Blurting, "you watched them make me into a whore.A "Darling," he'd murmured, kissing me, "I watched the most wonderful display of courage that night that I ever expect to see. They couldn't even break your spirit, when they beat you half to death. I'll be proud to say you let me be your husband." "Everyone must know what happened." I cried, unable to stop the tears that began to trickle down my face. "And everyone who matters knows what I do - that you were heroic." Only then did, I, blubber like a baby that if he wanted me, he could have me. He'd just held me caressing me as I cried myself to sleep. In the morning light, I knew what had to be done. I'd be damned if I'd let that bunch of thugs screw up my life. Taking a deep breath, I rolled up on my side and slid my hand inside his pajama bottoms. I was, both pleased and frightened to find him fully erect in my hand. Seconds later his eyes popped wide open. "It's time, darling." I murmured. When he hesitated, I whispered, "Please!"

A half hour later he'd rolled off me and held me while I shivered. "Was making love as much fun as when it was immoral?" His voice whispered from beside me. I knew he was trying to help me adjust. "It's only slightly less immoral when you're only engaged." I muttered, and determinedly, rolled back over to lie half atop him and kiss him good morning. I think I'd managed not to let my fear show when he'd lovingly taken me before and, actually, got a tiny thrill when I felt him aroused again. Now, his mouth opened and his tongue slid between my lips. I realized, once again, that making love in bright sunlight was a lot more delightfully wicked than at night. Feeling pleasantly dissolute, I squirmed around until I was fully atop him. Then scooting my knees up beside his hips and raising mine, I reached down to fit him properly between my legs. "You sure you're ready for this again so soon," he whispered. I couldn't help a shiver as a flash of man

131

after man penetrating me hit. Viciously, I shoved the picture back out of sight and concentrated on the remembered joy of this man inside me. I succeeded, as my body automatically opened to take him in. "You tell me." I murmured. He grinned. I laughed with Glee when he, with a leering grin, put his arms over his head and lay back to relax.

I lay atop him, trying to catch my breath and reveling in the feeling of my body slowly relaxing. "Shit!" I gasped as the phone beside the bed rang. "That damned - phone has a - death wish. Don't answer - it." I grunted. "It's Satur - day." Isaac chuckled. "Everybody on post knows we're here. Our Bird Dog's still outside." He reached over to lift the receiver. "I'm not - letting - ." I muttered breathlessly, lifting my head to watch him. "Tell them to go away." I saw his eyes widen. "Yes ma'am," he said. "Well - yes ma'am, she's here." "Yes ma'am." The last as he handed the phone to me. I shot him a murderous look but took the receiver. "Miss Scarborough," the voice said. "Yes." I answered trying to control my breathing. "This is Violet Richmond." Oh God!" I thought as she continued. "I'm afraid my husband has put you and Mister Hamlin in the uncomfortable position of practically ordering you to marry. I remember you well and don't intend to let him force you into anything you don't wish to do. I'm not sure he could but I just wanted you to know that if you need any help - no matter what you decide - I'd like to give it to you."

All I could say was "Thank - you - Ma'am," cursing the fact that my gasping breath was plainly audible on the phone. "I - well - we - I accepted - Mister Hamlin's - proposal - last night. I guess - we'll see the - Chaplain soon." "I'm so pleased - and apologize if I caught you at a - well a bad time." You sly old witch I thought. You can tell you did. "No." I said, sarcastically, "It was a very - good time. We were - well - exercising." She had the nerve to chuckle. "I see. Well, let me be the first then, to congratulate you. I hope you'll invite us to the wedding." I panicked. "Well, ma'am. I suppose - it'll be a very quiet affair." She was quiet a moment. "Miss. Scarborough," she hesitated another moment. "Please forgive me for butting into your business but a Chapel wedding would probably be better. You must be aware that your - relationship is common knowledge and on an Army post a quiet wedding makes for a lot of unnecessary talk - talk, that in your condition, is best cut off at the pass. If you stand up in front of everybody and dare them to comment, it'll preclude a lot of speculation later this year."

What the hell, was she talking about? I told her I didn't

understand. Her voice softened. Joanne, I hope you won't mind me calling you that, I've had six children and twelve grandchildren. I recognize the look. I started to ask you about it at the party but was afraid it might embarrass you." My God! She thought I was pregnant. "But ma'am!" I blurted. "I'm not -A Oh God! Was I? Sure I'd missed my period but with all that had happened I hadn't thought about it. Surely the doctor would have said something about it. Or had he? I remembered a remark when I was still doped up when he was reassuring me. I had tuned him out. He'd said not to worry that both of us were alright. I remember thinking it was good that Isaac hadn't been harmed. I lay there, stunned for a long time before Mrs Richmond, said, "Oh my lord! Me and my big mouth. Didn't you know?" I couldn't answer. I just dropped the phone and stared at Isaac. A frightened look flashed over his face as he grabbed for the receiver. "Yes ma'am," he said. After a long pause, a wide grin spread over his face and he said, "No ma'am. She'll be alright. Just a little shocked I think." Then, "Yes ma'am. I'm sure she'd like that. Yes ma'am. I'll take good care of her."

I stared at the ashen pallor on Jo's face. She'd jerked straight up atop me, and still impaled on me. I smiled at her. "Relax, darling." I whispered. "Girls get knocked up all the time." "Not me!" she cried. "Not - we're not even married!" I couldn't help a wider grin. "Well, if Mrs. Richmond has anything to do with it that'll be taken care of in a few more days. When she frowned, I laughed. "You've a date with her at two for a trip to Ktown. She thinks you need a proper wedding dress and she's already arranged for the Chaplain to perform a Chapel wedding right after services tomorrow. She says she'd be happy to be a matron of honor but wondered if you'd prefer Robin." "My God!" she groaned. "The woman's a steam roller." Then there was a look of panic as she stared at the clock. "Ten O'clock! I've got to get dressed." With that, she jumped up, a loud gasp escaping her as she had forgotten what she was sitting on. I laughed again. "I take it that a quickie wedding and shopping with the Colonel's wife meets with your approval." She frowned at me. "If you say another word," she growled "that thing," she slapped my semi-erection "Will never get warm again." I, simply, told that I loved her. She stopped moving and stared at me with a smile beginning to soften the frown. Reaching down, she took me in her hand and murmured, "well maybe I can spare the time to keep this thing from getting too cold." Her face erupted in a wide grin as she settled back atop me. A bit shocked that I could perform again so soon, I did my best to please her.

Saturday Feb 4 - later

I had dressed very carefully, making sure, that my outfit was dignified enough to go out in public with the Colonel's wife. As I approached her car in the drive, I nervously, tugged at my skirt. I couldn't help a blush as I thought of what she knew about me. As I opened the door, I realized I could have dressed a little more casually. She wore a very nice pants suit and flats, more suited to shopping than my skirt, blouse and half heels. She gave me a warm smile as she waved me in and remarked that I looked lovely today. A quick glance told me that no double meaning was intended and I fastened my seat belt.

As soon as we were on the road, she looked over at me and said, "Relax. No matter what anybody says I'm not a real ogre." I blushed deeper. Had I been that obvious? "I had best, apologize," she said returning her eyes to the road. "For being so forward about this whole wedding thing but there was a reason. By the way, don't think I'm pushing myself as your matron of honor. I just thought that on short notice you might need one." I told her I didn't mind but I thought I might ask Robin Laurence. She said that was fine with her. "The reason I thought of it was the reason of all this pushing. I'm going to be very frank. I've been quite irritated at the attitude of several of our officer's wives about your - well - relationship with Mister Hamlin. Even recognizing the reasons, I've been somewhat critical of the talk in public but that hasn't stopped it. As a result, I wanted to make quite clear my approval of both of you. I'm a bit old to really approve of your affair but still young enough to be, secretly, thrilled at the idea. I'm also afraid that the whole thing has brought out the mother in me. You see, I wasn't able to attend my youngest daughter's wedding. She eloped with a thoroughly disreputable - to my way of thinking - young officer. As usual, I was wrong about him. He's made an excellent husband and an almost excellent officer.

Anyway, I find myself being very - well wanting to be a part of a wedding. In addition, I not only like you, but am absolutely amazed at your courage and attitude." She looked over at me. "Now that you know what a busy body I am, do you still want to go through with this?" I told her I wasn't sure what I did was truly courageous - that I had been terrified and cried like a baby. She reached over and patted my leg. "Hush," she said. "From what I hear you are an amazing girl - pardon me. I am showing my age. Everybody under forty is a girl to me. I should have said woman. Anyway, it was my husband who used the term amazing. And when Albert is impressed with somebody, they have to be exceptional." To my utter astonishment and chagrin I felt tears begin to roll down my cheeks. Mrs. Richmond, immediately found a place to pull off the road and reached over to pull me into her arms.

I had been right. The girl had been holding her emotions in to the point she was about to explode. She cried like a baby as I stroked her and told her it was alright. "It's not," she blubbered. "It may never be. They ruined me! I'm ashamed to have Isaac touch me!" Then, the story of her ordeal gushed out of her as if she couldn't stop herself. I was appalled at the torture she'd endured - and amazed at the strength it took for her to handle it. When she had, finally, finished crying and hung limp in my arms, I told her so.

An hour later, she was again, managing to smile as we sat in the little German shop I liked. She paled, though, when the sales clerk brought out a short wedding dress - the sixth one we'd seen. We'd talked and she didn't want anything too fancy. "Oh God," she whispered. "I can't wear white." "Nonsense, Joanne." I whispered back. "You'll be telling everybody how proud of yourself you are. Besides, from the look of that man trap, Mister Hamlin will be drooling when he sees you in it." Finally, I was able to urge her to try it on. "When she came out, I had to grin. "I knew it," she cried. "It's too - well -A "It's perfect." I told her. "You've a great body. Why hide it?" "But it hasn't even got a back," she whispered. "Even better" I chuckled. "From the back, all that skin will drive the young guys wild - and probably a lot of the husbands in the audience too. Hamlin will leave that church knowing he's got the most desirable woman on the post." I grinned again. "From what you've told me, though, you might not make it to Berchtesgaden that night - maybe a gasthaus a few klicks down the road." It was a joy to hear a girlish giggle from her. She turned back to the mirror. "What kind of a bra could I wear under this thing?" I grinned again as the sales girl spoke up. "Fraulein, I bring that dress for the reason that you one of few Fraulein who can wear it. You need no bustenhalter. Dress has - how you say, Push up inside but not enough for many German woman." "You mean my tits are too small," she

136

grunted. "Nein," the girl said, quickly. "You have perfect - you say, tits? Many German Fraulein have too much."

"That was a hell of a sales girl." I laughed on the way home. Then I realized I had laughed without thinking. It felt so good. I looked over at Mrs. Richmond. "Ma'am I'll never be able to thank you for what all you did today." She smiled, serenely at me. "You just needed to unload some guilt," she said, quietly. "Guilt that wasn't yours!" I made a decision right there. "Ma'am, I'd feel honored to have you as my matron of honor. Robin can be a bridesmaid." "I would be honored," she said, "if you'll stop calling me ma'am. My name's Violet."

Sunday 5th Feb 1967

I couldn't help blushing as I, on came slowly down the aisle of the chapel on Sunday, my hand resting on Colonel Richmond's arm. He was resplendent in his dress blues with a whole chest full of medals. I felt as if everybody in the place was thinking "there goes that slut whose been shacking up with Hamlin". The slight intakes of breath when they saw my naked back didn't help. The article of clothing I had slipped off in the backseat of the Colonel's car meant that they were probably right. Colonel Richmond had offered, and I had, gratefully accepted his offer of "giving me away." Dad was still in the hospital back home and Mom wouldn't leave him so I had no family here. I stared straight ahead at Robin and Mrs. - Violet's smiling faces. When I turned my eyes to Isaac in his tuxedo, I saw adoration in his eyes. I blushed deeper. I wasn't used to adoration. Of course, it could be just plain old lust. I couldn't help a huge grin, and couldn't stop a nervous giggle, at the thought of him screwing me over and over last night after he'd given me his grandmother's engagement ring. We'd both been so aroused that I was still very - intimately tender. It had also been the first night that I didn't wake up screaming at the nightmare.

The ring was gorgeous but extravagant. The emerald must have been, at least, six carats and set in a very old, white gold, filigreed setting. When the Chaplain asked "Who gives this woman to be married?" The Colonel spoke up and said "Mrs. Richmond and I do." When Isaac held out his hand for mine, I had a sudden urge to jump his bones right here in the chapel. Instead, I turned and kissed Colonel Richmond on the cheek, then turned and took it. I stared, in disbelief at him throughout the ceremony. It was as if I had never seen him before -

137

certainly a stupid feeling since he'd been using my body for a month. That brought on another stupid grin. I wasn't sure which of us had been using the other. I'd certainly enjoyed having him use me - enough that I had initiated my own brand of depravity. I also, was perversely delighted at the thought of Violet springing the baby stuff on him. That reminded me that I had to check with that damned doctor to see if he had really told me that. I was so wrapped up in my thoughts that the squeeze of his hand, made me jump. The chaplain was looking at me and it dawned on me that Isaac had just "pled me his troth." "I Joanne Elizabeth Scarborough, do take you, Isaac Hamlin -A Almost panicked, to realize, I'd been staring at him like a damned besotted schoolgirl, as I blurted out the first line of my response. Panicked, I realized the words I needed had just flown out the window. "- do promise to have and hold and love forever and ever in sickness and in health until the end of time." I knew my face was scarlet but with memory gone, those words would have to do.

As we went slowly back down the aisle, he leaned over and murmured that he wasn't sure he could make it through the reception with me in this dress. Still a bit miffed at the spectacle I felt I'd made of myself at the altar I whispered back "Find us a private space and I'll solve your problem for you." Then with a wicked grin, I added that "it should be easy enough since I'm carrying my panties in my purse". Mrs. - Violet, sitting beside me in the car on the way over, had raised an eyebrow and chuckled as she saw me take them off. As a result, I was walking down the aisle in a chapel with nothing on under this decadent gown but my garter belt and hose. When we went into the basement of the chapel, with the rest of the guests outside waiting for the Chaplin to finish up, he tugged me into the men's room and pushed me up against the door. Grinning like a mad man he jerked my skirt up and his fly open. I lifted myself up to kiss him and my leg up to circle his waist as he impaled me. It was a frantic coupling, both of us fully ready for the act - and both of us exploding at the same time. After a minute of panting, he lowered me back to the floor and dropped my skirt. When I'd caught my breath, I slipped my bikini panties into his coat pocket. I told him to keep those for me awhile, and went to look at myself in the mirror. I couldn't believe it! Not a hair out of place. I felt like I had come completely undone. After a quick cleanup, I turned and gave Isaac a kiss. "Better get out of here before somebody finds us." He grinned, muttering that I was a brazen hussy and opened the door. I couldn't help a squeal of shock at the sight of Montgomery leaning against the wall opposite. "I had to turn two guys away" he said calmly. "Told them it was being cleaned. Your guests are waiting." I was too embarrassed to be really angry so I bit back the retort that came to mind.

As we headed back to the reception, Montgomery said that he'd wanted to have a word with us before we left the church. It turned out that Liam McPhearson was the one who ordered the hit on us. He was the leader of a breakaway segment of the IRA dedicated to violence against anybody or country that supported the British. Leonard Douglas was the Sein Finn's point man for public relations and had let it be known that "he understood McPhearson had been dealt with." I shivered. I knew how the IRA "dealt with" their enemies. He is also worried that, with negotiations going on now with the British Government, a serious attack by a known IRA member - even one not approved of by the organization - would disrupt everything. He knows that the IRA would get the blame no matter what. There's already a hue and cry about the attack on the plane this month. He swears the danger to you from McPhearson has ended and wants to help us find the rest of those missing missiles. The catch is that he wants a description and we've been instructed not to give it to him." Joanne, head down, asked how anybody connected with all that could be trusted. Montgomery scowled. "Well, I wouldn't but, then my roots go back to County Armagh. I might not be exactly unbiased". Jo looked up with a grin. "Hell, Arthur, the Black and Tans were at least as bad as the IRA." Montgomery managed a rueful laugh. "Yeah. But those terrorists were ours. Anyway, the Brits seem willing to trust him. They're sending one of their own to oversee his efforts. The problem is that they're not willing to send anybody with a clearance high enough to recognize the things."

Suddenly, I realized where he was heading. I glanced at Jo, quickly. She'd gone pasty white. "Not just NO but HELL NO!" I blurted. "You're sure as hell not going to send Jo to deal with that blood thirsty bunch of bastards." "I'm not, but Richmond will get orders to." "Well, he can, damn well shove his orders." I muttered, quietly now since a number of people were coming into the reception room. When Jo put her hand on my arm and squeezed, I scowled at her. "We best talk about this later," she whispered. "You're damn well not going." I growled back. She grinned up at me. "Didn't take you long to become a dictator, husband of mine." "Jo." I said, pleading. She lifted herself up

139

on tiptoe and kissed me, then grinning, wickedly, turned to Montgomery. "Sorry, Arthur. You just heard me promise to obey my husband. We're going on our honeymoon. Take a picture of the one from the airport and send it to them. You might throw in a picture of what was found in that warehouse too."

"Damn Mac! I know we're in a bind. That damned woman knows something. My informant could see it in her face. She seems not to realize what she knows but she keeps coming back to the pictures of the shipment." "Of course I know they shouldn't have screwed up but they did. They're nothing but a bunch of clods - clods not long for this world if my information is correct. Their own people are looking for them." "Yeah. I know none of our people would stand for doing her in. You'll just have to get somebody else." "Damn it! I can't syphon off enough to afford him. Get somebody else." "Yeah. I know. Just do the best you can."

5 Mar 1967 Sunday

I opened my eyes to a view of the Alps through the window of our rooms at the Army Recreation Center in Garmish-Partenkirchen. I couldn't help a sigh as I knew that today was our last day here. It had been a great week. My nightmares still came but, with Isaac beside me to wake me up they were fading in intensity. I'd learned to ski and we'd done everything any tourist would do - plus the ones that newlywed couples did too. We'd made trips to Rococo Churches, and to the tops of the mountain. I had to grin at Isaac's interest in the girls who'd hollowed out places in the snow at the very top so they could lounge in their Bikini Swim Suits and get a tan. It always amazed me how much the Germans loved a tan. We'd shopped in the town and, after our trip up the mountain, Isaac had insisted on buying me my second Bikini. I'd told him I'd never wear the thing, that even my bra and panties covered more than it did. He laughed and, sure enough, I modeled the thing in our room that evening. He insisted that this summer we'd go to Italy where I could wear it on the beach. "I've been told," he'd chuckled, "that down there, you only need the bottom part."

I turned to look out the window at the mountains with the snow all over them. Standing there almost naked, had seemed so incongruous but I didn't want him to see the grin on my face as I thought of it. I didn't want him to see that the idea turned me on. "It'll be a cold day in hell when I go out on an open beach with my tits naked. Besides, by then I'll probably be too big around to wear that piece of crap." I'd growled - not willing to admit that the thought made me feel delightfully wicked. "Well, maybe, you should get in some practice before then." He'd laughed. I'd protested that I didn't need practice to lie out so everybody could ogle me when he'd suggested sunbathing in our own snow hollow. I'd not been too adamant about it though. As a result, yesterday, I'd found myself, embarrassingly mostly naked in a lounge chair atop the mountain in the cold snow and warm sun, with my husband and the rest of the girls. Anyway, this morning the view was wonderful and I only turned away when I felt Isaac's lips on my shoulder. "If you like it so much," he murmured, "we can say to hell with work and stay awhile longer." Snuggling back in his arms, I told him that if we stayed away any longer they'd replace us with somebody who'd actually come to work - that it seemed like we'd been gone for months. "You needed some time to recover," he said. "And I needed some time to - forget." His look turned thunderous. I'd wondered a lot, if his having to watch what had happened to me wasn't worse than the ordeal itself. To change the subject, I told him I was starved. It was no lie either. This week I felt like I'd never get enough to eat. Maybe that damned doctor had known what he was talking about.

Breakfast was almost over by the time we got to the dining room, and there were few others there. We ordered, than settled in to eat a huge breakfast. Jo seemed to inhale hers. As we were relaxing over coffee, discussing our planned trip through the town, I noticed a tall man moving toward our table. I frowned as it became obvious that he was coming here. Putting his hand out toward Jo, he said, "Mr. and Mrs. Hamlin, I hope you will pardon me for bothering you on your wedding trip but I would very much like to speak to you." My frown deepened. The voice had a definitely strange inflection to it and the cadence belied the correctness of his English. I was just about to ask about what, when Jo extended her hand.

"I'm Leonard Douglas". He said, as Jo jerked her hand back so quickly she upset the water glass on the table. Ruefully, the man drew his hand back and said he was sorry his presence was distasteful but that he, really, must speak with us - that it would only take a few moments. I glanced at Jo. Her face had paled and her eyes were blazing fire. I wasn't sure whether she was trembling from fear or anger. Obviously struggling to control herself, she managed to grate, "Mister Douglas -A She took a deep breath. "I can assure you that I - we haven't anything to discuss." Douglas, paused a moment but continued. "Madam, what I have to say is important enough that I must risk your enmity to say it. I promise I will try and keep my presence here as short as possible." Then without a pause, he continued. "Madam, I hope you will believe me when I say that I would never associate with any person or group of persons who committed the crimes that you had to endure. I don't pretend to have always acted in a proper and legal way and, to my sorrow, women and children have, at times, been hurt as a result of my actions and those of my friends but never, deliberately and never, have any of us stooped to that kind of evil. Please allow me to sit. I do not wish to draw too much attention." Jo nodded slightly and he lowered himself into the chair between us.

"Thank you," he said. "Before I go any farther, let me admit to being capable of a certain amount of violence, when it becomes necessary. Your Mister Montgomery has, now, proof of that. In

142

addition, I did not need you to identify the weapons in question. We've known about them for some time and I have complete specifications for them. Further, we have discussed acquiring similar weapons for use such as that one was put. I won't pretend that we would not go to great lengths to foster the end of the British occupation of Ireland and reunification of the country but, our conclusion was that their use would be counterproductive and we refrained from acquiring them. It was a splinter group that did and as you probably know, half the world is up in arms about that one use and the incident has blackened our name badly. It has also dried up many sources of funds - especially in the US - that we have depended upon.

I know I am not getting to the point of meeting you but I wanted you to understand why I wanted it. As I said, Mister Montgomery has proof that the individuals that held you have been summarily punished, but there is a problem. The people they were dealing with are, apparently, very upset about the damage done to their plans. We don't know exactly who was involved but we suspect some governmental involvement – probably including your own. We have also discovered that in some way, you are deemed to be a hindrance to their plans and are to be disposed of." Jo appeared to be as shocked at his assertion as I was and he paused a moment to let us gather our thoughts, before he continued. "I have reason to believe that our information is reliable and, as a result, have taken the liberty of having a team of my people protecting you this week until I could appraise you of the situation. To emphasize the problem, your Military Intelligence protectors seem to be very new at this game. They have not once, noticed my people around them. Had we wished you dead you would have been so for several days." He smiled for the first time "or perhaps not Mrs. Hamlin considering your handling of the first group that attacked you."

My mind was awhirl. The IRA was apologizing for the attack on me, guarding me and warning me I was still in danger. They even admitted that they - well, actually a splinter group of theirs - had attacked an airliner and that their fund raising had been damaged as a result. Then there was "vindictiveness." What had that meant? Had they murdered the man who ordered my assault? The man must have read my mind for he said, "You should talk to Mister Montgomery about the details of our actions, but, believe me when I say you have nothing to fear from any of that group anymore." With that, he stood. "In the meantime, I have taken up too much of your time and will leave. Forgive me for bringing upsetting news on your honeymoon. My

143

people will continue to protect you until you return to your home. "fter that, it must be your own people for ours would be in too much danger from your security people." With that he stood and taking my hand, that I was too shocked to pull back, bent and kissed my knuckles.

Jo and I just looked at each other as the man left the restaurant. When we had recovered from his words, we discussed whether or not to go on out shopping. Jo shivered but said she'd be damned if she'd let anybody make her change her plans because of a threat. "No one will ever get me in that position again," she growled. "If I can't kill them, I'll kill myself! First, though, I want some answers." With that, we went back to our room and she put in a call to Montgomery's private line. "We've seen that man you wanted us to meet before we left," she said after a short wait. "Yeah." A pause. "Well, he said we were still in danger and that our helpers hadn't noticed any of his people around - and they had been." "Yeah. That's what I thought. He also said that you had some sort of proof that my earlier problem had been taken care of." Another pause. "I don't care! Tell me!" In a moment, she paled, and murmured, "Oh my God!" After catching her breath, she told him we'd be leaving in the morning and that our friends would be with us." I was about to blow my gaskets. "What? Damn it!" I muttered. She looked up at me, her face still pale but her eyes burning with satisfaction. "He said, and I quote, the animals that had originated the problem - there were six of them - had all their offending organs removed and were left to bleed out. He said he had been given the left over parts and had them in his possession. He was specifically instructed to give them to me if I wanted them." Son of a bitch! That oh so civilized man had castrated six of his own men - well maybe not really his own - and left them to die.

On the way back to Pirmasens, I vacillated between being feeling a vengeful pleasure in their murder and being appalled at that pleasure - as if I were less than human for it. Isaac tried to alleviate my fears and was more interested in the fact that I was still under a threat of death. "What is it that you know that causes somebody to suddenly want you dead?" I stopped cursing myself for being human and tried to concentrate on the more immediate threat. "It, obviously, has something to do with those missiles." I muttered. "But the IRA claims they aren't the - contractors. Hell! That sounds like a construction project." "Well, all the missiles didn't go to the IRA." Isaac pointed out.

144

I nodded, deep in thought. Six of them stayed with that shipment of arms. Maybe it was the one who wanted those other weapons who was behind this. I said so and we kicked the possibilities around all the way home - and were still doing so when Isaac drove up to his house.

"Damn it Isaac." I muttered. "There's something wrong with those two consignments. Something they both have in common. I've felt it ever since I first saw the second bunch of weapons. I just can't figure out what it is. What pisses me off is that I know that when I figure it out, I'm gonna be disgusted as hell that I didn't see it before." I wasn't prepared for him to laugh. "Come on honey" he chuckled. "Look at it this way. As your senior in the QASAS program, I haven't seen it either. You'll only be disgusted. As your macho boss, I'll be humiliated. Now, just what do you think you're looking for? It's only been a couple of months since you had to confess to Dawson that you'd missed the crew jimmying the Honest John spin rocket test. THAT was humiliating to you. I know Dawson acted like you'd been a complete fool but nobody else had ever seen that problem and they'd been doing it for years."

It still embarrassed me that I could have missed the fact that the inspection crew screwed up the testing of the spin rockets of ten Honest John rocket motors. The test of the igniter circuit continuity failed on all ten. They had seen this before every time they ran this test so they found that a little twist of the connector would clean off the connections enough that the rocket motor passed the test. I'd stood right there and watched them with only a vague idea that something was wrong. After all, they passed the test. The problem surfaced two days later when I was reading over the inspection report. Those ten motors were simply a small sample of over eight hundred motors and almost a third of samples tested had required "twisting the igniter wire at the connection." That meant that, statistically, a third of the eight hundred wouldn't fire unless their connections got "twisted." Unfortunately, "Twisting the igniter cable connector," before installation on the rocket was not in the field operating manual. I had to issue a suspension on all the Honest John motors in the stockpile worldwide until they could be re-inspected - and, then admit to Dawson that I'd screwed up. I wasn't sure which was worse in my mind. Somehow, I knew this was going to be a much greater embarrassment and for the life of me I couldn't figure out what was wrong.

As we moved our bags into the house, Jo was still quiet and

distant. I wondered for a moment if she was mad at me - or, worse, was she reliving the hours of rape and beatings she'd suffered. Then, though, I realized it was just the way she got when she was reviewing in her mind, a puzzle that, simply, wouldn't be left alone. Not for the first time, I realized that, in some ways, Jo was obsessive about puzzles. "Come on, darling." I murmured. "You know that it'll come to you if you leave it alone and that it won't if you keep wrestling with it." She looked up at me with a quick smile. "I suppose you'd rather I wrestled with you," she laughed. I couldn't help a grin and told her she must be reading my mind. Passing her hand over the front of my pants, she purred, "when sex is the subject, men's thoughts transfer from the brain to an area of their anatomy that is very visible."

It was time to get up and find something to eat. It had been a very pleasant hour since we'd gotten home and I lay on Isaac's shoulder reluctant to move. It was still a little amazing to think that only a little over a month ago I'd not given the males of our species much thought. Now I had not only given one of them my thoughts, but my body and my love and, in return, had gotten myself knocked up. As my stomach growled, I grinned something else that had changed. Back then, I spent a lot of time eating salads and worrying about my weight. Now I spent a lot of time wondering if it was meal time yet. "So, Jo, what's for supper," was the silent question. I had a yen for German. We'd prowled a lot of local shops the last few days and the thought of sauerbraten sounded good. I knew we'd bought a can of quick gravy for the stuff. I decided that a minute steak cooked in that would be just what I wanted. Now if I could only decipher the German labels to find the gravy. I carefully, rolled off Isaac's shoulder and slid out of bed. "You're going where?" Isaac's voice announced that he was fully awake. I shook my head remembering that he could come fully awake from a dead sleep at the drop of a hat. I told him I was hungry and was going to make sauerbraten. "If you go like that, your horny husband is going to make it impossible for you to concentrate on cooking." I turned and blew him a raspberry but couldn't help wriggling my butt at him as I slipped my robe on.

By the time I got my robe on and into the kitchen, Jo was rummaging through the cans we'd bought at the German supermarket and grumbling. "You'd think the Germans would be polite enough to label their food in English." Suddenly, she spun around, her eyes wide and her expression, gleeful. "Shit!" "That's it!" "It is?" I muttered, my attention fixed on the expanse of naked woman revealed as her

146

spinning body caused her robe to fly open. "Of course, ninny! The box markings were in English!" I frowned. "So? You'd expect missiles to be marked in English, even if the markings were wrong." Then it dawned on me too. It wasn't only the missiles that had been marked in English. Everything in the warehouse had been too. I hadn't really been surprised because I had already realized that all that equipment had come from the US. I hadn't considered how they'd gotten eastern block weapons but, had assumed, that it wouldn't be too hard for them to be acquired. As I thought about it the things were probably for some clandestine operation. As if Jo were reading my mind, she asked, excitedly, "Why would we mark Soviet weapons in English?" She had a point but she wasn't finished. "Besides," she cried, "I know where the damned things came from."

Yes sir! I know it's embarrassing. According to Douglas he's had up to five people watching them for over a week and we never noticed.

Yes Sir! If they'd wanted to they could have gotten them any time during that week.

That would be a godsend, sir. The people I have are green as grass and there aren't enough of them. A team would help a hell of a lot.

No sir! We don't know who it is that wants them dead or why? I can only assume it was the same people who wanted that shipment of arms. I can't, for the life of me, though, imagine why killing Scarborough would be of any benefit to them. Arms smugglers aren't known for vengeance unless there's something in it for them. To prevent exposure they'll kill in a heartbeat but not just for spite. It's too dangerous for too little gain.

No sir! It's not the IRA. Besides the warning and the protection, I have the private parts of, supposedly, the bunch of guys who raped Scarborough.

No sir. I think he was telling the truth.

Yes sir. I'll be expecting them.

147

Mar 6 Monday

It was almost noon by the time I managed to get to Montgomery's office. I'd had to check into Phelps's Surety Office at AWSCOM headquarters and meet the staff. I could tell that one or two weren't too thrilled about having a civilian as a boss, or maybe it was having a woman but I didn't have time to worry about that. My secretary, Fraulein Habermann seemed alright and I found, to my embarrassment, a hot cup of tea on my desk when I came in. I frowned and told her that I didn't need anybody getting me tea in the morning and that, besides, I preferred coffee. She gave me a look like my mother used to give me when I'd said something stupid. "I'm sorry, Frau Hamlin but in your condition, caffeine is bad for you. I'll get some caffeine free café for tomorrow morning. I apologize that I had none today". Shit! I thought. Was I going to be "mothered," to death for the next nine months? Oh well, an hour later, I had gotten a briefing on projects in process. I was pleased to see that the Siegelsbach debacle wasn't one of them. That, it seemed had been bounced back to higher headquarters. I wondered if Dawson was trying to explain his inaction to the COMZ commander. I'd told the staff to go on about their business till I had time to bring myself up to date, then I'd left for here.

When Scarborough came in she looked like she'd had a stressful morning. I couldn't help needling her a bit about the fact that a newlywed should really find some time to actually sleep. "Can it Montgomery!" She growled at me but her eyes were twinkling. "You're just jealous because no woman will put up with you." With that, though, her face turned, quickly, serious. "I'm sorry to be so rushed but I think you need to know that somebody in your outfit or one of the other spook outfits is behind all this." Then she leaned back, suspicion clear in her face. "Or did you know and were just leading me along?" I couldn't help my disbelief and it showed. "You can believe me or not, Scarborough. I've not the slightest idea what you're talking about." She studied me a long moment then leaned forward over the desk. "Well, whether or not you know is not important. What's important is that if all those weapons, including the Redeye II's come from a Stateside depot its one that's not listed in our files. Not only that, but all the munitions in that warehouse originated in Israel. It's material left over from their

149

ongoing, undeclared war with the Arabs. I know because I and Herman Walker inspected the stuff last June in Israel before it was, supposedly, shipped back to the states. Once I even overheard one of our handlers remark that – and I quote, trading good US stuff for this junk was a bad deal unquote."

"How do you know what you looked at was the same stuff in the warehouse?" I asked. "Because," she grinned, "Not only is it the same exact type stuff we inspected but I didn't trust the Israelis – actually the people I was working for – looking back, I'm convinced that it wasn't the Israelis taking our reports. We were never properly introduced to them – one name only. They, though, watched everything we did and maintained all the paperwork. We seldom got more than a glimpse of it. I didn't like them or their rules. The munitions went right from our inspection line to a freight container. There were no shipping documents for that either. Just to be sure I could identify those rounds if I had to I had a small stamp made. It was about the size of a pencil eraser, a round, black, circle with an S in it. I wasn't paying attention in that warehouse but that's what I've been puzzling over. I knew I was missing something and couldn't remember what. I saw it but didn't give it a thought. That same stamp is on all the interior ammunition packaging I looked at in that warehouse – except for the Redeye II boxes. Herman laughed at my paranoia and that stamp, then but he wouldn't be laughing now."

Damn! That was a hard concept to grasp because it brought up logical consequences that were uncomfortable to contemplate. Scarborough had leaned back in her chair to study me suspiciously, as I considered her remarks. I couldn't say that I blamed her. "Where did those weapons go after you inspected them?" She shrugged. "The containers were still in the warehouses when we were, politely, shown the door by another bunch of guys with only first names. All we did was identify and determine the visual condition of the materiel. I did the munitions and he, the rest. After that we came home and a few weeks later I got my orders for Germany." Both of us sat there, staring at one another for a long moment. "Well, Joanne," I said, finally. "I don't know anything about these weapons and ammunition. I don't even know much about the disposition of all that Egyptian equipment. There were a few remarks about it returning to the states but what happened to it was, apparently, very close hold. If what you say is true, it didn't go there but to that warehouse. If it were one of our operations, I'd hope that we'd have done a better cover job. I don't know about the Agency. The stuff, though, isn't going to be able to stay where it is much longer though. I understand that we and the Germans have reached some sort of agreement."

I sat there watching Montgomery and decided he really didn't know what was going on. It made my stomach growl. Suddenly, I realized it wasn't hunger. "You've got to pardon me a minute." I muttered as I got up and tried not to rush to the bathroom. Shit! I thought as I leaned over the toilet and dumped my guts in it. I'd heard of morning sickness all my life but never really thought I'd have to put up with it - hell of a time for it to show up. While bending over the toilet I had another irritating thought.

By the time Joanne got back to the office, I had put in a call to Washington. I motioned her to a seat on the couch, before it dawned on me that she was almost ashen. "You OK?" I asked as I waited for the connection to be made. "You look like you need to lie down before you fall down." "I'm alright," she growled, obviously angry. "It'll go away in a minute, I think." I managed to stop a grin as I realized what was happening to her - and just how disgusted she probably felt as it affected her control. Then she took a deep breath. "You asked me where those weapons went. I don't know but I noticed that all of them at that time had a GA lot number. I suspect they were all processed in the same place because the munitions in Israel all had Cyrillic markings. All the ones in the warehouse here were marked in English and, had a ND lot number. As I told you before I don't know of an ammunition facility with that lot prefix. If you find out where either GA or ND is you might get an idea of where they came from. I suspect it doesn't stand for Georgia or Germany just like ND probably didn't stand for North Dakota . Now! I know where those munitions came from and I know the lot prefix has been changed. The questions are why and by whom? I'll just bet that if you ask those questions all hell will break loose."

Just then the Roy Coniff's voice came on the line.

I sat on the couch, determined to control my rolling stomach as Montgomery began to talk, outlining what I'd told him. I was surprised he did it on an open line. He glanced over at me, and as if he'd read my mind, mouthed, "Secure line."

151

"Yes sir, but I think you need to expand the loop."

"She's here in the office now."

"Yes sir."

"Of course I know what it means. I would just like to know how it could have happened and why she's being targeted."

"Yes Sir! As sure as I can be with information from the IRA. I believe them, though."

"NO sir! I didn't think that. It almost has to be someone on the inside though - at least to the point of furnishing information and assistance. That stuff couldn't have gotten to Germany without somebody making it happen."

"Yes Sir. I agree. What about that bunch over in the basement uptown? I know a couple of the damned Girenes over there that are crazy enough to do something like this."

"If it's them, what do we do? Get out of their way? Hell! The entire middle-east could go up in flames. Besides, we can't as long as the contract on Scarborough exists."

"Hell. Douglas made it clear how lousy my crew is at protecting her."

"Yes Sir. I'd trust Troy and his crew."

"Well, Sir, we'll just have to manage till then."

"Ever hear of an ammunition installation with a designation of GA or ND? Scarborough noticed that all the lot numbers on that shipment had one of those designations."

"No sir. She doesn't know what or where it is."

"Yes Sir."

"Yes sir. Here she is."

With that he handed the phone toward me. I had to get up to take it. When I identified myself the sort of garbled voice on the other end said, "Hello Mrs. Hamlin. I'm Roy Coniff. I felt it necessary, after all you've been through, to congratulate you on your wedding and tell you we appreciate all you've done to help us in this affair. Let me assure you that this agency has had nothing to do with the problem's you've been facing − at least not that I'm aware of. I'll make sure an intensive investigation is performed. I wish I could state, categorically that no one in the government had anything to do with it − but I can't. On a different note, I'm happy you're beginning to recover from your - well - assault. I also wanted to tell you that I'm very impressed with your ability to think on your feet and your intelligence. I also wish a lot of my agents had your capabilities with firearms. Now, please believe that I'll do everything I can to get Arthur some help in providing you protection - even to the extent of moving you and your husband back to the states if you're willing."

Who the hell was this guy? I wondered. Whoever he was, I wasn't about to let those goons run me out of Europe. I told him so. I heard him chuckle on the other end of the line. "I was told that would be your attitude. Still, my offer holds. Considering your condition, keep it in mind. Sure you have no idea about those lot numbers?" I told him no, that it could be almost anything including North Dakota or Georgia but it could also be something as simple as German Activity or even George Allen. For all I knew it could just be a made up designation. He just said, "OK. Now let me talk to Mister Montgomery again."

I handed the phone back and settled back on the couch, my wayward stomach forgotten. When Montgomery hung up, I blurted "who the hell was that - and how did he know I was knocked up?"

He was slightly taken aback then chuckled. "Sorry. I didn't think to tell you. Roy is the CIA DDO - Deputy Director of Operations at the Confused Intelligence Agency and I've stopped wondering how he knows something. He probably knows what you had for breakfast. He works directly under Richard Helms at the Agency." He leaned back in his chair and frowned. "I suppose you figured out, from the conversation, that we were discussing just how all this clusterfuck occurred and who is responsible. According to him, who you can believe or not, it's an operation outside the realm of our organization or theirs. There has to be, though, somebody in the one or the other of the organizations involved and Roy'll turn over every stone he can to find out who it is - especially who is responsible in the contract on your life. I hope you'll believe me when I tell you that within our organization, nothing like that can happen without direct presidential involvement and never to anybody that doesn't present a direct threat to the country. Even more of a problem is the fact that not even a Presidential finding could be issued to justify an attack on a US citizen. It'd be political suicide. Anyway, Roy's having a team of guards sent over, professionals that, unlike my men, are trained to protect a person. Most are ex Secret Service people. Troy Marvin, who you heard me mention, was once the Presidents own guard. He can't get over here, though, until early next week. Until then, I'd appreciate it if you would keep a very low profile I'll add another two men to your detail but that's the bottom of my barrel."

His next action caught me by surprise. He took a box out of his bottom drawer and slid it across the table to me. When I opened it I found another Beretta in it with two loaded magazines and a shoulder holster as well as a fat manila envelope. "Take that to your husband and tell him that he's been reactivated. He's now in operations. Also tell him that, this time it's not a request that he take it." I didn't like that one bit and said so. He leaned back in his chair, frowning. "Due to your program's unique transfer policy, Joanne, we've used several of your people to gather information for us on occasion. Your husband has worked for us off and on for several years, mostly in intelligence evaluation roles. Even so, he was trained just like a real agent was. He's never, though, actually acted in an operational capacity. That's the weapon he prefers, one just like yours - though he complains about its stopping power. Those rounds are like yours and solve that problem. The envelope contains the same documentation you have, including his get out of jail free card. Now in actual, field operations, he's as green as you are but, between the two of you and my equally green agents, you should be able to watch each other's back until the cavalry, in the form of Troy Marvin, arrives next week. Any questions?" I decided that the questions I had to ask needed answers from my husband not Montgomery so I shook my head. He must have read my mind, though, because he grinned. "Go easy on him, Joanne. Remember, he's been bound by the same requirements you are now."

I suppressed a grin at the look on her face. She'd never be able to lie capably with a face that showed every emotion. "I suspect that Troy's in the process of planning something, probably for his direct boss, the CIA Deputy Director for Ops. I worried about getting the DDO involved in our problems but had no other feasible alternative. There's, obviously somebody else involved in all this besides the Irish boys. You'd better get your Surety shop set up the way you want it pretty quick. You may not have the opportunity after he gets here."

Wednesday March 8 1967

I was nervous, as I sat down with Isaac in the Colonel's office on Wednesday. I suppressed a grin as Isaac deliberately allowed his sport coat to fall open to reveal a glimpse of his new holster. Colonel Richmond frowned. "Just how many jobs do you two have?" he asked. "A lot more than I care for", I muttered. "We'll probably have a real spook to deal with soon." With that I gave him a quick rundown on our and the spook situation. He leaned back and sighed. "Life would be so much simpler if we were all required to wear uniforms." Then he pushed forward again. "I hope you two are about to give me some good news as to how the Surety and Surveillance offices are going to mesh with all the crap that's been going around."

I looked at Isaac and wanted to stick my tongue out at him when he motioned for me to "go ahead". "Well sir, now that I've had a crash course in Nuclear and Toxic Chemical Surety from the books in the office, I feel like a mother in law on a child's honeymoon. As far as I can see, the surety office has no power to actually DO anything. All the "doing" is done by the Storage and Maintenance crews. They are also responsible for all safety and reliability requirements. The Surveillance Division is responsible for seeing that they do their job. Their big headache each year is the SOI, the Surety Operational Inspection. The only thing I can see the Surety Division is responsible for is to see that all the above jobs are carried out by conducting inspections during the year and approving policies that they have little experience with - after they have been prepared reviewed and approved by the people who do. Their SOI, Surety Operations Inspection is pointed more toward administration and seeing that safety and operational demands are met. Either can get a commander fired if he fails them but for these units the SOI is the ball buster."

"That's the step your Surety Officer failed in last year." I couldn't help the growl after the tongue lashing I'd taken from the Communication Zone commander himself. It seemed likely that Siegelsbach depot will have to be closed due to Major Phelps screw up. "I'd like to know, Hamlin if your office knew of the plans being circulated."

I could see Isaac start to squirm. Finally, he simply nodded.

I bit back the tirade I wanted to unleash but Phelps had admitted to ignoring the complete staffing protocols because he was sure that his office was responsible for all safety and operational requirements. The asshole had even had the gall to remark that a little window in a wall wouldn't matter in case of a nuclear incident. He had seemed unable to comprehend that the worry was not so much nuclear but a much more likely ordinary explosion. Anyway none of that mattered. I suspected that the present Chief of Surveillance had not been in the loop either. The buck stopped at my desk. I should have noticed the incomplete staffing. I leaned back with a groan and asked what the two of them saw as present problems.

"Isaac and I have been going back over all programs for the last couple of years and comparing notes. As far as we can tell so far, there have been no other significant problems. The next big event will be the Surety Operational Inspection. That will be due late this summer so by mid-summer we should have our own exercise to prepare for them."

"Ok. So, assuming that I'm not relieved after the Siegelsbach affair, you think you can handle the job? Also what do you think of Lieutenant Sampson?" She shrugged, then frowned. "Unless Montgomery throws a wrench in the plan. As for the Lieutenant, well, is Surety the place you dump all your green as grass officers?" I couldn't help a chuckle. "We don't have a slot for an assistant Munitions Officer. Besides, since McNamara, no decent Officer wants the MO job since it's the one most likely to get him in real trouble. The present MO slot is an O-3 and the incumbent, Captain Reynolds, is a tanker and is keeping his head down until we get a new Junior Captain to relieve him. Sampson is lucky that Husterhoh Post has a permanent Officers Club Officer otherwise he'd be it. Since McNamara did away with the "Tail" in the military in favor of more "Tooth" we have almost no officers qualified to run any of our support services." I tried not to grimace. "That, of course, means that you Damned Ass Civilians, get to run rough shod over a bunch of clueless young guys who want only to play with the guns."

I closed my eyes trying to control my anger – and couldn't. "You know that I had a call from NATO just the other day upset because I hadn't sent in my listing for Local Nation civilian support for Logistics in time of war? What a crock! You'd think they could look out their windows and see that every civilian truck in Europe has a Military Number stenciled on their bumper for just that purpose. They are all committed to supplying their own troops, not ours! Without a US Transportation Battalion we'll be lucky to move anything in an emergency. We're lucky to even have a reserve Trans Company. Very few units over here have even that. If push comes to shove, we can have the entire Atlantic covered with supply ships but most of their cargos will end up sitting on the dock while the troops on line run out of everything. I happen to know that the Puzzle Palace in DC has been pressuring commanders to convince their DAC's to sign on for commissions in place in case of a war. They are seriously studying law to try and find a way to draft all of you into green suits when the bullets start to fly."

It was all I could do not to grin at the Colonel's dilemma. We'd gotten an intense push to accept commissions, mostly as field grade officers when we checked in theater. None of us who'd messed with the military for years could miss the transport problem either. All the support units for the army had been moved into the Reserve or National Guard and there was only one trucking company here in theater. If the line of battle was going to accomplish their job in coming wars, somebody would have to figure out how to move the guard units to Europe before the front line units run out of bullets and food. Reserve and NG Truck, Signal, Mortuary and Ration Supply units will never be ready for a "Come as you are war". Luckily, Joanne stepped up to the plate. "Well sir, it looks like your, Damned Ass Department of the Army Civilians have their work cut out for them. As for Lieutenant Sampson, he's green alright but, so far, I've not had to tell him anything but once. He's reluctant to make decisions about policy but I can't blame him there since I have no real idea how to handle a policy that doesn't relate to the facts on the ground either. The best I can do is to promise to try and keep you from falling on your sword."

Oh shit! My wife has reverted to her "Squatter" role. How could she -? Then I had to gape as Richmond burst out laughing. When he could control himself again, he gasped, "why don't you two go do whatever it is you Damned DAC's do and let me know if I need to bring my sword from home?"

Wednesday March 15

It had been an uneventful week since the Colonel's briefing. Siegelsbach would eventually close and Lieutenant Sampson was beginning to get over having to work for a woman – and a civilian at that. He was even taking some initiative in planning for the summer SOI. He'd even begun to ask questions, intelligent ones, once he found out that it wouldn't end in a blast as to how stupid he was for asking. Apparently Major Phelps had enjoyed throwing his weight around. Anyway, he'd come along well enough that I suggested he make a trip to Fischbach so he could see how the surety business worked in the real world. Since then he'd made several trips down there as well as one to Siegelsbach. Surprisingly, he'd even asked Robin for a date. Even more surprising was that she agreed.

Thursday Mar 16, 1967

I looked up as Peggy K came to the door. "Washington on line one, Sir." She said then turned to leave. I smiled. Only a DC call resulted in a personal heads up. All others resulted in a shout, of name and location. I decided I'd ruined a once very polite girl. I lifted the phone.

"Damn it Arthur! It's hard to believe that a damned Colonel out in the backwaters of the world could cause so damned much trouble that we've got Brigadiers wanting to jump in the Potomac without a life preserver!"

I had to chuckle. "It's nice to hear from you too Roy. How are all the other Confused and Incompetent Assholes taking this honor from our esteemed leader?"

"Well, you could put a gag on underlings that get POTUS upset that his pet projects are becoming political footballs. The man wanted to know what he can do about a damned civilian who can screw up the works so bad."

I was getting pissed. "You mean a woman who found a gang of thieves working for the army, killed a few, identified a stolen bunch of highly classified weapon that had been used to shoot down a British Airliner, was kidnapped, tortured, raped and was still instrumental in

160

taking out an IRA splinter group dedicated to kicking the British out of Ireland? Or maybe you mean her husband who killed the guy in the process of raping her? Or maybe it was her boss who threatened to drop a US Army Sargeant out of a helicopter from a thousand feet in the air after he had shot his balls off?"

There was a sigh on the other end of the phone. "Hell, Arthur, you're preaching to the choir. Even the man could barely keep the grin off his face while he hollered at State to make sure the whole thing got covered up and to get those weapons to the place they were supposed to go. State has assured me that there are no illegal weapons in Germany and that the President's plans are on target. There is only one problem left. Certain parties who shall remain nameless have realized that they have no idea in hell as to how to use some of the items and have demanded an expert to give them some training. As far as I can tell, there are no training manuals available yet and the only person who can fulfill that request is the same one that has caused all the trouble. There is an NSA Colonel getting ready to leave who will carry orders and whatever data is available for your expert to take to wherever she is needed. This is just a heads up for you."

I saw red! "Damn it Roy! My expert is just out of the hospital from the events I've described. On top of that she's just back from her honeymoon. She is demanding to see the evidence - grizzly evidence - I have that there are no longer any IRA threats against her. I know her! I'm going to have to show it to her or she'll turn over every pile of shit in the field to satisfy herself. We'll be lucky if she doesn't demand we put the heads on pikes over the main gate. She'll kill me for saying so but she's in no condition yet, either mentally or physically to go deal with a bunch of insurrectionists. There's also the fact that she's just taken over a job at AWSCOM that caused her predecessor, an Army Major, to be canned. If that's not enough, her new husband will raise holy hell over the idea."

"Well Colonel Holtman will have to get her to come around. He's a Spit and polish Girene and you know the Marines never fail in their mission."

I had to laugh out loud. "Roy I hope that Marine brings along some humility. He's going to be talking to a woman who's idea of spit and polish, is that polish is a perfect place to spit. If this guy wants to remember the Halls of Montezuma and the shores of Tripoli he also shouldn't forget the Chosen reservoir because what he'll be facing will be a hell of a lot scarier than an army of Chinese troops."

He actually did laugh at that. "Damn it Art, you make this girl sound like Annie Oakley. I chuckled. "Roy, this girl's more like Clyde's girlfriend Bonny. She told a high muckedymuck from MICOM exactly where he could stick his damned Redeye. She sent in a Nuclear Incident report on a squadron, headed by the son of a flying tiger hero. She was kidnapped by three thugs. She blew one's balls off and made swiss cheese of the other two with a pistol from almost forty feet away. She bit her own damned tongue while she was being raped and beaten, to keep from screaming. You think a damned marine with shiny shoes is going to impress her? If so I've got a bridge I'd like to sell."

Monday March 20

I was beginning to get the hang of working at a headquarters desk. You had to look ahead to possible problems and prepare for them – hopefully with a solution. A major one was a SOI coming up in September. A Surety Operational Inspection was a biannual event for all nuclear organizations and can and often does destroy careers. Between now and then repeated unit inspections will be held by AWSCOM, COMZ and European Command. A SOI was always a huge drain on command resources. A failure would not only reflect upon the command but would probably result in my joining the old AWSCOM Surety officer, my predecessor Major Phelps, on a ride back to the states.

I was up to my eyeballs in the reports of the last SOI from two years ago and making a list of questions to be asked of the two main storage sites and at headquarters when I heard a throat cleared. Looking up, Fraulein Habbermann was standing in the door. I raised my eyebrow. "I have a message from Mister H – well your husband, Ma'am. He says that he and you must go to Ramstein for a meeting at one PM and that he'll take you in his automobile as soon as he gets out of a meeting with the Colonel."

I sat back at my desk wondering what Montgomery wanted now? I had no doubt that it was he who had called the meeting. I had just finished my cup of coffee when Isaac came in. "Ready?" he asked. I nodded and grabbed my jacket.

Once in the car, he said that the Colonel had told him that we had a visitor from DC, a pretty important one. He wasn't told the subject but could guess that it had to do with our recent activities. I grinned and told him that even a dumb wife could have figured that out. He laughed then became serious. "Don't let this guy steamroller you." I grinned. "Darling, if I won't let my husband steamroller me, you think I'll let anybody else do it?"

In the Ramstein Support office we were shepherded into a conference room where Montgomery sat with a Marine Colonel in full Dress Uniform. He was introduced as Colonel Holtman, National Security Agency Assistant Operations Officer. "He has a proposal for you, Joanne." Interesting that he used my first name in a formal introduction. The marine drew himself up self importantly. I decided I didn't like him.

"It's not a proposal, Miss." He growled. "It's an order from the very highest level." He slid a document across the table. I glanced at Montgomery. He was trying very hard not to chuckle. I looked at the document. Sure it was an order signed by the Chief, National Security Agency, to the effect that Joanne Elizabeth Scarborough was assigned to temporary duty as directed by Colonel Holtman for an indefinite period to conduct duties as assigned by Colonel Holtman."

Truly pissed now, I gave him a bland smile and asked what this had to do with me. I'd never actually heard somebody Huruph before. "It's an order assigning you to me for extended duty, Miss Scarborough. If Colonel Montgomery and – Mister Hamlin – is it - will leave the room, I'll explain to you what you must do. I slid the paper back across to him. "If Mister Hamlin goes, Colonel, I go too. Besides that paper has nothing to do with me. It's been nice meeting you." I almost laughed as his face turned red with fury as he jumped to his feet. "Miss Scarborough, you, apparently don't know who I am." I smiled sweetly at him. "Of course I do sir. You're an officious asshole who thinks he can order anyone to do anything and they'll do it. Surprise! You're going to have to do better than a set of phony orders to have me listen to you rant but if you want to do that then, at least, use my correct name. I'm Mrs. Joanne Elizabeth Hamlin wife of the man you want to throw out of the room. Next, this is not a green suit I'm wearing so I don't even have to listen to you if I don't choose to. Finally, I not only don't work for you. Technically, I don't even work for the European command. I take my orders from the Ammunition Civilian Career Management Office at the Savanna Army Depot in Savanna, Illinois. They assigned me here and they can fire me if they want but you can't.

Now if you want orders cut for me you can call them and they may do it. Finally, if I don't like their orders I can always quit! Now would you like to sit down and act like a polite human being instead of an officious jerk? If so I and my husband and Colonel Montgomery will listen to what you have to say. Considering that I value my career, I'm inclined to help any way I can but I will not be bullied."

I thought the man was going to have apoplexy. He opened his mouth twice then, of all things, he laughed out loud. "Damn!" he said. "I'm glad my feet are under the table. I was told that spit shined shoes would just give you a better target to spit on. How the hell did that bunch of Micks manage to – Oh shit! Strike that. I'm sorry. That was an awful thought."

I knew my face had gone white at the memory of my ordeal. The man, though, was obviously mortified at having brought it up. Maybe he wasn't an asshole after all. I murmured that it was OK. "No it wasn't but thank you anyway." He took a deep breath. "Would it be OK if we started over with me apologizing for my idiocy and spell out the problem?" I took another breath and nodded.

My god! That was a hell of a woman. I shook myself. "First, we at NSA tend to think of ourselves as omnipotent – until we come up against a truly stupid error. May I assume that congratulations are in order – actually to your husband. With all our technological capability we overlooked something as simple as a marriage. Next, I did know of your ordeal and want you to know that we were all sorry and impressed – so much so that it was actually a subject of discussion at one of the POTUS briefings. Finally, there was a great deal of discussion of the wisdom of placing you in harm's way again. Unfortunately, we have a very high level training requirement and almost no one is available to the military who, not only knows what that weapon is but could teach inexperienced operators how to use it. Everyone assumed that a set of orders for any army personnel was all that was needed to satisfy the requirement." I had to chuckle.

"Now that I have been properly briefed upon the very real restrictions we were operating under here, I have to put it another way. We very badly need you to help us prevent a lot of unnecessary bloodshed with some of our – well, if not allies – at least interests in the middle east conflicts. Just how much do any of you know about middle east politics?" Montgomery sat back listening as Hamlin spoke up. "You mean Oil." I nodded but only in a peripheral sense. What do you know about the Kurds?"

Then I got it. "That's who we're giving the missiles to. I know they're the largest ethnic group in the world without a country and they've been fighting Iraq and off and on, Iran for years and Turkey in between. Also they have some of the biggest oil fields in the middle east. They practice a strange brand of Islam that is similar to the Shii's in an area dominated by the Iranian and Iraqi Sunni's." I thought about it a minute. "If I remember right, they tend a bit more toward secular rather than religious in everyday life. Most of this is all second hand knowledge but I'm pretty sure that boundary lines in that area don't mean much. They are only lines on a map drawn by the British after the various wars."

"Yes Miss. – Mrs. Hamlin. Most of the Middle east is Sunni but Iraq has a Shiite majority. Iran has a large Shiite population. The Kurds are a strange blend. In the south of Afghanistan the British drew a line across the area they designated as a country to carve out Pakistan. It went right through Pashtun lands. For practical purposes no country controls the Pashtun areas. Iraq ignores them and Pakistan refers to them as "Tribal Lands" Essentially, there are no real countries in the entire middle east, only tribal areas with county boundaries drawn through them. As a result, there will eventually be a huge religious war in the area. Right now the Shah of Iran ruthlessly controls Iran and Iraq – well if it hasn't had a coup today it will tomorrow. The Kurds are caught in the middle. Now you're right in that oil is becoming important to our country. Most of our shallow wells are drying up and the new ones require extreme drilling to reach oil sans driving up the cost dramatically. Cheap oil from the middle east helps keep our economy level."

"With all that, though, there is one factor now driving this particular situation. One of President Johnsons long held goals, no matter what you think of his politics and the various scandals surrounding his elections has been – help the underdog. It's probably political strategy but real none the less. Right now the Kurds are the underdogs in this area. It's for that reason that the arms captured by the Israelis were purchased and earmarked for the Kurds. They were hijacked, whether by crooks out to make a buck or an organization who wants the Kurds to remain vulnerable we don't know. The main thing is that we've got them back and they've been shipped. So far, we've met our requirement to arm the Kurds but when we looked around for someone to train them in use and maintenance of the Redeye type missiles we've come up empty. Your career program seems the most likely to help us meet the rest of the job – and you have the weapons that you can use to work out a training and maintenance scheme." I have in this folder a short description as to how the thing works in practice. I can authorize you to use up a couple in training if need be and can replace the one already expended and perhaps three more but that's about the end of the stockpile."

When he stopped talking, Isaac spoke up. "There's one ball breaker. Assuming that we decide she should actually go over there, she won't go alone. I'll be with her and so will at least one of Colonel Montgomery's body guards." "Impossible. It'll be hard enough sneaking her into the country little less a troop." "Well –". Time to get my two cents worth in. "HOLD IT GUYS!" My shout flipped three sets of eyes onto me. "Now, it's time to get real. I need some more information before I – I repeat – I decide on whether or not to do this.

First has anybody ever been to that end of the Mediterranean?" No reply. "Well I have and it wasn't a fun experience. Not only did I have a pair of Neanderthals for partners but no matter what I said, every eye turned to the men with me – and these were Israelis. Think what it's going to be like to a bunch of Koran thumping Muslims. A woman means nothing over there unless she's in a harem. I'll have a hell of a time just dealing with a bunch of men who think this is still the sixteenth century and won't see anything except the fact that I don't have on a burkha. I can't very well pull out a nine mil and shoot them to get their attention. That means that, much as I hate it, there's got to be a man along who's to be the nominal head of the training team."

"Next there has to be someone who can translate – not just into Arabic but into the local lingo whatever that is. Then, there has to be guards, at least two and they have to be solid as rocks because I'm damn sure not going to wander around the desert in a black tent. Sure as hell I'll be accosted at some time or the other and the guards will have to stop it without killing somebody."

"Finally, while you two military types debate, this civilian couple is going off to discuss the whole situation and figure out how to make appropriate arrangements with Colonel Richmond. We'll let you know in the morning what our answer is."

Tuesday March 21 1967

We talked little in the car on the way back to Ramstein the next morning. It had been a rather heated argument last night before I exercised my command authority and took off my dress. After that my husband was more interested in taking off the rest of my clothes than remembering what the fight had been about. Afterwards he, if not happy about my decision, at least accepted it. As we pulled into Ramstein, he squeezed my thigh and muttered. "Darling the thought of you going into that desert terrifies me." I patted his hand. "Now you know what wives all over the world feel when their men go off into danger."

Back in Montgomery's conference room he looked at me and nodded. I told them we would do their work for them. Montgomery smiled and Holtman let out a sigh of relief. With that he passed a folder over to me with big green Top Secret stamped all over it.

I hadn't believed Montgomery when he said that she would do it. Anyway, told them that Colonel Montgomery had people coming in that would provide body guards and that Mrs Hamlin's points about the situation on women in Kurdistan had been accepted by my office. A translator would be sent over and Mister Hamlin would also be added to the party. I then gave them a down and dirty brief as to the contents of the folder. "There is everything we have on using the Redeye II or, as the folks back home call it the Block III, as well as a draft set of instructions on maintenance procedures. Since your weapons won't have IFF they should operate almost exactly like the original Redeye. You will still have to acquire the target by flipping the level that will uncage the seeker and activate the gas bottle. When you get the acquisition tone you super elevate the muzzle about fifteen degrees and if the tone is still sounding pull the trigger. Theoretically, the thing will kill a target as it approaches but for practical purposes, it works better on a target going away. It's just the nature of the beast."

"Maintenance is more complicated but if you will watch the removal of the IFF you should have a good idea as to what can go wrong and how to fix it. We expect a lot of maintenance problems due to the fact of the desert environment and the inexperience of the operators. We expect more weapons off production lines for the rest of

169

the year but unless we can, somehow, find a way to return the damaged ones to here for service I expect several more trips to do the job and train the locals to do the work. Finally you will be travelling as Naval Lieutenant commanders from the staff of the Eastern Mediterranean squadron. Your staff will travel as Lieutenants and you all will carry diplomatic passports. That alone should provide a certain amount of protection as well. Appropriate uniforms will be provided. The arrangements are a bit flashy but we're hoping that their very openness will allay some suspicions – not to mention that it should give the Iraqi's something to think about."

We thought about sending you in through Iran or Israel but the Shah has begun to become a bloody tyrant with his secret police, the SAVAK running wild. Israel has problems with its own right wing protestors and Palestinian problem. POTUS knows that the Kurds are not much better but right now they are the underdogs and he is sick of all the back biting and killing going on in those countries.

He stood up and stretched his hand across the table. "Mrs. Hamlin, I wish we could do this some other way but I thank you for taking on the job. I will notify the office before I leave about your decision and they will begin arranging transportation and appropriate in country support. How long will it take for you to get yourself up on the weapons? Will ten days be enough? We expect to have the shipment on the road about then. Your surveillance chief at Fischbach seemed to think they could finish with the IFF removal by then." I looked at Isaac. He shrugged. I said that sounded like it would work.

Friday March 31 1967

With everyone pitching in, we finished the IFF removal in the Redeye II weapons. I even stole one day to assist, taking one into the other bay to disassemble it further than necessary so I could get a decent idea of what to do in case of failure. It turned out that the test set they'd sent us actually worked even if the weapon wouldn't actually fit in it properly. We had to fashion some heavy padded clamps to hold it in case of a motor firing. Luckily none did. Even more of a shock was that our modified weapons actually passed testing. We even wasted a Battery Cooling Unit by setting an IR flare up against our rocket motor barricade and activating one of the modified weapons. I had locked out the firing circuit but the weapon actually acquired the flare and gave all the right noises even when I elevated the nose fifteen degrees as the

170

operating notes directed. I set that weapon aside as a spare to be used for parts except in an emergency – if they ever got another BCU for it.

Monday April 3

It was 1000 hours in the Surety office and Sampson and I were going over the various necessary pre SOI events for the next few months. I was also preparing him for him taking over the office for a week or so if I had to be elsewhere. He looked up at me but it was a sign of his growing sense of situational awareness that he didn't ask why. Just then, Fraulein Habbermann came in. As I looked up I had the fleeting thought that I'd never really noticed that she was a truly foxy girl. I wondered that Sampson had not made a play for her. Of course, Robin wasn't crow bait herself but – "Ma'am?" I was so embarrassed that I actually chuckled at my inattention. I looked for an out. "Entschuldigen Sie bitte. Uh- Sorry. I was thinking of something else." She shrugged. "Your – Mister Hamlin asked that you come to the Colonel's office." I smiled and thanked her.

I was surprised to see Montgomery as well as Isaac in the office. Colonel Richmond pushed a packet across the table to me saying, "Colonel Montgomery has finally deigned to tell me that you are no longer my Department of the Army Civilians, who will be away on another vacation for several weeks. You two are now commissioned naval officers, namely Lieutenant Commanders Hamilton and Scarsdale. You both carry black passports giving you diplomatic immunity. He has not seen fit to give me an explanation for just about the worst set of disguises on the planet. Because of that, I have decided that he is in fact a card carrying member of the Complete Idiot Agency but have, never the less, lent him my conference room so he can explain all that to you."

Once in the conference room, I settled in a chair and remarked that I was afraid that the Colonel's assessment wasn't far off. "Unfortunately, your Stinger problem – and yes that's what all the political muscle is calling them now – has gotten tangled up in political posturing in the Middle East. First your weapons left Fischbach yesterday on shipping documents showing their destination as the Greater Antilles Army Depot."

I scoffed. "You've got to be kidding! I'd bet money that the

171

Greater Antilles doesn't even have an army – well I guess if you include Cuba it does. I doubt, though, that there's a single person on the planet that will believe that an ammunition lot starting with GA was made in the Greater Antilles. Hell I can't believe there's even an ammunition plant there – Shit! There's a good chance that there's no ammunition in the place at all. I'm afraid that the Colonel's description of a certain intelligence service was right on the money."

Ignoring Joanne's outburst, I continued. "Second, the weapons will be shipped through Turkey and arrive at their destination, Kirkuk next Monday. Two United States Naval Officers in mufti will be at the airfield to meet them. We have been assured that the Iraqi military will not be allowed to interfere. The weapons will be delivered by way of Turkey." At our questioning expressions he laughed and continued – "which the two officers will then accompany them to an area designated by the local Kurdish Military. Questions?"

I shook my head. "Am I to assume that we want the whole world to know that we're shipping extremely modern weapons of war to a minority tribe in the backwoods of Iraq? Also, I suppose everybody realizes that if the Iraqi Army hasn't attacked them yet this will practically force them to?" Then it dawned on me! "No! If they attack they are taking on the US Navy because two diplomatically immune Naval Officers are on the ground in the area. That has to be a confusing situation since, I assume, that no notice has been sent to them relative to the US interests in the situation." I looked over at my wife because we were going to be the focus of a whole lot of attention in this mess. She laughed out loud.

"You said out president was a slippery son of a bitch." I chuckled. This is all political slight of hand to establish a US presence in the area. You said he was basically a home front president. He really doesn't care what happens as long as he keeps everyone in that area of the world wondering what the hell the US is thinking. "That bastard is expanding the old English toast of "Confusion to the Enemy," to "Confuse friends and enemies alike." Suddenly another thought struck. "Hell! He expects a bunch of hit and run attacks by the Iraqi's until they can decide what to do. He expects them to use those new Soviet experimental helicopters that rumor has it, they have sent to the Iraqi's.

Also he is giving the Stingers a final operational test."

"Hell we elected a devious bastard. He's never let his right hand know what his left is doing. You sure he cares one bit about underdogs? He's hoping that someone in a US Navy uniform will be forced to kill the first chopper. He'll then be able to say that when he finds out who did it that he'll take extreme action. He'll probably put on a real show when nobody knows who that damned Naval Officer was because all of them will be present or accounted for."

"Also, just for the record, why would Turkey take part in this farce? They like the Kurds even less than the Iraqi's do. Come to think about it, why are we to be in "Mufti"? Why not in uniform if you want the world to know about us?

Montgomery smiled at Joanne. "Because they like the idea of a couple of US ICBM missile bases in their country – with the accompanying US dollars they will generate. Add to that, that one of the bases will be near the Iraqi border and that should reduce the Kurd menace to Turkey. Finally, the Turks may not like the Kurds but Iraq has made no bones about the fact that their secular approach to Islam is not acceptable to a true Muslim. They fully expect to have to, eventually have to fight both Iraq and Iran over that fact." It also means, I thought to myself, that the US will have to recognize their position with regard to what they consider "The Kurdish Problem".

"As for the Helicopters, what we have on them is in that packet on the table. They're supposed to be heavily armored and mount a 23mm cannon in the front. Our people announced that they wouldn't be available for use for another five or six years, yet, here are pictures of new and unknown choppers at the airfield near Samarra Iraq. Our assets believe that there are, at least, six of them. Some of those, though, may be Soviet M 8 troop carrying choppers. For now we're calling them XM 24 assault helicopter designated Hind. With that armor and cannon they almost have to be used as infantry support weapons. The cannon would be effective against Infantry Fighting Vehicles but would have little effect on main battle tanks."

No matter, though, both choppers are highly effective against ground troops and we've had reports that the newer one is almost impervious to .50 caliber rounds. Finally as to the uniforms – when you present those two black passports in Turkey and at the Iraqi border the world will know about it. Being in uniform would be like amateurs who don't know how to conduct clandestine operations. Of course they'll know about you anyway because of the black passport but would in that part of the world they expect other nations clandestine operations to stick out like a sore thumb like most of theirs do. After they've had a good look at you in western dress, you should probably get into less conspicuous gear."

I looked at Joanne. "I really don't expect you to wear a burnoose but a robe, sandals and a half face mask hanging to the side when not out in public should appease their sensibilities, even in tribal areas." As she started a protest, I held up a hand. "That's not an order. They want those weapons bad enough to put up with a woman munitions expert but it'll make your job easier. In addition, you'll find those sandals and loose robes are a hell of a lot more comfortable in a hot desert than tight fitting western wear. Why do you think that they still wear them after thousands of years?"

Friday April 7, 1967 Frankfort Germany

"Allah save me from incompetents!" the man screamed into the phone. "Of course I know the weapons have been shipped. I also know you were totally unable to stop that! Why is the damned woman still alive? She's got to be the key to all our problems. She's the one who was involved in the original shipping of the material. She's the one who handled the rocket maintenance. She's the one who led the raid on the warehouse. She's the one who killed your trusted team of thugs. She's the one who both the Germans and Americans rely on for how to handle the weapon information. Why in the name of God haven't you killed her as I instructed? Kill her, Damn It!"

"Sire, that's what I've been trying to tell you. She's disappeared along with that husband of hers. I sent a team to her house last night but no one was there. Our contacts tell me that they went on a vacation." I could imagine how the Imam was going to take that bit of news. I wasn't wrong. His scream nearly burst my ear drums.

"You fool! They just returned from a wedding trip! Why would they need another vacation? Find them! It's too coincidental that they and the shipment of arms disappear at the same time. Find them. Look for where the arms are going! That's where they'll be."

"You must find them and get rid of them. President Ahmed Hassan himself directed me just as I'm directing you. Those anti air missiles must not reach the Kurds. He's sending his deputy Saddam Hussein to the area to take charge of his agents there. Go to Kirkuk. Hussein's agents will aid you in your task. Do not fail! The personal price for you will be too high."

Monday April 10, 1967

As the good book says, "So it came to pass that" Well anyway, Isaac and I stood on the edge of a military vehicle park on the edge of Kirkuk when a heavily armed convoy of ten large very old British Army trucks pulled in and parked. Just in case anyone on the planet had missed our arrival at the headquarters of the Kirkuk military police, Mulla Mustafa himself was there to see his new acquisitions. As self proclaimed head of the "Kurdish State," he wanted to show off his coup. After greeting the Convoy commander an Army officer with, what appeared to be Colonel's pips on the collars of an Iraqi style uniform, he turned to us and motioned toward the "Sedan of State," an old but highly polished British Vauxhall. One of our guards, David Bakke was already in the back seat. The other one, Thomas Bouquet and our translator, with the unlikely name of Achmed Johnson were in the other vehicle behind us. We set off for what the Mulla called his top secret armory. It was only about ten kilometers out of town up against a low rock ridge sticking up perhaps fifty feet above the desert sand. It may be top secret but all around the horizon there were masses of people curious to know what all the excitement was about. I'd bet money that the Iraqi's knew all about his big secret.

I'd also bet that it was going to get their attention very quickly. We'd best get to work on training some local missileers. By the time we got inside the tunnel to a large room the heat had dropped at least ten or twenty degrees – enough that our sweat soaked clothes felt clammy. I was willing to concede that maybe, loose fitting robes might be in order for working here.

The Mullah's minions had been busy. A Redeye II lay on the table along with the grip stock and the Battery Coolant Unit. I shivered at the number of our regulations that had been broken in the process of Show and Tell. The Mullah was busy playing with the weapon and I felt it necessary to caution him that the thing was very dangerous. He looked up at me and smiled – a satisfied smile.

"Lieutenant Commander is such a mouthful I wonder if you would mind if I call you Mrs. Hamlin?" She raised an eyebrow. "If I may call you Mister Barzani." She replied, then added, with a twinkle in her eyes, "Of course Joanne would also be fine if I called you Mustafa. In that case, my husband would be Isaac."

I almost shook my head at my wife's brazenness. Still she had broken the ice very convincingly when he laughed out loud. "Oh, it's a shame," he chuckled, "that under the circumstances I can't add you to my harem, Joanne. From what I have heard about your prowess with weaponry, though, perhaps I would have a great deal of difficulty in that. You would probably foment an insurrection. Turning to the serious, though, I am not unaware of the danger of this weapon. It does

176

not appear to be one well suited to closed in spaces." Joanne laughed. "Well, sir, since the tail end is almost as dangerous as the front, you're very right. Anyone standing within ten or – well, three to five meters behind it will be, at least severely burned. In addition the warhead in the other end would cause great damage if detonated in a room like this. Few occupants would survive." She reached down and picked up the BCU.

"Sir, even this could cause severe burns to a hand that was holding it if it were activated. Luckily, there are a number of safeguards to prevent accidental discharge of the weapon. The BCU would be hard to activate without a deliberate electrical connection, except by throwing it in a fire. In that case a very powerful mini explosion would probably occur. As for the weapon, it is, while not entirely harmless as it is, can be considered fairly safe – except in case of fire. If that occurred, the proper response is to run like hell! Once the grip stock is attached and the BCU is inserted, that switch you have your finger on is used to activate it. Very quickly the heat seeker will spin up and look for a target.

Once that happens, you would hear a rising tone as the weapon signals acquisition. This means the seeker has locked on to exhaust heat from the plane of helicopter. At that point you elevate the weapon muzzle about fifteen degrees and press the trigger, that one below your finger. It's at that time that a rocket charge will fire and expel the missile from the tube. After ten or fifteen feet the rocket on the missile will fire and send the missile on its way toward the target. The reason for raising the muzzle is that the time lag between the firing of the expelling charge and the firing of the missile motor causes the missile to drop slightly. It could drop enough to cause the seeker to lose lock on the target. Elevating the muzzle too much could cause the same thing.

If the missile is not fired within a given period of time the BCU will discharge its electrical and cooling capacity and will have to be replaced.

"How long a time?"

I shrugged. "I don't know. The weapon is so new that much of the data on it is still being evaluated or, at least has not yet been passed on to me. The time I've heard about was around forty five seconds to a minute. I would think that with a helicopter shooting at you that would seem a very long time to be standing in the open. Remember the back blast I spoke of. Hiding in a hole and firing this weapon is not an option – another reason for your attack to come from the rear of an aircraft."

I took a deep breath. "Sir, I don't want to say the wrong thing but I'm curious. "As far as my briefing data goes, you are Kurdish. However I notice that to your men, you often speak a dialect that appears to be more like Turkish. I assume that there's a reason." "Very perceptive Mrs. – Joanne," He said with a grin. Do you speak Turkish?" I shook my head and told him that I once knew a Turk and recognized the cadence of the words. "Well, I am a Kurd but in this area the various dialects are very similar and my ideas and, those of my men, with respect to government tend more toward the secular than the religious. Most of them are actually from Turkey itself, hence the almost universal of Turkish in my camp. Other areas in which we are active are Sunni and more in tune with the Religious but even they are more of a modern bent than the Shiites. This is one of the problems with anyone operating in this area of the world. Out tribes have little respect for lines drawn on the map by the British long ago. Any other questions?"

When I shook my head he turned to a young boy standing beside him. "Well," he said, this is Naborn. He speaks very good English and will serve as your translator and, to use the British Army word, Batman. Anything you need just tell him and he will get it if it is to be gotten. He will also be one of your – will you call them gunners?" I couldn't help a show of surprise. The boy couldn't have been a day over twelve or thirteen. As soon as Mustafa left, the boy stepped around me to take up a position a step behind me on my left. I looked at Isaac and raised an eyebrow. He chuckled. "It's obvious who's boss here. Notice I didn't get a Batman." The boy immediately spoke up to me. "If your man needs a Batman, I will get him one." I smiled back at him and patted his shoulder. "It's not necessary Naborn. Mister Hamlin was just teasing me." The boy looked up at Isaac. "You allow that?" he asked, his astonishment obvious. I was confused. "I thought in your country that a husband can do as he likes." His frown deepened. "Yes Ma'am but in my family it is considered disrespectful to his wife in public." I was touched. "Then you must have a very wonderful family." I told him, patting his face. His face clouded over but he blushed as he looked up into my eyes.

As we went in to inspect our quarters, Isaac whispered, that I had acquired a young lover. I looked up at him in astonishment. His grin widened. "Next time you look at him, you'll find him looking at you in adoration." I frowned, thinking that the idea of a young boy's puppy love in a place like this made me uncomfortable. As we walked, I asked what he did in the Mulla's army? He dropped his eyes. "I'm not allowed to go on patrols. The Mulla says I'm too young. That's why I'm with you. He knows I speak the best English in the camp but also he knows that the cave is the safest place for me. I keep begging him to let me have a guy but he refuses. I ruffled his hair. "Don't worry Naborn, you'll be old enough soon enough. Just enjoy being who you are as long as you can. Growing up in this world is not something to be wished for. But for a skillful translator there will always be a need."

Tuesday April 11, 1967

It was zero eight hundred in the cave meeting room and already warm. I had to admit that my robe with a sort of head scarf called a Shayla, was more comfortable than my western jeans and shirt – not really cooler but it allowed the sweat - I had to chuckle at that. Mother always told me women don't sweat, they perspire. Got a news flash for you mom. I sweat like a pig. Anyway, in this dry heat it allows the sweat to evaporate and actually feels cooler. It also was not a confining as a Burka or Niqab and left my face and neck visible. Mustafa assured me that in a Shiite area it would be scandalous in most Shiite areas but here it was considered quite modest. He had urged the outfits and even the color. Isaac and my robes were white because his men considered the white robe a symbol of authority since he had his lieutenants wear them. He'd added that while his men would do almost anything he ordered them to do they would be very uncomfortable with a woman in western dress.

Well I now had four "students," one of which spoke passable English He was to be the interpreter. I introduced myself in the few words of Arabic I had managed to pick up in two days and told them that I was sure that their English was much better than my Arabic so "Naborn," here would be our translator. Then I had him tell them that if there was anything that they didn't understand completely to be sure and ask. My husband would also be ready to answer them also. I introduced Isaac. Then I began the down and dirty part of the lesson about the dangers of the weapon and what it could do.

After all were gathered close to the table, I explained the

179

various parts of the weapon allowing plenty of time for Naborn to translate. I had already pulled off the protective cap on the nose to allow them to see the seeker and explained that the thing was not nearly as sturdy as their rifles and could be damaged easily. After about an hour I was beginning to see their eyes glaze over and asked Naborn if they would mind taking a short break for tea or perhaps for prayers. I knew it was too early but thought I'd let them explain to the foreigner the basics of their worship. They opted for tea.

By the time the class was over that day, we had gone through two prayer sessions and lunch but we had covered the basics of firing the thing. For tomorrow, I intended to demonstrate the firing of the weapon itself. Mustafa had been intrigued when I asked if he could start a bonfire out in the desert and selected a position about a half mile away in a location atop the end of this sandstone ridge that would allow us to remain near the cave and yet protect the camp from the back blast and explosion.

I'd had to keep a straight face when a number of questions were asked but none directed at me. They all went to Isaac, sometimes with a sort of embarrassed glance at me. I guess women were ok in giving instructions but only men could answer important questions. When we came out of the cave the entire camp was bustling with one crew out on the ridge preparing the bonfire, another opening weapons containers and the rest, moving trucks and equipment back down the road. I remarked to Isaac that I must have made an impression on them about the danger of the weapons. Supper was turned into a celebration with Mustafa making a toast to the success of our mission.

STINGER
CHAPTER 20

Friday April 21 1967

After breakfast, served in Mustafa's old command car, we got out a stinger. I checked it closely to make sure we hadn't done any damage to it in handling then went outside. I was surprised to see that the entire camp had disappeared and another set up around the end of the ridge near where the bonfire was set. I stopped and looked over at Isaac. He was frowning too. Just then my "students" emerged from the tunnel each carrying a Redeye II. The light dawned. "Shit!" I grunted turning to Mustafa. It was no longer a genial smile I saw on his face but the face of a battle leader. "When?" I growled. He didn't pretend that he hadn't arranged for us to get involved in a real demonstration. "Three helicopters left Bagdad fifty minutes ago." He said. "They were informed that I had made camp at the end of the ridge and was lighting a signal for the tribes to gather around me so we could begin a march on Samarra. They have just passed into our province and should be here in about twenty minutes. The best angle for a surprise attack will be to cross over this ridge almost over out head and begin strafing the camp as soon as they pass over. From what you've said, that will put the tail pipes of the helicopters pointing directly at us, the ideal attack position for your weapons. We will see then just how good your instructions were."

I was furious but could see the situation from his standpoint. "A little warning would have been nice." I muttered. "And I suppose there is no one in the camp out there." He shrugged. "It's a lot more warning than my gunners will ever have again – and yes, it's a shame to ruin so many good tents but they can be replaced. Everything else has been moved into Kirkuk." "So you want me to start a war here." I muttered. That got a venal smile. "Oh no, I expect them to start it. Feel free to wait until they begin shooting before you fire – or not as you please. Your Students have no problem with beginning the war."

I looked over at Isaac. He sported a rueful grin and shook his head and went to get a Stinger of his own. It was my decision. I made it. Turning to Naborn I said. "Tell them to hold steady when the helicopters pass over. It will be very scary when they begin firing but don't panic – uh, be surprised into firing too soon. Naborn, pick our best man to fire at the plane on the right. The next best should take the left one. I will shoot at the center one. One of us is bound to miss so you get the one that's left. Everybody, after firing should go into the cave in case one or more are left and come after us. Can I assume that you've opened more boxes and have them available for such an occurrence?" He grinned and nodded. "Was I clear? Do you have any questions?" No Savaşçı Prenses." With that he turned and began instructing the other gunners. Mustafa burst out laughing. "I can't believe he did that in front of me!" He chuckled. "Did What?" I asked mystified. "In our country, we have the leader, sometimes called Shah or in Turkish Kral. The War Leader is the savaş lideri. Theoretically, the Savasci Prenses is the female war leader but since that does not happen here, she would be the war leader's other half, warrior wife or daughter. I suppose that he means that you speak for me."

Further philosophical discussion was interrupted by a roar of aircraft. I wasn't the flap-flap of a US Huey but more of a ugly roar. Suddenly three choppers screamed overhead 23mm guns blazing and ripping up the tents a mile in front of us. I managed to get my stinger in place and activated. The whine immediately signaled lock and lifting the nose, I pulled the trigger.

I was surprised that you could actually watch the missile home in on its target When Joanne's disappeared in the center of the flame from the turbine engine a split second later, the entire helicopter exploded in a scarlet fountain. Her students were, obviously startled but their missiles left the tubes only a second behind hers. There was a second major explosion and moments later a small one out over the desert. Somebody had missed. Joanne led the race into the tunnel but turned at once inside to count noses. Then she screamed, "Naborn! No! Run!" She was ignored. Her young Kurdish translator stood in the open as the third chopper turned and began racing toward him guns blazing. Just then he fired the Stinger. The ground erupted around him with 23mm rounds that stopped as the canopy of the third chopper disintegrating from the blast of the small warhead. It didn't explode, simply dove into the sand with a huge roar tumbling end over end for several hundred meters. The damned missile must have homed in on the blazing 23 mm cannon fire.

Ignoring the flying shrapnel explosion and metal from the tumbling chopper, Joanne ran for the boy. By the time I got to her she had his head cradled in her lap with tears running down her face.

Mustafa and the rest of her gunners rushed up also – just in time to hear him whisper, "Benim savaşçı prenses Paradise göreceksiniz." His head lolled to one side and he was gone. Jo held his bloody body to her snow white robe and bawled.

I was amazed to see the American woman, of obvious high rank, who had just performed like a true soldier, sobbing for an Arab boy without a real name and without any chance of being more than cannon fodder in our endless wars. I knelt down beside her and said I would take him. She looked up at me, tears still running down her face, "What did he say?" "He said he would again see his warrior princess in paradise." She asked his last name. I had to say that he didn't have one. Her face twisted in fury. "He does now!" she snarled. "He's Prince – uh - Savasci, Naborn Scarborough Hamlin." At my urging she released his body and I lifted him up. To the gathering crowd, I said, "Bu savaşçı Naborn, Scarborough, Hamlin çok savaşçı prenses tarafından adında. O insanları için hayatını verdi ve Allah'ın sağ kolu, cennette oturup bir kahraman.

Monday Apr 24 1967
It seemed that our presence with the Kurds was becoming an embarrassment. We were ordered home "by the most expeditious means". As a result, Monday found us climbing back into Mustafa's sedan on our way to Turkey. Just before we left though, Mustafa handed me a beautifully inscribed brass plaque inscribed with his words to his people, and the translation. "This is Warrior Naborn, Scarborough, Hamlin so named by his warrior princess. He has given his life for his people and is a hero who will sit in paradise at Allah's right hand."

183

Tuesday, May 2, 1967

I was buried in paperwork as the result of the Hamlin's foray into Kurdistan. It was a diplomatic disaster or a strategic coup – depending upon who was doing the talking. The striped pants crowd were furious while Roy Connif had been chuckling on the phone when he passed on the fact that Johnson agreed publically with State demanding to know who the Naval Officers were who committed such a "Crime." All the while he was grinning at the successful destruction of three of Russia's newest super weapon, the Hinds. That meant two totally different after action reports, the burning of two diplomatic passports and agreeing to try and find out who the "rogue" Naval Officers were that almost started a middle east war. I'd sent no less than eight classified requests for that information. To date no one had been able to enlighten me on the subject. The Hamlin's "Vacation" was up Friday and they had returned to work. To reduce questions, they had taken a roundabout route through Switzerland where hotel records showed that they had been staying for several weeks.

Even as I tried to keep a worried look on my face as I signed still another information request, I heard Frau Kraditch clear her throat. Looking up, I noted the frown on her face. "Colonel, there is a mister Leonard Douglas wishing to see you." It was my turn to frown. Recognizing the name, I couldn't believe he'd physically show up on a military post. Never the less, I told Peggy to show him in and hold all calls. The man she showed in was at least six feet tall with bright red hair.

I stood up as he came straight to my desk and stuck his hand across it. Even as I reached across the desk to take the hand, I managed not to grin at the obvious ploy of establishing his position in this meeting. Since he was a civilian, the outstretched hand established that he was, at least as important as I was. It was a trick I'd seen a number of savvy civilians use in a military office. I asked what I could do for him. He released my hand and backed up to close the door before sitting across from me. "In this case, Colonel, it's possible that I can be of service to you." I frowned at that, but to give me time to consider his offer, I asked if he would like a cup of coffee – then quickly remembering who he was, added "- or tea?"

That sounded wonderful but I was very nervous to be so much in public space on a US Air Force base. "Thank you no. I'll come straight to the point. "We have reliable information that your Mrs. Hamlin and her husband have had a price put upon their head. This happened before certain events in the Middle East took place. We have it on good authority that the task was offered to a young Cuban Guerilla named Carlos but the Iraqi deputy to Ahmad Hassan, Saddam Hussein preferred a more experienced man. We don't know if he settled on this Carlos or someone else. Carlos is reputed to have killed twelve men and charges $25,000 for his services – for two he charges double."

"Now, as to who has demanded the deaths of the Hamlins, we know that he is a very rich, probably Russian, arms dealer in Syria who was responsible for the diversion of the munitions shipment that Mrs. Hamlin thwarted. Rumor has it that his loss was almost a half million dollars on the transaction. Half of the payment has already been made and Hussein's Baath party wants it back. That folder on your desk has a list of the most likely ones responsible. It also has all the data we have on our guesses as to the most likely persons in your service that were behind the attacks on her and the diversion of that shipment."

"Now, before you ask the question on the tip of your tongue, my organization is not in accord with the policies of your country with regard to the Brits. My people, however are not, true terrorists and we don't want the world to think so. To the best of our ability we try to keep down civilian casualties. We feel, though, that we owe Mrs. Hamlin a debt for her treatment by our rogue members. We have, as you know, taken care of them but are afraid that their deaths will come back to haunt us, at least me, if it is successful. We actually, considered re-instating the protection we've provided in the past but felt it left us open to too much speculation. As a result, I am passing this warning on to you. I hope you are able to protect the couple, especially the wife. I'll admit to being just a little in awe of that woman. If I had a couple of ones like her, I'd have the Brits out of Ireland before Christmas." I had a thought and had to laugh. "Unless she decided that we were on the wrong side. God help us then. Oh well, with that I will leave you."

He got up to leave, then turned back and said that he hoped that Mrs. Hamlin's baby is a healthy one. With that he grinned and opening the door, walked out.

186

I sat back and stared at the closed door for a long moment before opening the folder he's slid onto my desk. An hour later, I opened my door and gave Fraulein Kraditch a number to call on the secure phone.

When Roy Connif answered, I explained what "Our favorite Irishman" had said. Then I read off the names of the potential bankers behind the contract on Joanne and the list of agents in his "firm" who might be potential turncoats. When he finished cursing, he said that Troy Marvin was still in country and that he'd put him and his crew back on security detail. I'd hear from him in an hour or so. "Believe me," he said, "no matter the official line POTUS himself would be very upset to lose Mrs. Hamlin. I wouldn't be too surprised to have him eventually, pin a medal on her – very quietly of course.

I frowned as I hung up the phone, then got up and headed for the Surety office. Fraulein Habbermann looked up from her typing. "Can I help you Mister Hamlin?" I shook my head and told her that I just needed to speak to my wife a moment.

Joanne looked up with a grin as I opened the door. Then, staring at me she frowned. "What's wrong?" I told her about Montgomery's phone call.

"Shit!" I muttered, throwing the pen down on the desk, I slid open my desk drawer. "How long is this going to go on?" I pulled out my nine mil. "Damn It! Im tired of this shit. Somebody's gonna look like Swiss cheese this time."

"Honey, we're not talking about some damned thug. This time it'll be a professional assassin handling the "Contract" on you." She looked up at me, daggers flashing in her eyes. "US!" she grated. "On us – as in both of us. I'm not going to put up with it. I don't care how good this Troy guy is, this time I'm going to make my own mess. The bastard better not miss his first shot because he's not going to get a second one." I watched the fury rise in her so that she was practically shouting. "You! Go get your own God Damned gun now and don't you ever go anywhere without it!" I had a terrible time keeping the grin off my face as I left the office. Fraulein Habbermann sat at her desk with her mouth gaping. Obviously, she'd heard my harridan wife shouting.

187

As I opened the door, a tall blond man stood in front of it. Obviously surprised, he said, "Mister Hamlin, I'm Troy Marvin. I'm glad I caught you and your wife together. I need to speak with you both." I couldn't help a laugh. "Mister Martin, if I remember right you're DC's gift to the body guard service. I think you should come down to my office with me and have a cup of coffee. Believe me when I say you don't want to talk to Miss. – well, my wife - just now. When she's gotten the desire to throw smash or shoot things out of her mind, she'll get her temper under control and be down to apologize for losing it. Then you'll be able to discuss protection reasonably"

Ten minutes later, we were sipping coffee when my outer door opened and Joanne came in. "Damn it Isaac – why do you make me lose" –? Then she spotted Marvin. She frowned. "Sorry, I didn't know you had company." She started to back up to the door. "It's alright, darling." I said quickly. "This is Troy Martin. You remember Montgomery mentioning him."

Damn! It took me a half hour to convince a skeptical Mrs. Hamlin that we protection types needed the work and that having our "protectees" running around taking out bad guys was putting us out of work. Finally she laughed out loud. 'Mister Marvin you must be Irish. I've not had so much Blarney shoveled at me in years. Well, I wouldn't want the Protectors Anonymous union after me. OK you do your thing but I hope you won't mind if I, at least, get to carry my own weapon."

May 5, 1967 Friday

"You look awfully young to take on a job like this." The boy, for that's what he was, smiled. He couldn't be a day over eighteen or nineteen years of age. The smile though, was not a nice one at all. "My friend and I are just, as you Americans say, starting out. He has successfully completed three contracts and I only two but he has another contract that is not yet complete. As a result, when the Iraqi called him he gave me the job. Now why do you want to pay so much American money just to kill an American Woman?"

This snot nosed kid irritated me his heavy accent and superior attitude grated. He, or more correctly his partner, came highly recommended and the Russian was paying for the job. I had to keep the grin off my face that he didn't know I'd tried to hijack his weapons for my brother and his Irish friends. If he had known, this kid would probably be taking a contract on me. As it was he was really angry that I hadn't been able to deliver the weapons to him. At least he'd finally agreed that he didn't need the woman alive anymore."

"You don't need to know the reason. It's enough that you know that my sponsor has half the money, ten thousand dollars, here for you and the other half to be paid when the job is done. When will that be?"

I didn't like this job. It seemed like a big rock suspended over my head. I especially didn't like combining jobs like this. Carlos had laughed out loud at the thought of two clients wanting to pay for the same victim. The killing part would be a lot easier than the grabbing part – ignoring the problem of convincing this big Irish clown she was dead when she was being spirited off to some Arab's harem. He was a weak link. He was sweating heavily just standing here discussing a murder. There was, obviously something very strange about this. This woman had to be someone important, or at least, important enough to have two totally different people putting hits out on her. Perhaps she was heavily guarded. Still, Carlos and I had discussed it at some length and decided that twenty thousand American – four times the rate for a casual execution - was worth the try. I shrugged, "an execution could be done in three days. To make it look accidental could take longer." I thought to myself, especially the kidnapping part and procuring a dead female to burn beyond recognition in an accident. The man just nodded and opened a suitcase of cash on the table. I waved away his gesture for me to count it. He turned and left. I picked up the phone and called Carlos.

I didn't tell Juan that I was a little worried about making two jobs into one. He was nervous enough. "Look Juan," I sighed, "this job could make our reputation. The Iraqi wants the woman so he can do his own dirty work. He'll probably sic his torturers on her or maybe put her in his harem until he tires of her. The Irishman just wants her dead. In both cases they'll add another five thousand US dollars for the man but he's not really a big deal. As for killing her, do it like we discussed. After you have her on the way to Iraq, simply pick a girl who looks like her stuff her in your hit's clothes. Then you film the killing and the burning of the body. Make sure she's not identifiable in the film and send it to the German Politzi. Blame it on the Irish. They're always good to blame a crime on."

Well, I already knew how I was going to do it. I'd watched the woman for a week and there were only a few times that she didn't have watchdogs with her. The trick was going to be getting them out of the way and her alone. The fake badge and uniform would get me onto the army post but that would add difficulty to both problems. I settled myself into the job of watching.

CHAPTER 23

May 12, 1967

I had heard the phone ring but had been pulling my hair trying to schedule preliminary SOIs for both Fischbach and Siegelsbach. I only looked up when Fraulein Habbermann called. "Mrs. Hamlin Line two. It's Miss Laurence at Fischbach. She seems perturbed." I chuckled. "Robin's always perturbed – with good reason. She has to deal with McLauren. It's a wonder she has any hair left." I was still chuckling as I picked up the phone. "What's he done now, Robin? Surely EUCOM's calmest, most capable Surveillance female branch chief can handle a simple mild mannered Scotsman." "Don't bullshit me boss. You know that I'm your only female branch chief and that SOB isn't mad at me. It was my predecessor who submitted a report that he didn't like. He's furious with you. He's on his way to the CO's office now so you can probably expect a call from Major Compton any minute." I chuckled again and thanked Robin for the heads up. Then I sat back to meditate. I was going to need all the calm I could muster to deal with Angus McLauren if I was to keep from shooting the bastard. I wished I'd worn slacks instead of this damned too short skirt and silk blouse to fight with him. Oh well, leaves my legs free to kick him in the balls.

Sure enough, when the phone rang, I told Fraulein Habbermann that it was probably for me. She picked it up and said, "Yes Sir" then she nodded to me. Lifting the receiver to my mouth, I said, "Yes, Major, when do you need me and what do I need to bring – a whip perhaps?" There was a snort on the other end. "It would be nice for you to come pretty quickly and the last would be a good idea." I laughed and said I'd be there in a half hour. Sighing, I stood and picked up my shoulder bag. As I went out the door, I said, "Could you tell the Chief of Surveillance where I've gone, please Fra-," I stopped and turned. "You know Fraulein Habbermann is a mouth full. Would you mind if we could call each other by our first names?" She looked up with a tremulous smile. "My name is Ingrid." "A beautiful name," I muttered. "Mine is Joanne. Feel free to use it whenever you think proper I've noticed that we're pretty informal around the Headquarters." With that I went out to the car, wishing we'd brought my little Porsche today. I would have enjoyed the trip over the mountains to Fischback in a car designed for switchbacks and tight curves. Oh well, Isaac's Mercedes would just have to do. Poor me! Such a come down to have to drive a Mercedes.

Damn! I was getting tired of looking over my shoulder all the time and carrying that damned piece around. I could damned well see why the people who had to carry the thing all the time wanted the light weight models – even if their low velocity ammo made them into little more than pea shooters. I opened the door and tossed my bag into the other seat. It was an unusual day for Pirmasens, bright and sunny with the temperature high enough that I was glad for Isaac's tinted windows. With that thought, I glanced in the rearview mirror to see Troy Marvin's agent's car come out the gate behind me.

I held a steady 140 Klicks down State Highway 10 to the turn off for the mountain road to Fischbach. As soon as I made the turn I glanced back at the highway. The agent's car wasn't in view. I started to slow until I realized a big gun was pointed at my head. In the mirror I saw a man in the back seat holding it. "Don't stop till you get around the curve!" he growled. Then he tossed a pair of handcuffs into the seat beside me. Then you can put them on.

I froze in fear. The memory of being tied spread eagled on a bed while a man beat me and another raped me filled my brain. "Watch where you're going!" the man demanded. His voice cleared out my brain. Fury replaced the fear. "I said stop!" he growled as we passed the last open stretch of road. I didn't know what had happened to the agents but it was obvious I was with the guy with the contract out on me. "Like hell!" I thought. I jammed my foot to the floor. "Damn it woman! Slow down!" "Like Hell!" I repeated out loud as I reached the first bend. "I'm damned if I'll ever let anybody have control over me again! Been there, done that! Shoot if you want. You're going to anyway. This time, though I'm not going to die alone!"

What the hell had I gotten into? The damned woman was crazy. Nobody ever argued with a gun. I pushed the muzzle against her head. "Careful, sonny," she laughed. "You're not a very experienced assassin or you'd never have let me drive. I've been beaten and raped by pros. I'm the one now who decides who's going to die. Pull the damned trigger if you want. Whether or not I die with a bullet or because I jerk the steering wheel and drive off the side of a mountain it'll be my decision not yours. By the way, better hang on. It's time to find out if a

Merc sedan can take a hairpin turn like my little Porsche does." With that I was thrown hard against the left door as the damned car lifted onto two wheels in the savage turn.

Damn! I really didn't want to kill myself. I felt like I'd pushed that damned heavy car beyond its limits. I'd thought I'd be able to reach my bag and get my piece but the centrifugal of the careening turn had driven me against the door and away from my weapon. It seemed like hours but was probably only moments before the right wheels landed back on the road. With a sharp left turn coming up, I slacked off the accelerator a bit. "Damn it, Bitch!" the voice in the back screamed. "Slow down or I'll put a bullet in you!" I forced a laugh. "Go ahead, sonny. Whenever you feel like looking at the gates of hell. I'll slow down when you throw that gun out the window. Hell! Then I'll even stop and you can try to kill me with your bare hands. I warn you though, I'm one pissed off woman and you can expect a hell of a fight." The sonny had pissed him off and now he was almost mad enough to pull the damned trigger.
But he didn't.

"Yeah, like I'm stupid enough to throw away my weapon so you can reach over into your bag and get yours." I said, holding onto the strap hard as the car swept around another damned sharp turn and began to climb up the mountain. She did a quick gear change and stood on the accelerator de gas. The engine roared but the auto didn't slow. It charged up the mountain like a maddened bull. The woman actually laughed. "Hell, grab my bag and throw it out too. Then we'll see how a macho man does with a woman half his size. Be damned careful, though. We wouldn't want you to jiggle my arm with a thousand meter drop on the left. By the way, you've only got about ten minutes at this speed. We'll either go off the edge or I'll ram this car into the gate post at Fischbach. Then we'll see how you do with a half dozen soldiers pointing rifles at you."
I thought it over. She didn't know about my knife and, after all, I did have almost a forty kilo's on her. As the auto charged up the straight climb to the summit of the mountain, I made up my mind. Reaching over the seat back, I grabbed her purse. It was big and heavy. Rolling down the window, I tossed it out. "Now yours boy." She demanded. I only hesitated a moment. How the hell had I lost control of

this situation. Carlos was going to never let me hear the end of it. I tossed out the pistol.

I grinned. I was pretty sure he didn't have another gun, probably a knife though. Oh well, a couple of cuts would heal. Besides, I had a feeling that he didn't want me dead. He wanted me for something else, almost certainly not something I was going to like. Oh well, I now had a fighting chance. I slowed the Merc as we reached the top of the mountain. There was a small flat area beside the road there. It was as good a place as any. "By the way, what did you do to my agent's car? You know they are CIA. They'll never let you have another day without looking over your shoulder."

"Colonel, there's a Mister Troy Marvin on the line." I looked up to see Peggy holding the phone. I picked up mine. "Colonel, our agents got stymied as they followed Scarborough – Mrs. Hamlin toward Fischbach. Somebody managed to get a bunch of sugar in their gas tank. The car quit just before they reached the Fischbach cutoff and Hamlin kept on going. She knew enough to stop and check on the problem. I'm afraid she had no choice. They managed to flag down a German Politzi and call in but they're still parked on the road. I've got a man heading that way now." After hearing Marvin's excited report, I said I'd be right there and told Peggy to get me a chopper for immediate take off. "Also send out a squad of MP's from both Pirmasens and Fischbach to cut off that road. If I remember right there's no exit from the road till you get over the mountain. Have them block all traffic. Nobody gets through till they've been carefully checked." As I was about to leave, I turned back. "Also contact Mister Hamlin and tell him his wife's out of touch and without her guard detail. Tell him she's on the road to Fischbach and may be in trouble. That's all we know now."

I was going nuts. It took almost a half hour to get a chopper in the air and by the time we got to the mountain road a road block had already been established. I had the pilot sit down and I commandeered two MP's to go with us. Then we lifted off and headed up the mountain. We were almost to the top when the pilot called back that he'd spotted something and began lowering the chopper to the road. One of the MP's jumped out as soon as we settled onto the pavement and ran to the bundle in the road. When he brought it back, I realized it was Joanne's bag with her Beretta still in it. I cursed at the thought that she was without any protection at all.

Back in the air, we kept climbing to the top of the mountain. This time it was me that saw the ominous stains. "There! I commanded "Put us down there!" I jumped from the door realizing that I should have brought a coat. It was noticeably cooler at this altitude. Sure enough it was a blood stain – a big one. So we hadn't passed a wrecked car and there was no dead body here. They must have gone on. I rushed back to the chopper and twirled my fingers on the way. The pilot was already spinning the rotor up as we jerked the doors shut. We headed on down the other side staying close to the road as we dared to keep from missing anything important. Just then the pilot called back and handing me a set of earphones, said, "It's Fischbach about Mrs. Hamlin." I grabbed the phones but all I got was static. "Reception's bad in this area, Colonel." The pilot shouted. "Couldn't hear all of it but it sounded like the lady was there."

CHAPTER 25

May 12, 1967

"Fuck em." I muttered as the car came to a stop. Quickly, she opened the door and got out taking the keys with her. She tossed them over against a rock. Calmly, she said, "If you want to ride out of here, you'll have to get them." With that she kicked off her medium heeled shoes and stood squarely in the road in nothing but her skirt blouse and hose. I got out pulling my knife from my boot. She laughed. "I see you didn't plan on a fair fight. Well, don't expect one from me either." Damnation! The woman didn't look the least bit scared. As I approached her, I tried to plan how I was to grab her without having to kill her. I might as well enjoy this. It wasn't often you got to beat hell out of a woman without all hell breaking loose. As I reached her, I faked with the knife and swung at her face with my fist. She wasn't there! I felt a Karate chop on the back of my neck that drove me to my knees.

As I thought, he was a gutter fighter with almost no training in any specialized martial arts. Still, I had to be careful. He had a knife and a long reach on me. I also had to control my temper because I was still imagining that night on the bed in that damned cabin. "Fight smart Joanne!" I growled to myself. He had at least six inches on me and at least that much reach. Add the fact that he was built like a tank so close in was bad. If he got his hands on me he could lift me off my feet and I was a goner. In my favor as he stood up and shook his head, was the fact that he, obviously, had a stiff neck and, like a tank, he lumbered. Also like a gutter fighter, he held his knife wrong. If he'd had it in a fighting position when he came at me, I'd probably have, at least, gotten a cut on me. He was, apparently, more used to back stabbing than actual fighting. I didn't get the impression of many brains. He'd been surprised that I got in the first blow and he was taking a long time to think about it. Maybe a bit more fuel to the fire would do some good. He hadn't liked that "Sonny" remark. "Kid, I think you need to go back to assassination school. So far you've made a hash of this one."

That did it! He lunged at me, drawing his knife back for a downward slash. I was ready. Jumping aside on one leg I aimed my foot directly at his crotch, knowing I was going to take some damage. Sure enough the descending knife went for my leg just as my foot met his testicles. He jerked and screamed, throwing off his aim. I caught a slice across my ankle but the blade buried itself in his thigh. He collapsed like a falling pine tree. Ignoring the pain in my leg, I didn't step back. Gritting my teeth, I jumped to my damaged leg and swung my entire weight behind the foot I smashed into his temple. He dropped the knife and grabbed his balls. I grabbed the blade and a baseball sized rock. This time the blow to his head felled him face down in the road. Taking the rock and knife with me, I limped back to the car and got the handcuffs then over to the big rock and retrieve the car keys.

It took me ten minutes to stop the bleeding in my leg and drag him over to the rear of the car. I damn near wasn't able to work the inert body into the trunk. Finally, though, I was able to close the trunk. Just before I did, he woke up. I shook my head at the fact that I hadn't split his skull. Then I had an idea. Ignoring the pain in my leg, I leaned into the truck and put the knife blade down between his legs. "Sonny, if you want to save your balls you'll answer a few questions." He tried to look mean but his eyes went down to the knife at his crotch. It only took a quick rip of his jeans to expose his most important assets for him to begin ranting. I really wasn't in any condition to drive but I didn't know how long it would take for help to arrive. I slammed the trunk and started the car. I drove very slowly down the mountain.

I was never so happy to see the Fischbach front gate in my life. As I pulled up the guard came to the window. I must have looked like hell for his eyes grew big and he asked if I was alright. I told him "Yeah but I need a medic." As he turned to run, I shouted for him to wait. He came back. "I want you to get Major Compton and Captain Buckholtz as well as a medic but I want it done quietly. I'll park the car in the motor pool. Tell Captain Buckholtz to put a couple of guards on Mister McLauren, preferably without him knowing. You have that?" "Yes Ma'am!" "Good. Make sure there's no big fuss but I could use the medic as soon as possible."

May 12

I hadn't realized that he'd gotten two swipes at me. A bevy of guards were surrounding my, would be kidnapper. It had been startling to find that I had two contracts on me, one for a kill and the other to put me in a harem in Iraq. Captain Buckholtz had sent two guards to bring McLauren here. I was finishing my report to him and Major Compton while the medic was bandaging up my leg when we heard the chopper. The phone rang. "Yes tell them that Mrs. Hamlin is OK, just a couple of small knife cuts. Really? No! No problem there. I'll send a jeep to the helipad."

He turned back to me. I understand congratulations are in order. I really think you should refrain from gutter brawls for the next few months." I blushed then exclaimed. "Oh God! Isaac!" He grinned. "Not to worry, Colonel Montgomery got him out of a meeting and he's on his way here. Apparently all your people can order up helicopters at the drop of a hat."

I jumped out of Compton's jeep in unseemly haste as we reached the motor pool. I let out a sigh of relief as I saw Joanne sitting on the table in the office. I had grabbed her shoulder bag as I left the chopper. Suddenly my fear turned to anger. I threw the bag onto the desk beside her. "How come you're here and your piece was on the side of a mountain?" She looked up at me with a cheeky grin on her face. "Because I let Juan throw it out of the car. Of course if you go back a little bit down the road from where you found that, you'll find his. It looked like an old M1911. If he'd ever fired it the way he was holding it, he'd have gotten the slide right in his eye. I'm glad to see you too Arthur." Damn that woman! I let myself slide into the only other chair in the room. "Who the hell is Juan?" She grinned wider. "He's the kid sitting in the other room with three big GI's standing around him. He took ten K to make the hit on me."

I filled him in on the facts as I'd gotten them and finished by telling him that we were waiting for his contractor right now. "You mean he just came out and told you who hired him?" Arthur seemed incredulous. "Well, I said, he did seem to think that if he didn't I might emasculate him but I have no idea where he got that idea. Or it might have been when I told him that the Irish Sinn Finn leader was a friend of mine." Just then two MP's showed up at the door with McLauren between them. At the sight of me his mouth dropped open. "Well, Angus, I came as soon as you demanded my presence. You want to tell me what it was you had to have so urgently?" Frantically he took in the people in the room. I nodded to Captain Buckholtz and a moment later, a terrified Juan was dragged into the room. "Juan baby," I cooed. Is this the guy who gave you the money?" He nodded wildly. "Good," I smiled, "now these two nice fellows will take you to see the Politzi who I'm assured, are waiting outside the gate. If you continue to be cooperative it won't be necessary to notify Mister Leonard at all."

Turning back to McLauren, who by now was pale as a ghost, I said, "I'm afraid that Mister Leonard is certain to find out about your part in all this. Also you may not know it but Juan in there was supposed to pretend to kill me for you. Then he was to turn me over to a high ranking Iraqi to play with. As a result Sinn Finn is not the only problem you have. You may prefer the protection of a US prison to any of the other countries who want to discuss your business dealings."

Just then the sound of another helicopter was heard. I sighed. I looked at Major Compton. "I'll go get him." He said. I looked over at MSgt Metcalf. "Would you mind if I use your desk, Top? My husband gets a bit excitable at the sight of my blood." Everybody actually laughed as he vacated his chair and I limped around to sit behind it.

"Where the hell is she?" I smiled at Montgomery. "I recognize that bellow. It appears that my husband has arrived." Just then the office door flew open and Isaac barged in. He rushed over to me and jerked me completely out of the desk chair. So much for hiding the bandage. Oh well the passionate kiss made it worthwhile. "Damn it Jo! Are you alright?" I couldn't answer because he was kissing me again. "I did gasp as my leg bumped against the desk. With that he looked down. "Shit! You're hurt. How bad?" I almost laughed. "Darling, please don't ask questions with your mouth full if you'd postpone the sex till we get home, I'm sure our audience would be a lot more comfortable." My words were a bit blurred since they had to pass around his lips. He did jerk his head up, though and glance around.

I bit back a chuckle as Hamlin blushed. Struggling for a stern face, I said, "Hamlin, to sum up, your wife was carjacked by a somewhat stupid assassin, outwitted him, beat him all to hell, made him give up the name of the person who hired him, arranged for the arrest of a high ranking MICOM official who was selling arms to anyone who could pay for them and put out a hit on her. She did it all that without having to ask her husband to protect her. Now if you can take your hands off her, I've got a few questions and comments to make." As Hamlin dropped his hold on her, Joanne settled slowly back in the chair with only a slight grimace of pain. I turned to her. "Now having said all that, I'd like to know why the hell, you thought it a good idea to throw your weapon away." I hated the cheeky grin that appeared on her face. "Because the alternatives were to slow down and let him grab me or drive off the mountainside at high speed and kill both of us."

She laughed. "I wasn't sure that Isaac's blood pressure could stand either alternative. I gave him two choices, losing his weapon and going hand to hand, or me killing both of us. We compromised by me agreeing to losing mine too and going hand to hand. Of course he cheated keeping a knife but that was almost a foregone conclusion. By then, though, I was pretty sure that he had an over imaginative idea of his capability – and I was right. He was a gutter fighter and up against a black belt in three different martial arts. I've gotta admit, though, that I didn't expect him to be fast enough to get in two licks with that knife. Give him a few more years and decent training and he might be formidable." I muttered that he wasn't going to have either.

May 13

"Yeah Roy. That's the story. Aside from a couple of scrapes with a knife she's fine and McLauren is in the guardhouse. He was so arrogant that he still doesn't believe that we can make a case against him. He claims to have powerful friends – and even asked that they be notified. I've sent you the list and assume you'll be able to use it wisely." He chuckled. "Oh yes! I've already got a team on each of them. I expect that we'll be able to come up with enough dirt to put them all in a cell. Also I've notified the Director about the situation and he's done some calling around. I think that some of our foreign contacts will be getting some unwelcome news soon. Keep Troy and his crew on her for now but I think in a few days, at most a week, the danger to her will be passed. By the way, If you aren't going to put her to work for you, I could find a spot for her. The DCI was very impressed with

201

her."

    I laughed. "Forget it Roy. She's made it quite clear that spook work is not a part of her career plans. Besides, she's knocked up and already starting to show a little – probably about three months."

CHAPTER 27

May 18 Thursday Bagdad Iraq

   "Sir, he wants you in his office." I looked up at Ashram, our office manager, surprised. There was no doubt who "he" was, Ahmed Hassam al Bakr. Strange, usually he just came out into the outer office when he wanted something. Never the less, I knew he had a visitor and he was the boss, so his office it was. As I opened the door, I recognized Mister Rommel, one of our main arms suppliers.

   "Have a seat, Sadam, Mister Rommel has brought us some disturbing news. Have we a fatwa on an American government agent?" "Oh! Oh!" I couldn't help a twitch. Taking a deep breath, I nodded. "Not really a Fatwa, sir, we asked for an agent to capture the woman who – interfered with – our activities against Mustafa. He was to deliver her to us here." Ahmed turned to Rommel. "Is that who we were discussing?"

   "Yes sir. I have news and a notice. The kidnapping failed and the agent, really an assassin, was captured by the woman in question. He seems to have had two jobs. One was to kill the woman and the other to kidnap her. Now it seems that she is considered a friend of the Sinn Fein and any further attempt on her life will as it was put, "bring repercussions." Finally, I have been notified by my suppliers that such any such attempt would have the effect of drying up any further actions on their part. They specifically mentioned any dealings with me with respect to your organization."

   With that, the man got up and headed for the door. Ahmed turned to me, a frown on his face. "Tell me you did not try to have a US Government employee kidnapped." I had to apologize and explain that it had seemed the proper thing to do at the time since she seemed to be an expert on the new weapon Mustafa had acquired. I thought we could learn much about its capabilities and limitations." Ahmed's frown didn't leave but he nodded. "It might have been worth it – then. It is not now. Make sure that any activities relating to the woman in question is terminated immediately and all records of them destroyed." "Yes sir." Then he added, "Now!"

August 1 1967 Tuesday

It was hard to keep a straight face as I came into the conference room to meet the SOI team. Colonel Richmond was, obviously having the same trouble. All eight members of the SOI team had their mouths hanging open at the sight of a female Surety officer, especially one with a large round lump under her skirt – all except one woman. She had a sneaky smile on her face. I glanced down at the roster - Major Pamela Deering. I couldn't help a wink at her. She'd, obviously done her homework. She grinned wider and pantomimed drawing a one in the air beside her head. I'd have to warn Sampson to watch out for her. He'd come a long way since he'd come into the office. He'd been green as grass but never had to be told something twice. Also, he'd spent a lot of time at Fischbach with Robin and she'd obviously spent a lot of time bringing him along – in more ways than one. I'd pretended not to notice the large diamond engagement ring on her finger. I wondered if his family was rich. Well, wool gathering time was over.

The Colonel introduced his staff and Colonel Perkinson introduced his. I made careful note of the faces matching them up with my roster. I gave each a quick numerical score. Perkinson got a zero. I pegged him as a lush and titular head only. There were two majors, Deering and a Lyle Williams. She got a 1 and him a three. Three Captains, appeared to have a lot of smarts, each getting a three. They were John Johnson, Joseph Barbour and Alexander Fernan. Finally, there were two Warrant officers, CWO Atkinson and WO2 Vermier. Atkinson got another 1 and Vermier a 2. None of the team was impressed by a pregnant woman and a shave tail lieutenant. I managed to look overworked and as instructed, so did Ben Sampson.

In my experience most SOI teams assumed that the unit personnel they visited were incompetent and if you looked too capable they put you down as a smart ass. I'd told everyone involved in this thing to give them what they expected to see. I was going to have to warn everybody about Deering and the Warrant Officers. They all had put up with a lot of prejudice and were fully aware of the people they ran up against. It didn't pay to try and bullshit them.

Aug 10 2067

The last test of the SOI was over and Isaac and I were celebrating at the O club when Deering and Atkinson from the team came in. She saw us and smiled. I gave Isaac a quick look and waved them over. "Are you sure we're not interrupting?" she asked. Isaac spoke up and assured her she wasn't. She looked at me and raised an eyebrow as she and the CWO sat down. "I think you've a question you'd like to ask." I laughed. "Confirmation perhaps." Her grin came up. "What kind of a spook are you." She laughed out loud. "How do you come up with that term?" I leaned forward on my elbows and took a sip of wine. "SOI inspectors are totally committed to see how many quarter turns on a screw is made. They are totally unworldly in dealing with the world as it is. They only understand what a manual says it should be. You spent ten days, looking at personnel records and personal evaluations. The chief spent his time watching my chief inspector in almost everything she did. Now according to the record he's happily married and a father of four so it isn't lust."

" And what do you conclude from your observations?

I chuckled. "I watched a couple of recruiters looking at potential – well, in your business you probably call them assets and evaluating them and their organization to determine the best way to use it. Now, I think you have a question."

I had to laugh. This girl was damned good. "Well, the first thing that comes to mind is that should you be drinking wine in your condition?" Her grin widened. "Probably not, but I truly hate doing what everybody tells me I should do." She shrugged. "For instance, I always wear my seat belt, or did before I got round as a basketball. Only a stupid person doesn't. I don't mind my boss telling me I have to but would hate for the government to tell me I had to. I hate smoking but if the goody two shoes movement intensifies, they're going to try and make everybody stop. If they do, I'll probably begin smoking a bit just to spite them." I almost had to cackle. "Why the hell are you working for the government with that kind of attitude?" She leaned forward suddenly serious. "I have one of those jobs that we have to make up the rules as we go half the time. When I'm wrong all I have to say I'm sorry. By now you should realize why Isaac and I keep telling Colonel Montgomery to stuff it when he makes noises about working in a different field. Believe me when I say that no spooky outfit would want me working for them. Next?"

It was my turn to lean forward and lower my voice. Alex and I are both amazed at the way that young shave tail handled himself during the inspection. I know his record. He knew nothing when he came here but six months later he didn't bobble a single test. Your doing?" She leaned back in her chair and took another drink of wine.

"Don't under estimate that kid." I said in a low voice. "He might be a good candidate for your recruit of the month. "You're right. He knew nothing when he came here but not a whole lot less than I did. Most in our business have a pretty low opinion of Surety Officers. We sort of learned together and he never made the same mistake twice. Also, he has been damn near plastered to our Surveillance Chief at Fischbach – in more ways than one." I had to chuckle at that. "She hasn't mentioned that ring on her hand yet but I'm quite sure that they've reached some sort of accommodation. Anyway, Robin is a truly great branch chief and most of what he's learned about things that go boom he got from her."

Just then Isaac joined the conversation. "And, in case you've forgotten the beginning of all this, neither Joanne nor I, am the least bit interested in being recruited into any new endeavor. Very soon she was going to be very busy taking care of a job and a pair of new arrivals. I'm going to be very busy with another job and taking care of the caretaker."

The rest of the evening, Alex and I spent an enjoyable time with two very interesting people. I hadn't been too surprised that her replacement at Fischbach had been so competent. Their career program was known for turning out talented people. The real surprise had been the young Lieutenant. By the time the inspection was over I'd made it a point to check over his record. The idea that a new shave tail with barely six months experience in Surety could put together such a performance was almost beyond belief. I grinned to myself. She and Hamlin didn't know yet that a future assignment more ideally suited to their talents and proclivities would probably be coming their way in the near future. She, at least would almost certainly enjoy a job with almost no rules. I wasn't too sure about him.

Aug 13 Sunday Evening

It had been a long and enjoyable Sunday I almost purred as I snuggled up to Ben in my big bed. He had finally worked up the courage to entice me into that bed last night. I felt my lips curl up. It was a good thing he didn't know just how easy I had been to entice. I had been beginning to wonder if I'd been wrong to think that he wanted more than a platonic relationship with me. Apparently, though he was just unusually shy. I wondered if I was his first "conquest" since leaving the point. I knew that he was an enigma to most of the female population at AWSCOM headquarters for his lack of interest in them. It was obvious though that he'd had some excellent bedroom teachers though from the performance he'd put on last night and several times today.

As I sleepily considered all this, it dawned on me that he was still wide awake and, unlike my languor, he was still tense. I frowned and lifted my head. "Ben?" He turned his head to me. I managed a shaky grin and nibbled on his chin. "You tired of me already?"

Oh my God! How could Robin think that? Surely she knew that I couldn't think of anyone or anything else when she was around – or, for that matter even when she wasn't. Hell! I'd blundered my way through the SOI wondering what I'd forgotten while my mind wandered to her. "Sorry Love. I've been worrying about something."

Love, huh? That sounded promising. My curiosity, though, was aroused. I asked the obvious question. He sighed. "It's those two on the SOI team, the woman major and the Chief Warrant." Not very romantic to wonder about them when he had a naked woman laying half atop him, I thought. "What about them?" Another sigh, "It was the questions they asked. Hardly any of them dealt with Nuclear surety of safety – not even about procedures. They kept asking about Isaac and Joanne, about their duties and activities – even her attack and their so called vacation. Now you and I both know they've been involved in some strange happenings but have been too smart to ask about them. In fact, I'd bet money that they weren't even actually members of the SOI team."

I had to chuckle. "Joanne told me the first day they got here that the woman, Major Deering, at least, was a spook. Didn't she mention it to you?" He shook his head. "All she said was that we should watch

208

them and be careful what we said and did around them. The thing that worried me most, though, was the number of pointed questions they asked about you." That got my attention! Something very hard pressed against my hip, though was more attention getting. I decided to table the other problem for a later discussion – much later. I kissed him and smiled, remembering daddy's warning so many years ago. "Daughter, when a man's thoughts drop below his belt, his brain gets turned off. Don't let yours do the same." As Ben rolled over atop me, I thought to myself, "Why not?" Seconds later, I gasped in delight and decided that thinking was grossly over rated.

"Mister Hamlin we just came from the nursery. That is as fine a pair of kids as I've seen since my last was born. May I assume that your wife handled the birth as well as she has handled all the other events in her life over the last few days?"

"Of course sir, just as you'd expect from her. She even carried her weapon into the operating room in case she had to defend me against assassins while she was delivering." I deliberately had spoken a bit loudly outside Joanne's room door. I had to grin at the shriek that came from inside.

"Colonel," I shouted," send your wife in here so I can tell her the real unvarnished truth about that ass hole I married. If they'd really let me have my gun I'd have shot him in the balls for what he did to me."

Albert grinned at me and nodded toward the door. As I stepped inside Joanne's room she let out a sigh. "Thank God you're here Violet. Maybe I should call you Mrs. Colonel Richmond so you could shoo all these damned men out of here before I go mad. I'm so fed up with all the testosterone I'm about to scream. The doctors say everything's fine while I hurt all over. Isaac has said how proud of me he is till I'm ready to hit him, and he didn't think to bring any makeup over so I look like death warmed over. I practically had to fight Robin for my own kids before she'd let them go." Still she couldn't hold the frown any longer as Miss Lawrence stuck her tongue out at her. "They are adorable though aren't they?"

I had to laugh. "For you information, I left Mrs. Colonel Richmond at home and as for the twins, yes they are. Have you settled on names for them yet?"

"Yeah! We named the one who'll probably be as obstinate as his father, after our own fathers Robert and John. The other one who will no doubt be as beautiful and brilliant as me, we named after my mother and my best friend, Judith and new best friend, Violet. The doctor thinks they're both going to be tall so I'll probably be the shrimp of the family, but I'll tell you one thing −", I raised my voice so my husband who was ignoring me could hear. "There aren't going to be any more six pound twins. I'm gonna find some little stud − maybe a midget - to knock me up the next time." A voice from the hall yelled, "I heard that!" "Remember it!" I yelled back." With a groan I grabbed my stomach. My diaphragm wasn't up to screaming at my husband yet.

Just then the nurse brought in two vases loaded with yellow roses. "These just came in." she said. "I thought you wouldn't mind me bringing these while you still had company."

As the nurse set the vases on the table and handed her two cards, she grinned. "I wonder who-". She paused as she pulled out the first card. Then she laughed out loud. "Damn that Irish bastard!" She gasped grabbing her stomach again handing the card to me. "Congratulations! If I could induce their mother to agree, I'd like to recruit her two new fighters into the Mob. They'd probably rout the Brits single handed - Douglas Leonard" I shook my head as she opened the second envelope. "You seem to turn up admirers in the damndest places."

Looking up I was astonished to see her crying. Silently, she handed me the second card. "Congratulations to the mother of Prince Naborn Scarborough Hamlin upon the delivery of his two siblings of which he would have no doubt been very proud - as are the people he gave his life for - Mustafa" "Strike that! The damndest Admirers in the damndest places. Don't you know anybody who isn't a revolutionary?" She ignored me and just held up her arms. Lawrence, tears sliding down her cheeks, immediately brought the two children to her and placed them into her outstretched hands. Cuddling them to her she let her tears flow for another child. Lawrence, unselfconsciously took my hand and we sat beside her as she mourned one loss and gloried in the gift of two others.

www.ingramcontent.com/pod-product-compliance
Lightning Source LLC
Chambersburg PA
CBHW051504170626
46811CB00002B/650